CREATIVE WRITING FROM WALES

Edited by Heather Killingray

First published in Great Britain in 2001 by
YOUNG WRITERS
Remus House,
Coltsfoot Drive,
Peterborough, PE2 9JX
Telephone (01733) 890066

HB ISBN 0 75432 704 3
SB ISBN 0 75432 705 1

FOREWORD

This year, for the first time ever, Young Writers proudly presents a showcase of the best 'Days Of Our Lives . . .' short stories, from up-and-coming writers nationwide.

To write a short story is a difficult exercise. We made it more challenging by setting the theme of 'A Day In The Life Of Someone From The Second Millennium', using no more than 250 words! Much imagination and skill is required. *Days Of Our Lives . . . Creative Writing From Wales* achieves and exceeds these requirements. This exciting anthology will not disappoint the reader.

The thought, effort, imagination and hard work put into each story impressed us all, and again, the task of editing proved demanding due to the quality of entries received, but was nevertheless enjoyable.

We hope you are as pleased as we are with the final selection and that you continue to enjoy *Days Of Our Lives . . . Creative Writing From Wales* for many years to come.

CONTENTS

Ysgol Crud Y Werin

Ffion Enlli	295
Sera Williams	296
Sioned Owen	297
Alex Annis	298
Caren Durant	299
Dylan Rosa	300
Robin Hughes	301
Sioned Mair Williams	302
Marc Williams	303
Dafydd Jones	304
Sharon Roberts	305
Adrian Garner	306
Catrin Roberts	307

Ysgol Cystennin

Niccola Howard	308
Georgia Colman	309
Louise Owen	310
Catherine Williams	311
Carly Bebbington	312
Danny Russell	313
Jodie Russell	314
Tom Williams	315
Thomas Kirby	316
Sarah Ryder	317
Charlotte Campion	318
Wesley Earl	319

Ysgol Dyffryn Trannon

Ffion Evans	320
Lisa Jones	321
Bryn Jones	322
Jonathan Evans	323
Daniel Williams	324
Kathy Mills	325
Jamie Robinson	326
Carly Harris	327

The Stories

A Day In The Life Of The Classroom Gerbil

Hello, my name is Scuttle and I live at Tunnel 1, Cage 1, Class 4C. I am a classroom Gerbil and the children love me (I like them too). But anyway this is a typical day in my life.

I was woken up by a slam of the door shutting and was very dazed. I scampered out of my tunnel and looked outside of my plastic bar cage. I saw a very crooked old figure with a raincoat and I squeaked with curiosity. But, my curiosity faded, as she was only the teacher (Mrs Rosen). I scuttled back into my tunnel and fell asleep again.

I was awoken again by children speaking happily. School had started. A very small girl was coming over to my cage; it looked like she was about to give me my breakfast. She opened my cage and put my delicious breakfast into my bowl. I waited until the girl was gone and started eating, piling it down in great lumps. But suddenly, I noticed that the little girl had left the door of my cage open. Should I open it and go out into the world on my own? Or should I stay in my cage and carry on a peaceful life as a class gerbil? In the end I decided that I would make a run for it, climb out of my cage and be free. So quietly, I slivered over to the open cage door and climbed up the plastic bars. One more bar and I would be free. I've made it!

It was hard getting across the classroom floor and out of the door of the classroom. When I had finally got out of the classroom, I hid in the corner until a child opened the door so I could get out. Finally (after about an hour) someone finally opened the door and I scuttled through quickly.

It was very chilly outside and so I had to find a tiny little space by the wall where I could sleep for a bit.

Finally I woke up . . . but I was in my cage, in my tunnel nice and warm. How did I get back here? Maybe it was just a dream or somebody might have taken me back to school while I was sleeping. Anyhow, it was an exciting day, wasn't it?

Harley Cheyenne Johns (10)
Blaen-Y-Cwm Primary School

A Day In The Life Of . . .

Woof! Woof! It was 7.30am, as usual I was getting very excited as Gareth let me out into the garden and said ‘Good morning boy’. By the way, you’re probably wondering who I am? I’m a very large, three-year-old golden retriever named Tasz, who loves fun, games and of course, my food. I like lots of company, long walks and I really love it when Gareth strokes, pats and cuddles me. My speciality is being crafty and then being able to get back into Gareth’s good books when I do something wrong.

On this particular hot sunny day, Gareth and his family went out locking me in the living room on my own as usual, or so they thought! They had forgotten to shut the window. Once the family had disappeared from the bottom of the driveway, I jumped onto a box, onto the table and then out through the window. I landed on a soft heap of dirt, got up and sniffed around. Suddenly I lifted my head; another dog walked slowly by, looking rather forlorn. I ran after him as fast as I could and discovered he looked identical to me. I asked, ‘What’s your name?’ He replied, ‘Mania,’ and then started to tell me how his owners had abandoned him. ‘Follow me!’ I said and running side by side, I took him back to my home.

After I had shown him around the garden, we got back in through the window. I love to impress and so I showed Mania how to lie on Gareth’s bed, play with the washing in the basket, chew a pair of slippers and play with an orange from the fruit basket. It was so much fun, especially as I know I shouldn’t be doing these things!

Time passed quickly and before we knew it, Gareth and his family were returning home. They were amazed to see me lying there quietly with another dog.

‘Where did he come from and what’s this?’ said Gareth as he took a piece of paper from Mania’s collar, which read ‘Mania’ and underneath ‘abandoned’.
‘How sad,’ said Gareth. The family had a long talk and decided that Mania could stay.

Resting my head on my paws I thought, ‘Now we can have twice as much fun! What a good day in my life this has turned out to be. I wonder what tomorrow will bring?’

Gareth Hancock (11)
Blaen-Y-Cwm Primary School

A Day In The Life Of Neil Armstrong

I woke up at 1am on July 21st. It was only three hours before I was to be the first man on the moon. How was I to know that in three hours my whole life was going to change? We went over the list for the last time. I said to Buzz, 'Good luck.' I was shaking in my suit. We didn't know what was going to happen. We left the shuttle in the cramped lunar pod.

We were all nervous. All I could think about was my wife and kid back home. We started to speed up as the moon's gravity pulled us in. I was sick in the shuttle. All of a sudden there was a bump. We had landed on the moon. We opened the hatch. I climbed down the ladder.

I took the first step and said, 'This is one small step for man and one giant leap for mankind.' We did little things like seeing how gravity affects things. After two or three hours we went back to the lunar pod to get ready to take off.

We started the rockets. It took only a short blast to get us up. We didn't know it but the ship would fall apart when we got back to the shuttle all I wanted to do was to see my family again. And that was the best day of my life.

Samuel Sutton (11)
Bodafon Primary School

A Day In The Life Of Owen

In the morning I wake up and play on my PlayStation, then I get changed and watch TV. Later on I go and play with my friends and we play on our bikes. In the afternoon the ice cream man comes. We buy one and then carry on playing, doing skids on our bikes. Then I go in for lunch. After that I play football for about an hour, then I do some skids on the hill. Later I play basketball with my friends for ages, then we play until tea. Next comes my Game Boy. I watch loads on TV and finally, I go to bed at nine o'clock. I'm glad to be Owen.

Cathal McCabe (9)
Bodafon Primary School

A Day In The Life Of My Hamster

I am Tibby, a hamster, and this is a simple day of my life.

Like every other ordinary day, I get woken up by my human. I try to get back to sleep but the music that she listens to is booming mad. When she leaves at half-past eight, I get a nice quiet sleep. In the middle of the day I get up for a little something to eat, but yet again I go back to sleep just like any other hamster would.

At half-past seven in the evening when I wake up, I have a little something to eat and drink, then my owner comes up to the room and she holds the ball to my cage and I happily go in for my daily exercise. I saw the treats bag on the floor, so I quickly rolled over and tried to nibble it through the breathing holes, but I am too slow and my owner comes and snatches the bag away. After my roll around, my owner gets me out and gives me a cuddle and a stroke down my back. Then she puts me back in my cage.

Through the night I run in my wheel, nibble my food and run all about the cage, but halfway through the night I am put in the bathroom 'cause I am being too noisy. That is a simple day of my very simple life.
But I *know* it will be repeated tomorrow!

Maxine Silver (10)
Bodafon Primary School

A Day In The Life Of A Frog

I was swimming around in the glimmering water, when suddenly I saw I had little wriggly things. They were legs! I had grown legs! Yippee! I knew then that I would soon be a frog and I could hop and hop around my pond. All my friends had grown legs before me and so now I was really happy.

When I was little I had not grown quickly at all. I knew one day I would grow and I have my pond, which is very big, so I can swim around in the fresh, sparkling water. Although my life as a nearly grown frog is happy and great, there is still much danger that awaits me - the fish and birds that are huge and like little tadpoles! Mrs Willma has two very big fish that I have to dodge. Then suddenly *help*, the fish was trying to eat me. *Help!* The fish was holding on to me but I was trying to escape, twisting and turning around and found I went over and over again until I let go. I quickly swam away into the darkness of my home.

I told all my friends and family and they thought I was really brave. My friends also said that they were glad I had grown legs. Well, that was a scary but quite exciting day of my busy life as a tadpole, with legs.

Rebecca Thomas (10)
Bodafon Primary School

The Match

I had woken up in the morning when it was time to go to the match. We had got in the Landrover and set off. Brooklyn was sitting in the back sleeping.

We were there. We got out. Posh was going onto the field while I got changed. Brooklyn ran around the field with a football. He was kicking it expertly. I was in goal when Brooklyn was shooting the ball. He was good at it.

I was number 7 mid-field. It was time for the match now. Brooklyn was waving and supporting me. He was shouting. It was half-time by this time. I was waiting for the next half to start and we just got a drink.

It was time to go to the match in a minute. We just got some food for Brooklyn because he was hungry. We had a little play. He was shouting everywhere. He always loves watching me, he never misses me play.

I always let him do what he wants. It was time for the second half. We won 3-2. We got in our car, Brooklyn fell asleep and we set off home.

Thomas Cartledge (9)
Bodafon Primary School

A DAY IN THE LIFE OF A ROBIN

One cold winter's morning I was perched on a branch singing. I started to get hungry, so I went to get something to eat. Firstly, I went to the farm that was close to where I was. Then I started pattering my feet on the ground, but there was no hope, so I went to the seaside to see if there was anything to eat. I started pattering my feet again and this time a worm came up, so I caught it and then ate it. Suddenly a robin came swooping down from nowhere. I called loudly, 'What is your name?'
She replied, 'Rita the robin.' Then she called back 'What is your name?'
I said, 'Ricky the robin.'
She called me to her nest, so I went with her. When we were flying, a vicious black cat jumped out and tried to catch me and Rita. We dodged out of the way but the cat kept on jumping up and trying to get us. Then finally we used our wings and got away. We flew to the top of our bush where we could hear singing coming from far away. I started singing, then lots of other birds started singing as well. In the end it was a choir of different birds. What a lovely end to the day. I enjoy being a robin.

Dominic Nickson (10)
Bodafon Primary School

A DAY IN THE LIFE OF A HEDGEHOG

I was wondering whether to cross the road or not, because my great granddad once did and sadly, he didn't make it across to the other side. I gathered up all of my courage and was going to cross.

Luckily, children wanted to cross the road to go to school and so a tall figure came with a big, tall stick saying 'Stop' on both sides. As soon as the tall figure held up the sign, the cars stopped, so I thought I would cross while I had my chance.

I went over the road and the tall figure noticed me. She stared at me and stayed there. She still held the sign up and let me go across while the cars were still stopped. The tall figure stared at me as I crossed the packed road filled with cars. As I went past the tall figure, I smiled at her and she smiled back at me. I stepped up the step. She put her tall 'Stop' stick down and the cars drove away.

I was so pleased that I had made it across the road and my mum, dad, brothers and sisters will be so proud of me

Charlotte Beswick (11)
Bodafon Primary School

A Day In The Life Of Lucky, The Horse

I was lying down in my soft bed of hay sleeping, when that annoying girl came skipping up the drive. I don't like her because she kicks me in the sides when she rides me. I was hurried up and a heavy saddle thrown across my back. The bit almost made my mouth bleed. I was feeling OK but she mounted me and kicked me harder than ever. I galloped, jumped over the fence and up the mountain.

My plan was working, the one I dreamt last night, until a large quarry halted me. I looked down at the rigid cliffs that sloped down to the stony ground. I quickly moved back but the girl pushed me on. I dug my heels deep in the muddy ground.

I turned around and galloped home, rolled over and dropped her off my back. I untangled my girth and bridle and snuggled down in my only place for dreams - my bed of hay.

I never had to be ridden by her again. Another girl came to see me, she was the best rider ever. We galloped over lush green mountains and she even stayed late to take care of me. I knew I'd have the best time in the whole world each time she came walking up the drive.

Angela Narey (11)
Bodafon Primary School

A DAY IN THE LIFE OF MY SISTER

My sister Rachel Patricia Sargent always wakes up at 7.30, gets dressed and goes to school. But not on Saturday - she wakes up at 8.30 and is dressed and ready for dancing. She pushes herself to the limit, always dancing ready for her exams. Her biggest achievement in dancing is passing a test where only one girl out of a hundred passes. And for acting, she played the part of Annie and does most of this in one day. She practises for her exam, then straight after she goes and does Annie.

Rachel's most amazing day was probably going to Manchester to dance in an academy. All the way there she was calming herself down ready for her big exam. When she got there, there were a hundred girls trying out. They went in two at a time, usually with a friend and Rachel was one of the last. Just before she went in she said to me 'I'm going in.' She went in, the music started and she started to dance her little heart out. She smiled, gave it her all and came out so proud of herself. She said, 'I've done my best, that's all I can do.' I was so proud of her but all we could do now was wait for her results. When her results came, she opened the pack carefully and pulled out a certificate saying 'Honours'. My sister started shouting 'All that practice has paid off and I've passed the impossible.'

Matthew Sargent (11)
Bodafon Primary School

A Day In The Life Of Princess Diana

As I woke up I got my posh clothes on, like my lovely crown with jewels all around it. I put on my lovely dress to keep me warm.

I went to the NSPCC and gave them a cheque for £555.50. After that I went to the hospital to see if everyone was OK. I talked to an old lady and she said, 'Lovely day isn't it?' I said, 'Yes it is.'
I went to take William and Harry for a walk around the park and back. I came back to Buckingham Palace. After that I went to see the Queen for tea. She gave me some scones and a hot cup of tea. After that I went home for the night. I got my night-gown on and I was reading my book in bed thinking who I will help tomorrow, like the RNIB.

David Illingworth (11)
Bodafon Primary School

A Day In The Life Of My Pet Cockatiel, Eddie

I woke up with my sheet over my cage. I rooted around for some whole seeds to eat. I squawked for Dominic to come and let me out, but no one came, so I decided to have a little snooze for a while. Well, I thought it was for a while. The next thing I knew, Matthew and Dominic were downstairs with me, I had my sheet off my cage and the TV was on.

On the TV there was Ant and Dec, I think they are very funny. Matthew changed my seed and water, I had a quick drink of water and a peck of seed and then Dominic let me out of my cage. I stretched my wings and flew around the room a few times, nearly crashing into the window. I came zooming in to land on the window sill, I whistled to a swooping buzzard circling around. It made me feel quite sick and dizzy. I wobbled and fell off the window sill and I screeched as I fell and hit the table with a bang!

I was knocked out for what seemed like forever, but when I woke up I was lying on the floor of my cage and spiky woodchips were all over the floor. I was feeling dizzy but I lifted my cage door up and scrambled out. Dominic's rabbit, Reg, was in the room, so I decided to have some fun. I jumped onto his back and went zooming around the room. What fun! Suddenly my day was over. What a thrilling experience, being my own pet for a day!

Dominic Elias (10)
Bodafon Primary School

A Day In The Life Of Tiger Woods

I awake on the day of the Masters' Final. My heart is racing and I have butterflies in my stomach. I wave goodbye to my mum and dad, heave my clubs into the car and set off for St Andrews Golf Club.

When I arrive I get caught up in a stampede of press and photographers. I finally escape and make my way to the first tee. I am really nervous and that is probably why I hit my ball into the trees. I am not distracted by the huge crowds at all. All I am doing is keeping my head down and keeping my eye on the ball.

Surprisingly, time goes by so fast and I am soon on the last hole of the St Andrews Golf Course. The tension is very high and to win the Masters' Trophy I need to win this last hole. I hit my tee shot and my ball flies through the air and glides onto the green. Everything depends on my last shot. I swing back my club just a little bit and hit the ball. It starts to roll and slowly goes into the cup. Yes! I had won. I was ecstatic. When I got the cup I held it up high. This is the happiest day of my life. I have achieved my ultimate goal and all my dreams have come true. My emotions run wild. They overpower me. I have reached the pinnacle of my talent.

Daniel Galston (10)
Bodafon Primary School

A Day In The Life Of Romans

What it is:
You go to a place called 'A day in the life of Romans'. You dress and live like a Roman. All the clothes are there for you.

What you do:
There is a Roman Theme Park and Roman swimming baths. There are all sorts of Roman activities there. Great!

How much:
Adults - £100 each for a week
Children - £70 each for a week
The food is free but drinks from the bar aren't.

How they look after you:
You call room service in the morning and a Roman maid comes and serves you.

Where it is:
It is in beautiful countryside where there are gorgeous scenes and walkways. As well as being a Roman, you can walk by the lovely streams and fields.

Roman History:
If you want to send your kids to a kid's club you can, but in a Roman kid's club they learn all about Roman history. They draw and have all sorts of activities.

Food:
In the morning, afternoon and evening, there will be a nourishing meal - a Roman meal. Tasty, healthy and scrumptious.

Roman baths:
There will be a masseur to massage you and a lovely pool with a sauna, steam room and jacuzzi.

Gym:
There will be a gym where you can get fit and get away from Romans.

What the rooms are like:
They have a comfortable bed, a TV in every room, a settee and a kitchen with all the utensils. You will also have a washroom and balcony where you can sunbathe.

Amy Webb (11)
Bodnant Junior School

A Day In The Life Of My Dog

I wake up and stretch with tiredness. I get up for my delicious breakfast of chicken and beef and I lick the bowl clean. It is a sunny day so I take a stroll in the garden and bark up a tree a few times to scare some birds, but the best thing of all, I scare a cat!
I jump out of a bush and bark out loud which gives the cat the fright of its life. It has started to get really hot today and I sit in the shade, then lay down and relax. My throat gets really dry and I am hot in my thick fur coat so I go to my mum and dad and they pour some water in a bowl. It is nice and cool and sparkles in the sunlight. It is too hot to go for a walk to the beach, so my human sister puts her paddling pool out. As she is putting the hose in and the water starts to spray out, I get excited and jump in. It is really freezing. I yelp and jump out with shock.
Well, that is my day.

Jenni Blythin (11)
Bodnant Junior School

A Day In The Life Of Emily, My Niece

I've just had my feed and I brought it all up so my mum had to change me. I've heard I'm having my pictures done today.
I'm finally here in Boots with my mum and my Auntie Sam. My mum holds me first but I keep looking at her so the photographer can't take pictures of me. Now Auntie Sam is holding my bum. Just to annoy the photographer, I keep slipping down but he puts me back up and makes me laugh and smile. He finally gets a snap of me.
We leave Boots and go to the newsagents. Auntie Sam buys loads of sweets and I think she's a greedy pig.
We go to my nanny's house and I sit in the sun with my new brolly on my pram. I fall asleep, but I'm only pretending as I am hoping I don't see my nan. She looks like a big, big monster!

Samantha Williams (11)
Bodnant Junior School

A Day In The Life Of Limp Bizkit

On Saturday me and my friends were practising our band. Stuart was playing the drums, Jamie was playing the guitar, James was playing the guitar as well, Ashley was on the DJ set and me singing.

When we were rapping, this man from the singing studio heard us and wanted us to play live on TV. He said we could be a proper band.

The next day we went to practise at the studio. When we had finished we had a concert on Saturday. We had to do lots of practice. When Saturday came there were millions at the concert. Our manager said we were fantastic. The boss of the company said that we made millions from the people that came.

DJ Leathal gave Ashley some tips on how to scratch the deck.

After two years when we were 21 years old, the government started to complain about the swearing in the songs and we were put in prison for starting riots in the crowds.

James Parker (11)
Bodnant Junior School

A Day In The Life Of A Spider

Once there were two spiders, one called Rain and the other called Drop and they both lived in the grass. One day Rain and Drop decided to go for a walk. They came to a big wall at the bottom of the garden and there they met another spider called Dinky. He was smaller than Rain and Drop. Then they heard a noise at the front of the garden, but it was too close to them and Rain was too slow, so he got sucked up by the mower. Drop started to cry but then a small voice from behind said, 'I'm here, I'm here!'
In joy, Drop ran over to Rain then they went home and had a party and lived happily ever after.

Natalie Dyke (11)
Bodnant Junior School

A Day In The Life Of My Mum

My mum wakes me up with a soft whisper, 'Wake up.' Read on and find out more . . .

'Wake up,' she whispers. She walked into the bathroom and washes her hair - it glows like gold. She rushes down to get us breakfast and dries her hair. Then she walks softly upstairs to get dressed. She puts on a blue silk top and black pedal-pushers and the sun shines on her face.
When she is dressed she goes back downstairs and puts on a decent amount of make-up. Then she packs up to go to University. She rushes around whilst trying to eat some toast.
'Here's your dinner money.' She speaks like an angel.
She blows kisses from heaven to me and then picks up the keys gently. She asks us kindly to get our coats and then go out. She says,
'Have a nice day, I'll pick you up. Love you, goodbye.'
She is just too late to catch the train, so she waits for the next one. She smiles at the people around her. 'What a nice day,' she thinks to herself.
The train pulls up at the station, she lifts her heavy bag and walks onto the train. She sits down and her golden, soft hair flicks softly onto her face. She gets out her National Curriculum book and reads in her head.
Before she knows it she is at the station, so she packs up and gets off the train. She slowly walks to the bus stop and waits for the bus.
'Here it comes,' she says.
She climbs on the bus, shows the driver her pass and finds a seat. She sits there for four minutes then gets off to go to the University cafe for something to eat. Then she goes to her first lecture, history. She demonstrates her project and looks like a dove, speaking softly.
'Mary, are you coming?' she calls. She walks slowly towards the bus stop again and here she has to do what she has done already.
Finally, she arrives home. She picks us up, takes us home and then she cooks and cleans. She is really clever. As she is doing her work, she gets a cup of tea from me. She is the best, she is really the coolest.

Diane Young (11)
Bodnant Junior School

A Day In The Life Of A Spider

My web is silk to catch my food. I think you've guessed what I am - of course, a spider. Here's a day of my life:

I wake to tinkle of dew on my web thinking, it's a fly for my breakfast. I rush out but there's nothing there. The night before, the wind had damaged my web. 'Best get to work,' I mutter to myself.
That takes me to 12 o'clock and buzz . . . I'm stuck in the web. I'd caught a lovely juicy bluebottle for lunch.
'Mmmm . . . tasty!' and with a cry, I've eaten it whole!

Well, there you have it - a day in the life of a spider.

Gareth Jackson (11)
Bodnant Junior School

A Day In The Life Of My Dog, Max

What should I do today?

I will get up in an hour and mither my mum for a sausage. Then I will go out to play in the garden with the ball and then go and play in my pond (try to catch frogs). After that I will go inside for a nap for an hour and then I will have my dinner (my favourite - chicken and lamb). Then I will wait for Ruth and Jane to play football with me and I sometimes bite them, but not often. After that I will go for a walk, a really long walk and will come back in for a drink. Then I will have my tea and play outside for a while. Then I will settle down to bed and dream about what to do the next day and who to bite.

Jane Davenport (11)
Bodnant Junior School

A Day In The Life Of My Mummy

My mummy wakes up at 7am and gets showered. She then says goodbye to Paul and waves him off at 7.45am. She wakes me up and tells me to get dressed and have a wash.

My mum puts her make-up on and her uniform and then she cleans my trainers. After that she goes to work and she is on her feet all day because she is a beautician. When she comes home she makes us tea, then we watch television and talk. Then we go to bed and sleep, ready for another day when my mum will shine again.

Now that's the story of my mum. What a hectic day she has!

Hollie Williams (10)
Bodnant Junior School

A Day In The Life Of A Bee

In the early morning light we are woken by the queen bee buzzing around our hive.

I get up and report to the honey hive room, awaiting my morning duties.

'Collect as much pollen as you can during the morning and you may then have the afternoon off.'

I buzz out of the hive looking for flowers. There are so many, I don't know where to start. Blue, purple, yellow, red, green and orange and the smells are exquisite.

I land on so many that I am weighed down. I take it back to the hive and I am now free until 8pm.

I buzz around looking for something to do. Yes, I have it, there's a football match. Bees versus wasps. I know what to do! I fly down and buzz around the goalie. He is so scared, he runs off. One to bees, nil to wasps.

I then try to find something else to do or someone else to annoy. Suddenly I feel two hands clasp around me. I wriggle free but get stuck in a jar. It's bees one, wasps one.

I finally get free and I am so annoyed that I lash out and sting a little girl. I fly away before I do something else I regret.

I have 10 minutes before I die. This is the punishment all bees have for stinging something or someone. Ten minutes left of fun.

Bees 2, wasps 1.

Stephanie Sparkes (11)
Bodnant Junior School

A Day In The Life Of My Best Friend

My best friend is really special to me. She is really special to me and she is a really good friend. Her name is Fay and we see each other every day. We have been together since we were two years old but Fay's mum and my mum have been together since they were two years old.

We get ready for school, then we meet each other by the gate in school. Then we walk into school together. But today, Kate had walked in with Fay and I was upset. She had taken her away from me and she is not my best friend anymore.

Laura Wardell (10)
Bodnant Junior School

A DAY IN THE LIFE OF MY MUM

My mum is wonderful. For one day I'd like to be just like her.
In the morning she'll get up and have her breakfast. When my brother and I step out of the door, she'll tidy up all the bedrooms, she'll wash the dishes and clean the clothes, she'll iron and take the dog for a walk.
She's got brown hair, brown eyes and she's quite small. She looks after us day and night, when we're ill and when we're healthy.
When we get home from school, she gets dinner on the table. After dinner she cleans up the table and baths the babies. After that she puts them to bed and tidies up downstairs. Then she sits down to watch the television.

My mum is the best mum and that's why for one day I'd like to be just like her.

Laura Pullen (11)
Bodnant Junior School

A Day In The Life Of Spike My Dog

My dog Spike will wake up and stroll into the front room with his eyes nearly closed.

When I get up Spike jumps for joy and keeps licking me for about five minutes and then he goes into the kitchen to see if there is any food in there.

Then my mum will come in with my breakfast and Spike will sit on the floor with his paw on my knee waiting for me to give him some.

After that Spike will run outside to see if there is any cats that he can chase and bark at. Spike just loves cats. He will come in through the back door and stop to see if there is anything in his bowl that he could eat.

Then Spike will play with his lion teddy bear. He likes to bite its eyes and nose off. But the best thing Spike loves to do is bark, he will bark all day and bark all night, he just loves to bark.

After that Spike will first go to sleep in the front room but then he will get too hot and then he will move into his bed and fall fast asleep there.

I love Spike very much!

Nicola Hughes (11)
Bodnant Junior School

A Day In The Life Of My Mum

My mum is very kind, she's got green eyes. My mum is always busy. To start the day she will wake me up and make my breakfast, she will then walk me to school. We have to walk a long way because we live at the top of the hill in Meliden. She will walk back and tidy up. When our house is tidy my mum will do some washing. My mum will walk to school to pick me up. Most days we walk home and other times we will get the bus.

When we get home my mum will cook tea. When we have finished she will wash the dishes and dry them, so really my mum works very hard. I wouldn't like to be her.

Emily Wilkinson (10)
Bodnant Junior School

A Day In The Life Of My Brother

My name is Mark Wilford Roberts and I am always in mischief. I am two, nearly three. I live with my mum, dad, Christina and Chelsi.

I wake up at 7 o'clock and I have cornflakes for breakfast. (Sometimes I have a different breakfast). I take my two sisters (Chelsi and Christina) to school with my mum. My dad goes to work and sometimes my mum works.

When my mum goes to work, my dad and I go to my nanna Sue, nanna Tyler or Alison.

I eat a lot of crisps and cakes and sweets, I do brush my teeth. I have a big dinner sometimes.

I play with my toys and my favourite game is Star Wars.

When Christina and Chelsi come home from school I get excited. (Sometimes my sisters have homework).

I have a big tea with my two sisters. While I'm watching TV my dad comes home. I get my pjs on at 7 o'clock and go to sleep.

Chelsi Eardley (11)
Bodnant Junior School

A Day In The Life Of My Mother

In the morning my mum wakes me up at 7.15am and makes me my breakfast, and we talk on the way to school and she kisses me goodbye.

She goes to my nanny's and stays there and goes for a little stroll around town until 3.20pm which is when she picks me up, she always gets me good delights after school.

On a Monday she gets me a wrestler. She gets me then that much there's none I need. When we get home I either play on my Nintendo or watch TV while she polishes my shoes because I have scuffed them at school (sorry Mum).

She cooks tea and gets me a pudding and then she watches TV with me and makes me supper. She then sends me to bed and goes to bed just after me.

Patrick Clough (11)
Bodnant Junior School

A Day In The Life Of My Mother

My mum is the best, she cooks and she cleans. She tidies my room whenever it's a mess.

She is one in a million.

She wakes me up at 7.30 and gets dressed. She makes my breakfast and her own. She gives me my dinner money and sweets for school, makes me sandwiches for when I am not dinners. Whenever she is not well she phones my grandad and he takes me to school.

When we are at school she does the cleaning which includes, tidying my room, her room and my brothers, feeds the animals, washes my clothes, cleans the windows, does the hoovering.

But on Monday she has her day off. She studies art at college. When we come home the house is spick and span. She is like a spider always busy and on the go.

When we think she has done too much we always buy her a present once a week, which is normally a small bottle of brandy.

She is the best. I don't know how she can fit all that into one day and just can't understand how she can put up with me because I am always asking her for things.

Although she is not like most mums, she can do things but not as well as most people.

She is the best.

Carolyn Gaskell (11)
Bodnant Junior School

A Day In The Life Of A Soldier

I wake up in the morning and start training with my mates. We climb up a climbing wall, cross a river and loads more stuff and then we have a break for about five minutes. We train if there's a war, we put all our kit on and we practise shooting targets and we practise camping out and we kill animals to survive.

Once the alarm has gone we were sent out to war, and I got stuck under a pile of wood. I survived it and I was awarded one million pounds and a medal. I never went to war again.

Chris Knowles (11)
Bodnant Junior School

A Day In The Life Of My Niece!

Hi, my name is Shannon Olivia Toner. I am two years old. My favourite colour is pink. I love the Tweenies and Jellikins. My favourite food is crisps and toffee popcorn.

My best friend's name is Rosie.

On Sunday 20th May, I went swimming with my auntie and my mum, I loved it and I enjoyed the monorail so much my mum kept asking the man if we could go round again and again.

I then got tired and we went home for tea. I had potatoes, peas and carrots, then I went to bed.

Hayley Toner (11)
Bodnant Junior School

A Day In The Life Of My Mum

My mum wakes up at seven,
With smiles from Heaven,
She wakes me up,
With her hair like a hedgehog,
She makes my cup of tea and breakfast,
She puts on quite a lot of make-up,
We rush to work and school really fast,
She works really hard selling cards and toys,
She gets smiles from little girls and boys,
She picks me up from school in her car,
She doesn't have to come very far,
We go home and have our dinner,
We watch TV and have some fun,
Because my mum's work,
Like an angel is never done.

Charlotte Roxburgh (11)
Bodnant Junior School

A Day In The Life Of A Cat

I am going to be a cat for a day in a life of something. I wake up and cry at my owner for food. Then after my breakfast I have a half an hour nap! Soon after my nap I want some more food so I cry even more than the last time.

Then I go adventuring in the drive where I hopefully will find a mouse. Then I see a small little tail behind the bin bag, so I run after it and get it. I always like to use them as presents for my owner. After I have shown my owner I climb a tree, it was the tallest tree in the garden. Later on I go into the streets where loads of flies are, I love flies and I love chasing them.

Then, 'Woof' I heard a dog. I looked around and saw a Dalmatian running towards me with his jaws right open so I run as fast as I can home but halfway I am out of breath. I hear my treats being shaken by my owner, that means it's time for me to have my treats. That got me charged up so I ran as fast as I could home to have them.

Afterwards I settle down for the night asleep on the sofa. So that's my day in a life of a cat.

Adam Jones (11)
Bodnant Junior School

A Day In The Life Of A World War II Soldier

He gets up early to fight for his country. He has to be aware of all German aircraft, they bomb anyone and anything. As soon as night falls they will come, a big angry wail sounds, bombs drop. The RAF take-off, shoot down the Nazi planes. The children cry with fright as bombs go off down the street. Then the all clear sounds, everything is alright 'til another day.

Lee Hinton (11)
Bodnant Junior School

A Day In The Life Of A Dolphin

As waves splash on the rocks, under the sea is a happy dolphin. It's me, I'm a dolphin for the day. I'm jumping in and out of the water tossing and turning. This is fun. Then I get a rumble in my stomach. I'm hungry. Fish, I'll go and catch one. Yummy.

I come to an island where the puffin birds play. The island has palm trees where the monkeys play tricks. Grass where the adder snakes slither. I carry on swimming against the waves and with the wind on my face.

Oh no, I'd better be quiet. I've come to a group of sharks, look at their teeth, they are sharp and pointy, just waiting to chew me up. Phew, I'm glad they didn't hear me.

I come to the shore, a nice beach full of children laughing and shouting.

There's a little boy drowning, I'll go save him.
'Help' said the little boy.
I'm glad I saved him. Oh I've got to head back now (to the cliffs).

I said goodbye to the beach. I swam past the island and travelled for ages until I got to the cliffs. Suddenly I turned back into a human, even though I can't be a dolphin I'll never forget the day I had in the life of a dolphin.

Katie Taylor (11)
Bodnant Junior School

A DAY IN THE LIFE OF A WATER DROP

As I turned the tap off, *squeal, squeal* it went. There was one last drop of water halfway in the air and as it touched the sink it went *splash*. It was sliding down the sink, then suddenly disappeared.

Scramble, scramble it went slivering down the drainpipes. Down, down, down it went through the open doors.

It has travelled and travelled for many days, but still it could travel for ever and evermore.

Danielle Bell (11)
Bodnant Junior School

A Day In The Life Of A Dog

Every morning all dogs wake up and do the same thing, they stretch, go to their master, lick their face to tell them to wake up and let them outside. When they are outside they chase next-door's cat away, wake up all their neighbours with a bark, do what they have to do, bark two times to be let back in, have a drink of water, lie down in a nice, warm basket for a sleep.

In the afternoon all the dogs' masters have gone shopping. When they come back the dogs can have their dinner, later the dogs watch TV and after that the sleepy dogs go to sleep. The next day the same old thing happens.

Tara Baillie (11)
Bodnant Junior School

A Day With Jane Davenport

I respect my girlfriend Jane Davenport. She has ginger hair and blue eyes like me. She is in 6PW and I really admire Jane.

Jane is like water droplets on ice-cold water. Yesterday we went to the park and the cinema, it was like we were on the planet Mars, it was the best day of my life.

I gave Jane a goodnight kiss, it was like we were floating in the night light.

Mark Canaven (11)
Bodnant Junior School

A DAY IN THE LIFE OF A WHITE TIGER

Hi, I'm Patch! I'm a white tiger. My mum calls me Patch because I have a black patch on my right eye.

I live in a zoo in the sunny state of Florida. I had to be separated from my mum when I was two. I'm three and a half now. The half makes all the difference because I'm nearly as old as my brother.

One day, last week, I escaped. I'll tell you, if you want?

Well, I woke up and stretched out. My keeper, Mrs Jones, fed me my breakfast. I had a joint of meat. After my breakfast I have to perform in a show.

I had to do tricks like playing dead or rolling over. After that I normally sit in front of the audience and look pretty! After that Mrs Jones would take me to my cage I have shows to do every four hours so I need my rest.

I hate living in my cage. It's not peaceful like the jungle. It's like I'm trapped, I just want to be free! I want to chase the birds, I want to see the wonderful plants with tropical colours, I just want to get away! It's horrible everyone watching me. I feel like I'm in prison.

I drifted out of my cage into the jungle called the city. There's a jungle, well a forest so I walked there.

After a while I heard a voice. My keeper's voice. 'Patch come on!' I heard her say about ten times. I purred loudly as I ran to meet her.

She took me back to my cage, my home here in the zoo!

I know now it doesn't matter where you are as long as you're with your loved ones.

Alicia Johns (10)
Croesyceiliog Junior School

A DAY IN THE LIFE OF A POP STAR

A day in the life of a pop star I thought as the teacher asked me what would you like to be when you grow older.

I never thought of it before but I thought I might be in luck today. I was! On the way home when I saw the postman walk past I said, 'Have you got any letters for me?'
Then he said, 'What's your name?'
I replied, 'Jessica,' and he gave me a letter and I opened it, it had a letter inside saying,

Dear Jessica,

Would you like to have a day as Suzanne as she's fallen ill? The date to come if you are coming is November 24th 2001 in Manchester. Someone will pick you up.

Telephone if you coming, 0773050821.

I shouted, 'Yes, 2 days before my birthday,' then I told my mum about the letter and she rang the telephone number.

A few hours later a man knocked at my door and took us to Manchester. I had quite a good time, I sang and had a chat with the gang. I was upset when I had to go home because I had so much fun.

Jessica Moore (11)
Croesyceiliog Junior School

A Day In The Life Of An Actress

One day I sat down reading the newspaper and on the front cover it said that a play is on today but they still need a main character, but it had to be somebody who was between the ages of 16 and 21. I'm 18 so I thought to myself maybe I should go to the audition.

When I was at the audition I had to wait for half an hour, then all of a sudden I was called in. I was very nervous and I didn't know what to do, they made me sing a song and just read one and after that they asked a couple of questions about myself and told me that I had got the part of playing Mary.

That day I had three hours to learn all my words and then only five hours to actually rehearse, then the big moment came, I was to go on. I was not prepared, my legs were still shaking. I went on the stage, after I had said my first sentence I was fine.

When the play was over I went to buy a programme, the show was called 'Rock Nativity', then I went to a fancy restaurant with a few other people who were in the play as well.

That night I had ten calls off people who wanted me in their plays. I turned down two plays and I accepted eight plays but luckily they didn't want me until next week. That night I went to bed feeling proud of myself, and my acting continued.

Ali Jenkins (11)
Croesyceiliog Junior School

A Day In The Life Of A Horse Jockey

I got up at 7.30 in the morning, as today was a big day. I got changed into some old clothes and put my nice clothes for the horse jockey championships, in a carrier bag.

I walked to the stables to brush and tack up my horse, Milky Way. Milky Way is a creamy colour with a light brown mane and tail. As I was putting on his saddle I heard footsteps.

'Who's there?' I shouted as I turned.
'It's only me,' replied my cousin, Hayley. 'I only came to wish you luck and help you tack up.'

When we had finished, about 9.00am, we put Milky Way into the horse box and I got in the car. Hayley told me she'd be in the audience, with the rest of my family.

When I arrived I saw my family. 'This is it, the championships,' I thought as I went to the changing room to change. After that I went to the stables and got Milky Way. I walked to the starting point, heart pounding and hands shaking.

The atmosphere was amazing, bright lights and cameras, I mounted my horse and just seconds later the whistle went, I gave Milky Way a whip and off we went, wind all in my face. We were in fourth place and we came to a jump, we cleared it well. I gave him another whip to go faster.

We were coming to the finish line but three other horses were in front. 'C'mon Milky Way, we can do it!' I shouted as I gave another whip. We sped up to second place as we crossed the finish line.

We got a drink and all the cameras were on us, and a tear rolled down my cheek.

Soon after, I got home and my family congratulated me. It was absolutely amazing.

The next day a letter came through the door, it said, 'We are happy to award you first place, as the other jockey has been disqualified as he went out of the ring towards the end.'
'Yippee!' I shouted as I told my mum. It was the happiest day of my life.

Lucy Jones (11)
Croesyceiliog Junior School

A Day In The Life Of A Designer Of Clothes

One day I woke up and I realised I wasn't myself because I was grown up, then I realised I wasn't in my bed. I found out it wasn't the year 2001, it was the year 2015, and I was one of the most famous people in the world.

When I got dressed in one of my suits and had my breakfast a limo was outside waiting to take me to work. When I got there I thought to myself, 'This place is huge.' I went into my office. I decided to design something - a bit futuristic.

When I had finished I went to one of the people who helped make my clothes to ask her which material to use. She said, 'Leather.' Everyone started operating the machines. When the first one was made in my size I took it home and then went back to my office and started making up my new catalogue.

It was going to be called 'Clothes of the Future'. It was going to be called that because it will have clothes from the future, my company's name is 'Clothes'.

Then it was time for lunch. I went downstairs to the cafeteria, it wasn't very busy because most of the people who work for me had already had their lunch. I only had a sandwich and some crisps because I was going to go out for dinner tonight. When I had finished I went back upstairs to finish my catalogue.

After I had finished it was time to go home. When I got home it was seven o'clock. I changed so I could go out but then the phone rang. It was my boyfriend, Rich. I knew it was him and he asked me if I wanted to go out. I said, 'Yes.' He said he would pick me up at eight-thirty. Rich had dark hair, blue eyes and a sense of humour.

When it was eight-thirty he was outside waiting. We went to the movies, we saw 'Never-Ending Teardrop', it was very depressing. Then we went to a restaurant, I had chicken à l'orange, it's my favourite. The restaurant was a French one.

After dinner he took me home. By then I was tired so I went to bed. When I woke up the next day everything was normal but I will never forget that day.

Emma Jarrett (10)
Croesyceiliog Junior School

A Day In The Life Of A Man United Ticket Holder

Today I am going to see Man United play Arsenal, it's going to be tough but they will do well. I reckon Man United will win 2-1 so I'm going to place a bet on that score of course. So fingers crossed I'm going to win.

I'm going to buy a football kit, but first, to the bookies. In one minute I saw some stupid bets, like 58-0 to Arsenal. I mean that would never happen. It should be the other way round, 58-0 to Man United.

Well here I am at Old Trafford, the place where dreams come true, where everyone wants to play. The time is 10 past 2 and the match starts at 3.00 o'clock so I've got 50 minutes, time to have a drink and party!

Here I am once again back at the stadium. I'm in I 16, *so come on Man United!* You're going to stuff them like little teddy bears and chuck them in a freezer.

So here I am at the football match and it's 1-0 to Arsenal and, oh! Man United have scored, it's 1-1. The atmosphere's electric and, it's another goal for United, 2-1, fantastic. What a fantastic day.

Mark Eccleshare (11)
Croesyceiliog Junior School

A Day In The Life Of A Ladybird

One day in the open countryside I was on the top of a bluebell drying out my wings after the rain.

All of a sudden I saw a big object run past, then it swooped me up. I tried to fly but I couldn't, then I realised, *it was a human.* Its hand opened and the light shone bright. I was standing there shaking, I was petrified but it didn't seemed to want to hurt me. I climbed to the top of the thumb to fly away but the human caught me, I tried again and I got away, I flew as fast as my tiny wings would go.

The human boy started to run after me and tried to catch me with a net. I was getting very tired. I saw some bushes so I flew straight for them and hid.

I was in the bushes hiding and catching a breath of air, my heart was pounding. I have been chased by a human before but never with a net, I was petrified.

I flew back to the group and told them what had happened, they were all shocked but then the oldest and wisest ladybird came out and cried, 'That happened to me once but I got trapped in a bottle.'

It soon got dark and all of us fell asleep. I fell asleep under a rotting log where it was warm. I woke up the next morning with the other baby ladybirds crawling over me and they brought me food. I thought that was very nice. My wings were stiff and I couldn't move.

I liked living as a ladybird and I hope I stay here forever.

Cally Tinton (11)
Croesyceiliog Junior School

A Day In The Life Of A Whale

Myself and my family had just come back from a day out, it was eleven o'clock and I was really tired. I went upstairs and flopped onto my bed.

On my wall was a huge poster of a blue whale, every night I would stare at it until I fell asleep, so tonight was no different.

'I wonder what it would be like?' I said to myself. About one second after that I was in a deep sleep.

The next day I opened my eyes and I was surrounded by a blue silky sea.

I couldn't believe my eyes, I rubbed my eyes a number of times, trying to wake up from what I thought was a dream. No matter how many times I did so I was still there.

In one way I felt excited but in another I felt really scared.

I rubbed my eyes again and to my surprise I felt a rubbery, slippery, smooth surface touching my face. I no longer had a hand but a fin.

By this time my heart was pounding and I was very afraid.

I was now a fish, or so I thought. I swam to the surface of the water and looked at my reflection.

I was a whale!

I could hear other whales calling and I could actually understand what they were saying.

Another surprise was that I could reply.

'Now is my chance,' I said in my mind.
'Now is my chance to experience a day in the life of a whale.'
'It is time to get our food,' said a whale who I assumed was my mother. She didn't say it in the same way though.

The whole pod of whales went out to gather their food.

After that we went to sleep, we were all leaning against our mothers. Morning came and I was getting used to my fins and gills. Although there were other whales around, I still felt lonely as not one of them had made friends with me. Things changed quickly though. I was playing by the coral when a younger whale like myself came over and introduced herself, her name was Lavender.

We had got along quite well and were racing back and forth to the bottom of the sea, we were having lots of fun.

Like the night before the pod of whales had to go and find their food. Lavender came with myself and my family, we caught a lot more fish with extra help.

Myself and Lavender had become close friends during the day and I was sad because I knew I would have to leave. However I was there for another couple of hours and I was going to enjoy every last minute.

Lavender and I went to the surface and started to lean into the air. As I reached the water I felt myself falling, my fins couldn't hold me up. I crashed down on a hard surface. I was back in my room.

Was it all a dream?

Amy Jones (11)
Croesyceiliog Junior School

A Day In The Life Of Suzanne Shaw From Hear'say

We had just finished the auditions for a new band, I went home not knowing my life was going to change. The next day Nigel came to tell me if I had made the final five or not.

He said 'You are the only one who split the judges decision, so they have sent you something.' He gave me a small bag, I opened it and I couldn't believe my eyes. It was the keys to the Popstars house.

'Welcome to the band!' said Nigel,

'Oh my god, oh my god, you're joking!' I kept saying.

The judges went to the other nine people, to tell them if they had made it or not.

For five of them, their dream was about to get shattered. The final five had to move into a secret location house for three months until we were revealed to the world.

We all set off for London not knowing who we were going to be living with for the rest of our fame and fortune. The first to arrive was Danny and Noel, shortly followed by Myleene and when Kym and I arrived the band was finally together in our new home. Nigel gave us a quick tour of the house and then left.

A few days later, we went to the Top of the Pops studio where Jon interviewed us.

'So what is it like, sharing a house with four people you hardly know?'

'The worst thing is that we are surrounded by cameras - 24/7. I said 'I thought it would be hard sharing a room with Danny but it's not, we get on so, so well!'

'What do you think of each other?' Kym said 'Noel's the comic of the band, his cooking is wicked and sometimes he can be a mega idiot,'
Noel interrupted, 'Kym is mad and her feet really smell, Danny is my best mate and Suzanne is wicked, she makes me laugh all the time,' I said.

'Noel can cook loads of food, when I sit down, he will shove his hands in my face. No one can stay in a room on their own, we just all pile into one room.'

We got back home at 11.00 o'clock, Danny went down to the chip shop to get us all some chips.
'I never knew being a popstar was going to be this hard and tiring' I said as I fell onto the sofa.
'Yuk what's that smell?' Everyone looked at Kym who was sitting on the arm of the sofa nearest my head, waving her bare feet around.

'What?'

Noel kicked Kym and her trainers out of the room,
'I'm gonna buy her new trainers, her ones that she has got on smell!' said Noel.

After not even one minute, we all piled into one room and ate our tea.

I never knew pop stardom was going to be so hard and no one knows us yet and when they do it's going to be a lot harder.

Emily Davies (11)
Croesyceiliog Junior School

A DAY IN THE LIFE OF A DRAGON

I woke up suddenly with a cough and a blast of fire. I wonder what I should have, deer would be a nice start and for the family, human.

With a big flap of my wings, I soared into the sky and started to circle the land below.

I could not see any humans but two, sweet deer. I killed them both with two swipes of my claw, I devoured one deer very fast as I knew the family would wake soon, I soon got home and started to roast the deer.

The family soon woke with the smell of the roast deer. After everyone finished the meal, I went down to the river to have a drink, suddenly 50! 50 men appeared on the horizon, I shot like a rocket to the family.
'Take the family and hide, 50 well-armed men are coming!'

I stood my ground when the men came, they charged with their swords and picks. One sword man came up, I did a fire blast, it melted the sword and armour. I did it again and again and again, they were all wearing nothing and with a couple of flashes, they were all dead in a neat pile,

'Honey we don't have to go hunting for a while,' he remarked, 'we've enough food here for months!'

Neil Jones (11)
Croesyceiliog Junior School

A Day In The Life Of Andy Cole

Hi my name is Andy, I got up at 7.00. I got dressed, got my boot bag and went out of the door. I opened the door of my Ferrari, got in and drove off towards Old Trafford. When I got there, I changed into my training kit and went to the pitch.

On the pitch I saw my friends, Fabien, David and Ryan and I saw that David Beckham had a new hair cut.

'David what have you done to your hair?' He did not answer. Today was the day of the World Club Winners cup final, it was Manchester United vs. Las Vegas. It was to be held in Cardiff! The time now was 8.00. The coach was waiting in the player's car park. We got in. On the way we had a game of cards. Fabien won.

It took one hour to get to Cardiff. When we got to the stadium, it was 9.00. We went to the cafe in the stadium and had some breakfast.

Kick off was 10.00. It was now 9.30. We all went into the dressing room. The team was up, this was the line up.
1. Fabien, Bartez 2, Gary Neville 24, Lilwes Brown 6, Jaap Stam 11, Ryan Giggs 16, Roy Keane 8, Nicky Butt 7, David Beckham 18, Paul Scholes 9, Andy Cole 9, Dwight Yorke, Yes! I'm playing.

We got changed and went on the field with such pride. The whistle went. Las Vegas were playing excellent. 10 seconds into the game and the ball was in the back of our net. We started playing our best. At half-time it was still 1-0 to them, we played our hearts out. There were two minutes left in the match, David crossed the ball, Dwight missed it and I headed it, the keeper missed it and I scored 1-1 with a minute to spare. Then they shot and missed, Fabien took the goal kick and it was in! The final whistle went!

'We've won!' we all shouted as we did back back flips and clapped our supporters who'd cheered for us!

Brett Mahoney (10)
Croesyceiliog Junior School

A DAY IN THE LIFE OF MICHAEL OWEN

I wake up and was going to get dressed and have my breakfast. I was ready for my football session so I took my BMW to the football round. When I got there my best friend, Robbie Fowler said,
'Alright Mick!' I said,
'Fine.'

So Gerrard Houllier took us onto the ground and we practised really hard for three whole hours because we had a big game at Brazil and they're the best team in the world.

The game was on Saturday, it was Friday today, so I was really up for it. I went home to have my lunch spaghetti pasta with a chilli sauce so then I went to bed to keep my energy up for the game tomorrow.

So I woke up, got my football kit on and drill top, we were playing at the Millennium Stadium, we were getting ready for the big match and all the team was ready.

Daniel Maynard (11)
Croesyceiliog Junior School

A Day In The Life Of An Astronaut

5, 4, 3, 2, 1 Blast off! Bob, Bill and I set off for a journey to the moon.

The burning flames of our thrusters were gushing out like a waterfall.

We zoomed into the darkness of space faster than the speed of sound.

There is no gravity in space so we floated into a long narrow room where the food was kept. We had a little snack and strapped ourselves back into our seats. Then we set a course ready for our journey to the moon.

The night sky looked like a boy's face with sparkling freckles on it. The stars shone brightly as we moved closer and closer to the moon, our destination.

We were going to land on it and Bill was the man to manoeuvre the space shuttle. He had had years of experience and he had landed loads of space shuttles before.

It was a perfect landing! We were all dressed in our space suits and we waited patiently for the door to open . . . even though we were nervous, we were anxious to get out and onto the moon.

When the door had opened, we leapt out onto the moon. It was amazing. I felt as light as a feather because there wasn't hardly any gravity.

We explored the surface for rocks, we could take samples from. We could take these samples back to earth where scientists could examine them.

We went back into the space shuttle, after we had finished everything, with the best experience anyone could ever have had.

5, 4, 3, 2, 1, blast off! Bob, Bill and I set off for the journey back to Earth.

Kieron Window (11)
Croesyceiliog Junior School

A Day In The Life Of An Egyptian Pharaoh!

As the chambermaid walked into the tomb to do her daily chores, she noticed the pharaoh was lying on the floor, with a broken vase next to him!

'Aaaaaa!' screamed the maid, 'The pharaoh's dead!'

'Don't be foolish' boomed a voice from outside. The pharaoh's son strolled in looking very responsible.

'I'm not joking, oh great one!' stuttered the chambermaid to the pharaoh's son.

'Call for a doctor immediately!' ordered the pharaoh's son. Soon after a man came and looked at the pharaoh. He was not dead but knocked unconscious by one of his ancient and valuable vases on the wall.

'Clean that mess up right now!' said the prince, quite shocked that a family heirloom had been broken in such a way.

The maid swept quickly as not to annoy the prince and walked out of the tomb with relief. The doctor picked him up and put him on his shallow bed, and there he examined him carefully, he was not bleeding.

The prince sat on the throne and ordered slaves to work hard. He enjoyed it very much and did a good job following in the footsteps of his father. He had a succulent feast of roast chicken and pork with vegetables from his father's own gardens and drank the finest wine in all of Egypt!

He had his father's jester to entertain him as well. Except for his father's unconsciousness this was an excellent day!

He went to see his father every thirty minutes. This luxury lasted for eight hours! Eventually his father awakened and they nursed him well.

'Have you enjoyed your time in my place, son?'

‘I certainly did, it was absolutely great! Your jester is hilarious, your wine had an unbeatable taste and your meat and vegetables are great!’ said the prince.
‘I’m so happy, you didn’t hurt yourself badly father!’

‘So am I.’ Then the day ended with everybody happy and the Pharaoh king again!

Gareth Emanuel (11)
Croesyceiliog Junior School

A Day In The Life Of A Crocodile

I was in a huge, smelly brown lake and the guard keeper threw huge pieces of meat in. The guard keeper was shouting 'Enjoy your dinner!' while we were scrambling to our dinner. I'd eaten already but I was still hungry. I saw a young boy, I sneaked up to him through the tall grass. Grab! I missed. I was lazing around in the water when I saw a family. I sneaked up to them, 'Grab!' I had something, oh bother, it's only a bag!

However in the bag was a bar of chocolate, a flask of orange and a bag of crisps. When I was a human, it was easy enough to get a bar of chocolate, bag of crisps, or a decent meal. I wish I was a human boy again!

'Ahh! My tail! Where is it? - I've lost my tail. Someone please help!' Behind me were some other crocodiles laughing at me.

Oh I wish I was a boy again! Yeah! Yes! I'm a boy again. I'm really a boy, then I realised I was in the middle of the crocodiles. I screamed! I quickly jumped out and thought a crocodile has a very tough life.

I decided I just want to stay as I am!

Sam Cox (11)
Croesyceiliog Junior School

A DAY IN THE LIFE OF A GO-KART DRIVER

'I wish, I wish to be a go-kart driver,' I slowly fell asleep. The next morning I found myself sitting in a go-kart, in the pit lane.
'What the . . . '

'Go!' said the starter. I revved my engine up. Whoosh! Went the engine! I was going at least fifty MPH, I twisted the steering wheel left then right.

I went around the track sixteen times. The sound of the crowd was electric. I was now in third place, we all knew on the tightest corner, not to take it at one hundred MPH. The leader spun and hit the person in second place.

'Yes!' I won the race. I raised my left hand in the air.

I pulled into the pit stop. Just before I got up, I vanished. I found myself eating my toast in the morning.

'Wow I should wish for that more often!'

James Gallivan (11)
Croesyceiliog Junior School

A Day In The Life Of A Professional Netball Player

I woke up one morning in my hotel room. I was in Florida, America. Today was the day that I would be playing for Wales in a netball tournament.

It was a scorching hot day, I got up, showered, got dressed, brushed my hair and placed it up in a ponytail. I walked quickly downstairs to get my breakfast, to find my teammates were already there. I got some toast and ate it quickly.

I was so nervous, in came our trainer, Jo.

'Right, the taxi's arrived.' We grabbed our bags and jumped into the taxi, just finishing my last piece of toast.

When we arrived at the grounds we would be playing on, we felt more nervous than ever. The minutes passed until it was time to start. We were playing against a team called the 'White Tigers,' but they looked like a weak side. Aimee made some brilliant goals and we won 6-2.

We had a drink of ice-cold water to cool us down. Soon after we were up for our fourth match, we had beaten all of the teams we had so far played by at least four goals. We could tell this game was going to be a tough one. But in fact, we beat them 3-2.

We all felt on top of the world, we had got through to the final! We had a short rest. Our trainer, Jo, walked up to us.

'Well done girls, great! All you need now is to win this match and we've won!'

We walked on with pride. The whistle went. We started off in the first half with three brilliant goals but unfortunately they had already scored two.

The second half had started and straight away I scored a goal to make it 4-2 to us. At the end of the match it was still 4-2 to us. The whistle went . . .

'Yes! We've won!' we shouted. We ran (with the energy we had left) up to collect our medals. We picked up the gigantic gold shield. The roar of the crowd was deafening and we walked off with grins on our faces hoping to be back next year.

Emily Harris (11)
Croesyceiliog Junior School

A Day In The Life Of An Architect

One day I went to work. I am a architect. I design buildings. One day I was in my office designing a building when I heard a loud bang. People were using dynamite. I said that they had gone crazy. I went out and I said 'What are you doing?'
You said, that we should blow this up'
'I did not say that.'

I said that you can blow it up when I am there. So after we had cleared all the rubble, we started to build the house. The house is worth £250,000.

It was huge! It was like the biggest house ever, I even had a £4,000 swimming pool in the grounds of the house, and I am proud of the house, and I enjoyed building it.

Jennifer McWalter (10)
Croesyceiliog Junior School

A DAY IN THE LIFE OF A POPSTAR

I was sat down on the settee when I had a call to say that we were singing tomorrow night at an Award Ceremony. We were all jumping up and down because we didn't know if we were going to get through or not, we had to get all our clothes ready and lots of other things. We were all excited!

The next day we were all ready at six o'clock. We left during the afternoon just in time. We were all driven there in a limo.

It was the first time I had been in such a huge car. It was thrilling! Altogether there were ten seats, a telephone and a TV in the corner with a CD player under it and anything you could think of.

Finally we were there, as soon as we were there we had to sing because we were first up, we had to sing 'Pure and Simple.'

I felt very nervous because it was our first song. About half an hour later, they said that we had won the Award. After about two hours we went home with not one . . . two . . . or three awards but four.

Laura Kirkham-Jones (10)
Croesyceiliog Junior School

A Day In The Life Of A Tiger

One day I switched on my TV and sat in the chair. Out of nowhere a bright flash leapt out at me. The next thing I knew I was in a disco, I looked around and nobody was human. They were all animals, like pigs, elephants, dogs and lots more others.

I went to scratch my head and my hand was all furry, I went into the toilets, looked in the mirror and I was all furry, my face looked like a tiger. I was choked and shouted 'Ahhh!'

As I walked out of the toilets, a panda walked past me and he said 'Hello - how are you dude?' I said, 'Fine thanks' and walked off.

When everyone went home, I followed them to see where they lived, I followed them right into the middle of the jungle and everyone went in their homes so I sat down and started to feel hungry. I got up and ran with all my might and caught a passing deer. After I went down to the river and had a drink of water, it was very cold. When I lifted my head up I saw on a stone, a shining thing and it was glowing. I picked it up. It was a stone with a gold stripe on it. I put it in my hand and held it as tight as I could.

The ground started to shake and with a big flash and bang, I was sat in the chair watching television.

Craig Button (11)
Croesyceiliog Junior School

A Day In The Life Of A Worm

I was in my hole and I could sense and feel a banging sound so I went up to the top of the hole and Bob, the owner of the house and garden was building a bird house.

I knew there would be trouble this afternoon so I came up the hole about midday and all I could hear was tweet, tweet. It was a bird so I turned around and . . . I realised I was flying. I looked up at the sky and I was in the bird's mouth.

When I had been taken to the nest, I tried wriggling out but I couldn't, the bird was too fast for me. After a while the bird fell asleep, now I could escape.

I crawled out of the nest and fell out of the doorway. Bob saw me and put me in his worm farm. After a while Bob took me out of the farm and put me in the nest. I hid under the sawdust and fell asleep.

When I woke up, I saw my mother and father, but they were dead. I looked around me and everything was red.

I started to wonder where I was. I took another look and there was a berry and two dead worms and me.

I tried to get out of the red thing but it was too slippery. I thought for a moment and realised I was in the bird's stomach. When I woke up I found myself in a bird shooting field on a bird's back.

The man below shot the bird I was on and I fell to the ground and I fell in front of two flowerpots and there I met Bill and Ben, the flowerpot men. They gave me directions to the end of the garden.

When I got there, I nearly got stood on by a boy about 5 years old. I started to cross the road, as I did - Squash - I had got run over by a 4 x 4. I tried moving again but I couldn't.

Ross Tudgay (11)
Croesyceiliog Junior School

A Day In The Life Of A TV Presenter

Yesterday it was Friday. I had a lovely, relaxing day pampering myself in the Hilton, a hotel in Wembley but today it's back to normal. This will be my fifth series.

I am a TV presenter and I host a show called Get Your Own Back. In fact, I should be on my way.

Beep! Beep! I heard a car horn, it must be my taxi. 'Come on Lisa,' the taxi driver called. I dashed off and twenty minutes later, I found myself sitting in a dressing room.

Lauren brushed my hair over once again then I walked through the hall way and into the huge, double doors.

I felt excited because I liked being filmed in front of everyone and I like to see the expressions on the children's faces. Last week an audience came in and the first words I heard were 'Woh! Isn't this amazing, it's huge!'

Today a boy called Craig, he was very friendly and trying to get his own back on his dad, trying to gunge him. A girl called Amy was attempting but determined to win back the embarrassment on her older brother.

Amy told me she was a bit nervous. I told her that I felt like that, the first time I was on television and I'm still like it now.

'Let the games begin!' I announced. Cheers came from the audience as Amy and Craig raced against each other while Amy's brother and Craig's dad were dressed as frogs. Amy was winning! They both had to try and throw pretend flies in a huge bowl shaped like a lily pad.

Now Craig was in the lead, he won. There were a few more games and Amy only won one.

This was the last round, it was a question round. Amy answered them all right. Her brother was gunged. 'Hah! Hah!' she said to her brother, 'I proved you wrong!' She was that pleased she even invited me for lunch at an Indian restaurant to celebrate.

'This is the end of the show, see you next week with our other teams, bye,' I ended the show.

I finished off my day eating a chicken korma curry, my favourite. What an end to a lovely day.

Kelsie Cantelo (11)
Croesyceiliog Junior School

A Day In The Life Of Tina From S Club 7

Beep! Beep! Beep! Beep! I hit my alarm clock onto the floor with such a thud, the floor shook.
'What time is it?' I whispered softly. It took a few seconds for my eyes to adjust to the golden sunlight beaming in through the bedroom window, but as my eyes came into focus, I saw my clock read 6.30 a.m. so I stood up, gave a huge yawn, walked over to my chest of drawers and took out my favourite sparkly silver and gold crop top and my electric blue shorts.

I slopped into the bathroom, got dressed, cleaned my teeth and was just starting to brush my long black hair when I heard 'Teeny! Tina! Hurry come on!'

'OK Jo, I'm coming!' I roared back to her. When all the band was ready, we raced down the stairs and into our private show room. Our exclusive camera man positioned us on to the creaky wooden platform and started snapping and clicking pictures of us for S Clubbers magazine.

As I stood on the hard wooden platform, I thought about the concert tonight and went over all the words of our songs and dance routines.

At lunch we all had chips and pizza for our meal and chocolate pudding for desert. My pudding went down in lumps, I was so excited about our big concert, I could barely eat my favourite dessert.

Soon 8.00pm came, I was so excited, I couldn't wait! The next thing I knew, we were all stepping out onto the huge purple stage in front of hundreds of adults and children. The roar of the crowd was deafening. We stepped onto the stage with such glorious pride and started to sing.

After the concert we went to dinner at the Ritz and had soup, wine and banana split.

When we had finished our exquisite three course meal, we drove home to our apartment in our scarlet limousine and went straight to bed, feeling very tired after such an exciting and thrilling day.

Laura Baker (11)
Croesyceiliog Junior School

A Day In The Life Of An Actress

Toot! Toot! 'Script' went the taxi driver.
'Check,' I said.
'Foundation, for those bags underneath your eyes.'
'Check,'
'Clothes.'
'Check,'
'Is that it, Ms Catherine Zeta Jones?'
'Oh oh hang on a minute, I need my waterproof eyeliner and mascara for scene thirteen,'
'The argumentative scene.'

I was rushed into the taxi cab and off I went. You see, I got home really late last night, I was really shattered. We are doing a play called 'The True Face.' It is being filmed in Hollywood.

Out the cab I got and into a little buggie where a man I had never seen before drove to where I was supposed to be.

Wardrobe first, then hair, then make-up and then studio. I had to wait for three hours, just to do my first shoot. I might as well not of bothered to come at six o'clock in the morning.

On the set at last, with no breakfast in my tummy. Still starving as I was, like a proper actress I didn't complain.

'Lights, camera, action!' shouted the director. Nothing would stop me now. I would just keep unravelling my script. Until the director shouted 'Stop.' I stopped, I paused, and thought, why did he stop me?
'I think we should have this scene done in dimmer light' ordered the director, 'back here at seven tonight.'

Seven at night. I was back, we did the filming but there was a little interruption in the middle. I was home at last! Reading my script at one o'clock in the morning. 'Oh it definitely is hard work being an actress!'

I climbed into bed and immediately drifted off to sleep.

Catherine Chalk (11)
Croesyceiliog Junior School

A Day In The Life Of A TV Presenter

On Friday morning, I had to be at the television studios for five o'clock, no later, I had to have my make-up put on by artists and my hair done by professionals.

It was the first time for me and Ali producing our own television show live together. We'd been learning our words all night, last night and the morning had come around quickly. We got used to the cameras and we met the crew before we went on air.

The first programme I announced was 'Tom and Jerry.' We sat on the sofa in the studio because we were waiting for a visitor to talk to us on television.

It was Linford Christie, he was going to talk to us about the record breaking programme. Ali and I chatted to him on air, he said the new programme will be starting on the sixteenth of June and was on at five thirty five in the evening. Ali thanked him for coming in and was looking forward to seeing the new show.

The next programme was Bill and Ben, the Flowerpot men. While the nation was watching it, Linford left in his limo.

There was a long day ahead and still quite a few programmes to be announced. I read out some letters sent in by the viewers.

We launched a new competition, it was to design a school uniform and whoever won it, the uniform was made for their school.

Ali announced the next programme 'Goosebumps!'

We talked to the cameramen and had a look at how we were presenting the show because it had been taped. It looked OK but we criticised ourselves a bit before we were back on air.

The day was coming to an end and we didn't want to go home, we were enjoying ourselves so much.

The last programme we announced was Home Farm Twins. After that we ended the show and I said,
'Next week the original presenters will be back and all the shows will be to schedule, starting on Monday.'

We said goodbye to the crew and hope to see them in the years to come. Then Ali and I made our way back to the hotel to catch the coach back to Wales in the morning.

Lauren Savigar (11)
Croesyceiliog Junior School

A Day In The Life Of Victorians

'See you later, Mum. I'll be back by half six' I called out.
'No later Amy,' Mum shouted.

I ran down the garden path, covered in blossoms and honeysuckle, all over my trousers.

Five minutes later, I arrived at the gym, I don't know why but it all looked different, completely strange.
'Oh well,' I said to myself, 'I'll look anyway, if not I'll go home.'

I went in. The hall kept on changing on its walls. First like space, then World War II, then World War I, then it said Welcome to the world of . . . The Victorians. It felt like I was flying through the hall.

'Arhhh!' I screamed, 'What's happened to me!' I was dressed in a long black skirt, grey shawl and long plaits either side of my head, bang! What was that?'

Someone ran past screaming, 'Make way, Queen Victoria is coming!'

Then suddenly I thought about Mum and how long I'd been missing.
'What if Mum's called the police to have a search party out for me?' I asked myself. I got all worked up, then I had a great idea'
'I'll wish.' I said to myself.

'I wish I could go home, I wish I could go home, I wish I could go home.' Bang, a puff of smoke took me back to my path.

I whispered to myself 'I'm never going to that gym again, not unless it's a different one!'

Susan Brooks (11)
Croesyceiliog Junior School

A Day In The Life Of A Horse

Yesterday me and my owner competed against hundreds and hundreds of horse racers and successfully got through to the finals. Tomorrow we will be competing against the winners.

It was the next morning and I didn't feel well. I thought, 'That cannot be, I'm competing today.' I heard a car and managed to stand up and take a look. It was Nelly, my owner, and she had come to pick me up. I laid back down and thought, 'I'm not going to let her down,' so I got up again and walked towards her and said 'Neigh.' Nelly turned around and looked at me. We were eye to eye until Nelly shouted,
'Hello beauty, how are you today?'
I didn't reply but what I did was swing my tail from side to side. Nelly said, 'Come on, let's go.'
Nelly opened the thing that I called 'the choker', because it was small and cramped, plus it had little tiny holes. Although I didn't like it, I had to go in. All of a sudden the engine started and we set off. Finally, Nelly got out of the car and opened the choker and said,
'We're here!'
I got out and said to myself, 'It's beautiful.'
We went down and they said, 'Take your positions.' Nelly took me to a box and shut the door. Suddenly the whistle went! We started to race! I was third out of fifteen horses. I thought to myself, 'It's my tummy not my legs.' Then I darted round the course, past the others and through the finish line. Then I neighed! I've won!

Kelly Ham (10)
Croesyceiliog Junior School

A Day In The Life Of An Egyptian Princess

One day I was an Egyptian princess called Jasmine and my mum, who was a queen, started to become ill. It was horrible. I wasn't allowed to go and play with the lower class, as my family called them. I had to go with people of my standard.
I lived near Cairo and we have hundreds of pyramids near where I live. My mummy and daddy got me lots of gems and jewels. When you're a princess or a queen, you have to wear a crown with lots of jewels on it.

Everything was being made ready for a ceremony. I wanted to go home. Everyone was telling me what to do and were saying,
'Look at the princess, I wish I was her.'
I thought and said to myself, 'Well, you can if you want!'

My best friend Toni was in the crowd jumping and shouting. I walked down the steps of our palace and everyone moved. Then I thought, 'Why are they moving?' But I remembered what I learnt at school and my own thought, I'm an Egyptian princess. Then a little girl didn't move. Her mum was really scared, so I picked her up and took her to her mum. Her mum went on her knees and bowed. She said, 'Thank you princess.'
My mother called me back to get dressed into different clothes. She told me that I was having a party, for I was eighteen, so I got ready for this occasion.
The party started. I walked down the steps and everyone gasped and gave me compliments. I was having a great time until midnight, then I was home by 12 o'clock. I looked in my wardrobe and the clothes I wore that day were there. To get my head refreshed, I went to bed and - 'ssnnoore!'

Kirsty Robathan (11)
Croesyceiliog Junior School

A Day In The Life Of . . . ?

I got up at 5 o'clock in the morning. I got dressed. While everyone was asleep, I crept downstairs and made a quick cup of tea, collected my money and went out. As I was walking down the path, I remembered the keys for the car were not in my pocket. Now I was a bit annoyed. I would be late to tip my load, so I went back to the front door. It was hard to open as I had put Sellotape round to stop the wind coming through. Eventually I got through and got the car keys. I drove to the yard. When I got there I went to the toilet, then I filled my tank up. I got in and looked at my papers. The papers said: 'Cambridge, trailer 26'. I set my timer and put the engine on. I went and found trailer 26 and reversed into it until the back end of the cab was level under the hook of the trailer. I got out and wound up the trailer legs. I got back in and drove out of the yard. I got out and locked the gates, then I got back in and drove off.

I drove and drove and drove until I came to Cambridge. I unloaded the trailer and went for a cup of tea. I went back to the lorry, got in and drove and drove and drove until I got home. When I went up the steps to my house, what did I see? The front door keys!

James Buchan (10)
Crossgates CP School

A DAY IN THE LIFE OF A BABY

I woke up this morning and I was crying a lot. I found my dummy on the floor. I put it in my mouth, got out of my cot and went to explore. I came to a long, tall hallway. Everything seemed so strange and I went to investigate. I came into the kitchen and my mum picked me up and put me in my highchair for my breakfast.

Later on me and my mum went to the park. She picked me up and put me in my pram. She pushed me all the way to the park. My mum picked me up again and put me in the swing. She pushed me once or twice, then she put me back in the pram. Then we went back home.

My mum put me in this room which was surrounded with toys. I went closer to the toys. I grabbed a doll and put it in my pocket.

It was dinner time. I got in my highchair and ate my scrambled egg. Once I had finished my dinner, I went to explore the bedrooms. The first bedroom I came to had a four-poster bed and dressing table. I remember I had put a doll in my pocket. I took it out and put it on my mum's bed. As I was coming out, my mum saw me. She picked me up and put me in my cot and read me a bedtime story. After she had finished reading, I curled up and went to sleep.

Kirsty Doman (10)
Crossgates CP School

A Day In The Life Of Garfield The Cat

I shot in the house in the morning and yelled for my breakfast. My owner, Charlotte, came down the stairs, picked me up and gave me a cuddle. She opened a tin of cat food and scraped it into my bowl. I ate it up quickly and with a full tummy, hopped outside. I smelled a mouse and followed the scent to a paddock and pounced on it. Unfortunately, it got away. Then I found Tigger, she is my friend. Charlotte is her owner too. I jumped on Tigger and we had a play fight. We ran around chasing each other. Tigger and I ran into the house and Tigger ran upstairs. I ran into the lounge. I jumped onto the sofa and lay there sunbathing. I went to sleep and dreamed about having lots of fish for lunch and running around in the patches of long grass. Suddenly I woke up. I could hear the sound of Charlotte's mum calling me for my lunch. I couldn't wait! I leapt off the sofa and landed on the slippery floor. I nearly slipped over. I ran on the carpet of the study and through to the kitchen. I scoffed my cat food and ran outside. I loved climbing the trees, trying to catch the insects in the air. By the time I had finished playing, it was time for tea. After tea I curled up on Charlotte's bed and fell fast asleep on the blanket.

Charlotte Adderley (9)
Crossgates CP School

A DAY IN THE LIFE OF FUDGE

I am Fudge the pony. I am ten hands three. My body colour is skewbald. My owner is called Sabrina, she is very kind to me. I have a lovely field of my very own, it has lots of dark green grass. Every day Sabrina catches me and brings me into my stable and then she brushes me. I like being brushed because it tickles me a lot. Then, when she has finished, she tacks me up and we go out for a country ride over the hills. It is very tiring so we have a break at the top of the hill. On the way back down we have a gallop. Then on the way down in one of the fields there is a water tank where we always stop so that I can have a drink of water. When we get home Sabrina puts a sweat rug on me so that I don't get a cold. While I cool down Sabrina gets me some oats to eat. After she's given me my food and I've finished, she brushes me some more and gets me some water, then turns me out into my large green field for a well deserved rest.

Sabrina Stephens (9)
Crossgates CP School

A Day In The Life Of A Snake

One day the sun was burning down in the countryside. My skin was hot and my body was sticky and sweaty. I saw some tall grass and I decided to wriggle through it. When I got out the other side I saw a rat, so I chased after it. When I caught it, I hissed and ate it up in one gulp. Yum, yum!

All of a sudden I saw a giant's foot. It was about to squash me, but I quickly moved out of the way. Then I saw a big tree with hundreds of leaves on it. Then I saw a tree that had fallen down and it had made a hole in the ground. I slithered through the hole and I made it my home. I found a leaf and put it on the floor, then I found some sticks to put them around the leaf. Suddenly the broken tree was rolling down the hill. When the tree stopped rolling, I quickly wriggled out of the hole onto the ground. Then I saw another snake. The other snake was dark and light green. The snake talked to me and said,

'Do you want to have a snake race?'

I shot off! When I was very near the finish, the other snake was also very near the finish. We both drew. Then we decided to go back to our homes.

Rosie Patto (9)
Crossgates CP School

A DAY IN THE LIFE OF AN ANT

One day the ground was shaking. I looked up and there was a giant's foot coming right at me! I'm sure that's the one who killed my brother last weekend, so I quickly got out of the way. Then I saw a gang of ants. They were trying to lift a huge stone and I decided to help them.

'This is exhausting,' I said. Then it tipped over. It rolled down the hill.

'At least that stone has gone. We wanted to shift that stone for years.'

I looked round. I saw some trees and a giant's home. It was huge. I was buried with long grass. I crawled up the grass. Then I jumped on the ground where there was no grass. It was concrete with platforms on it. I was at a school. Suddenly, all the children came out and I ran because I did not want to be a squashed ant.

I met the gang of ants. They said, 'Don't climb the bricks because the giant will get you and squash you as they don't like ants. Then I heard a noise. I looked round. It was a lawnmower! I ran and ran. It was very close to me. I ran home and I never went out again.

Kate Harris (9)
Crossgates CP School

A Day In The Life Of An Ant

I woke up this morning in the same old ant hill. My name is Flick and I've dreamed of life outside of the ant hill. I went to the bar last night and the princess asked me to dance with her. I did but I didn't know it was the princess!

Someone in front of me started to annoy me. Paul hit Dross (my friend in the ant army) and a fight started. The princess ran out of the bar. I switched places with Dross but I did not know we were going to war against the colony of green beetles. We were on our way to war and we were singing. When we were there, I fell through a hole and went back to the colony and we won! But we did not know the General was going to kill us. He tried to drown us all. We built a ladder out of bodies. I dug a hole and I became a hero! I married the princess and had a thousand children! Our children went swimming every day.

Brett Price (9)
Crossgates CP School

A Day In The Life Of Penny, The Horse

I am Penny. I am a chestnut horse with one white sock and four white spots. I am blind in one eye. I am twenty-five and I'm 16 hands. I have got a huge field with lots of green grass for me to eat. My owner is called Lucy, she rides me up the golf course. When we get back, Lucy brushes me down. Then she feeds me on oats, barley, chaff and sunflower oil. My rug is cosy. My mane and tail are smooth. I am frightened of the roads.

I have two other friends, one is black, the other grey and a bay horse. I like my friends. I like playing with the other horses who are called Fudge and Ebony. I have a saddle with gold crosses around it. I have got a big brown stable with lots and lots of straw and hay. There is food for me to eat. It is warm in my stable. Lucy always keeps me clean and rides me up the road. I live in a big field up at a farm called Underhill. Children come up to see me with carrots and apples and feed them to me.

Heidi Lewis (9)
Crossgates CP School

A Day In The Life Of A Squirrel

One cold and bright morning, I awoke and climbed to the opening at the door. All of the trees were white. What has happened outside? What has happened to my world? It had been snowing. What's snow?

'Snow comes when it is winter and it gets very cold up in the sky so it freezes. The water and the rain become snow and it lands on the floor and makes it all white,' said my brother.

'I am hungry,' I said.

'Good job that I collected some nuts,' said my brother. 'It would be very hard foraging for food. The nuts I collected are in the base of the tree.'

'Oh good,' I said. So I scrambled down the tree and ate some nuts and then I went to climb and play and swing in the trees in the forest. One hour later I went back to the tree. I was bored so I ran off to explore and play in the park.

I saw some tall creatures with hair and one had a funny thing on its head with a feather on it. I went back to my brother and he said that they were humans and that they were dangerous. I ran to my bed in the tree, had a snack and went to sleep on the leaves.

Joshua Dunn (10)
Crossgates CP School

A DAY IN THE LIFE OF A RACE HORSE

Speedy, the race horse, was lying down on a comfy pile of hay in his cosy stable. He wasn't alone though, he had always had his friends Black Bullet, Misty and Silver living in the stables next door. They were also race horses and next week they would all be competing in an important race.
Ding! The bell went, the race horses woke up, yawned and steadily got up. Speedy was taken for some water and food. He quickly drank and strode off into the beautiful field. There were hedges and flowers and it was warm and sunny, a perfect day for a good practice.
The master lifted himself up onto Speedy. They trotted slowly at first, then got faster and faster. Speedy was enjoying his run and was heading for his first practice jump. Up he went! But the back of his legs hit the fence. Smash! He collapsed onto the floor! His leg was broken and bleeding. Men came running up to the horse. Speedy was in great pain and it was difficult for the men to help him up. Eventually they managed to get him onto his feet. Speedy limped sadly back to the stables. His dream of winning the race was over.

Stuart Eyre (10)
Crossgates CP School

A Day In The Life Of A Farmer

Got up at six and checked the in-calf cows and heifers. It is going to be a dry day. Arrived back at the house to have breakfast. Main job to be done today is sort out the young heifers. Some will remain at home during the summer, others will go to rented land. This job takes up the remainder of the morning. Quick cup of coffee around midday and a call to the vet to arrange an inspection for the cattle that are to be moved to rented land. The cattle staying at home are moved up the hill, being driven on foot followed by the quad. When I returned, jumped on the MF and started cleaning out cattle pens. Stopped at one for lunch and checked the in-calvers again.

Number 59 was calving and having trouble. Away quickly on the quad to get ropes and the wife, as workman hasn't turned up. Success! Managed to pull a big bull calf. Finish cleaning pens out, this takes me up to tea-time. Later, with the help of the rest of the family, we return the heifers back to their pens to await a veterinary inspection.

Off on the tractor to find the chain-harrows so that a start can be made on the silage fields. A neighbour's lad came to help; a nice break to watch Coronation Street. Back to it. I may just catch the 10 o'clock news if I'm lucky.

Edwyn Powell (11)
Crossgates CP School

A Day In The Life Of Lucky

I was standing on top of my hutch. It was like I could see the whole world. It was an amazing experience. Then my enclosure door opened and a person came in and put new food in my bowl. A little while later, another person came in and changed my hay. It's *so* much more comfortable. I dug my way under my house where no one could find me and so I was protected if there was thunder and lightning. I ran round fast and stood on my hind legs.

The people had given me a large run with lush grass and plenty of dandelion leaves to eat and I can have a large space to run around. Every night the people come and give me some greens. I hope it's not cauliflower because I do not like its rubbery taste.

The hutch is also nice because it stops dogs getting me. They look after me and make sure I'm safe every night. I hope they will always be my owners because they are nice.

Well, now I'm running around my pen because I don't want to go back in my hutch. I jumped under my hutch but my owner caught me and put me away.

Sam Lewis (11)
Crossgates CP School

A Day In The Life Of Neil Jenkins

With the thousand point mark behind me, I've decided that it might be time to hang up my boots and spend more time with my daughter. Today it is the Barbarian match. Graham Henry has told me that I'm one of the players who is starting the game.

As we reached the stadium, a sea of red shirts filled the streets. Everyone was cheering when we went past. We arrived at the stadium and the fans were surrounding the bus.

Waiting anxiously to go onto the pitch, we could hear all the singing around the stadium. The commentator said, 'Give a big, warm welcome to Wales,' so we ran out onto the pitch. We sang the Welsh National Anthem. Soon it was 7-0 to the Barbarians. We were charging with the ball when Robert Howley passed the ball to me. I ran with it and before I knew it, I was on the ground celebrating. I had got us back in the game. We were really trying hard in this game because the Barbarians were a hard team. Near the end of the game it was 38-33 to us when the Barbarians had a try. The man stepped up to take the kick and with a really hard boot it went right between the posts.

We'd lost the game. We were tired and disappointed, so me and the boys decided to go for a few pints. Later that night I decided I might just stay another year!

Daniel Stokes (11)
Crossgates CP School

A Day In The Life Of Jeremy McGrath

He awoke early in the morning and had his breakfast, put on his gear and had a short ride on his Yamaha 250. He had a long day ahead of him. He was going to the European British Championship in Sheffield for a very important race.

He set off for the airport in his van. The engine was loaded onto the jet and the jet set off for Manchester Airport. The journey from America to England took ten hours and another two hours to Sheffield. He had a long sleep while his mechanics prepared his bike. He walked the track and started his bike for a practice. He sped along the track like it wasn't there. Soon the practice session was over. His fans swooped in for his autograph straightaway as he appeared in front of them for the last time before his race. The horns were blowing, the crowds were shouting! It was time for his race.

It started well, the Kawasaki rider was always just behind. He sped across the jumps with his Yamaha 250 and turned too sharply and crashed. His fans cheered him on. He couldn't let them down. He got up and carried on. He overtook everybody and the fireworks shot up as he did the winning jump. He had won!

Christopher Davies (11)
Crossgates CP School

A Day In The Life Of A Shoe

This is called a day in the life of me, the shoe, so I will begin my story.

I have got stringy laces and I never get a rest, not even at night because Jasper the dog tries to chew me up. But luckily, with his big growl, it wakes my owner up. My usual routine every morning is to be worn to school. We only live a few minutes away. There are all sorts of different shoes like me. My make is Clarks shoes. It is a very tiring job.
We went to London, well one of the cities, and we were walking for hours and the bottom of my soles were worn out. I will be thrown out soon and there are these nice flashing trainers he bought yesterday. His sister woke me the other day and she made a big hole in my sole and she got me dirty and wet. I had to be washed and my owner took my laces out, which I think were the best part of me. In the end, guess where I ended up? With the dog Jasper!
That is the life of a shoe (well my life anyway).

Amy Richards (11)
Crossgates CP School

A DAY IN THE LIFE OF VICTORIA BECKHAM

I got up one morning and looked up at the daily timetable. First I go shopping, then watch David play football. After that I sat down, had a cup of coffee, then jumped into a warm shower. Just before I left the house, the phone rang. It was my mum, She wanted me to go round to her house for lunch but really she wanted to see Brooklyn. He was her favourite grandson, well at least he was, until he was sick all over her! Now I am off to the shops to buy Brooklyn and me some new clothes. I have just purchased Brooklyn a new Manchester United football kit just like David's.

When I was shopping, I bumped into Mel C. She was buying some new shoes, so we went for a coffee and a chat. We had a good chat and then I went to get Brooklyn changed into his new clothes to watch David play football. When David came home he was disappointed because Manchester United had lost against Liverpool. He had a shower and I put Brooklyn to bed. Later we went to bed.

What a busy day I had today and I fell straight to sleep.

Sadie Lewis (11)
Crossgates CP School

A Day In The Life Of A Dog

I am a Gordon Setter. I am black with brown patches and my owner is Adam. I live in a big house with a big garden for me to run and play in. He gets up and feeds me and he plays fetch with me before he goes to school.

He stops at the shop and gets me my favourite treats which are all different colours and tastes. When he gets home he takes me for a long walk where I run and chase birds and rabbits. I love splashing and running in the big puddles. My favourite part of the walk is the part with the jump which has a big puddle on the other side. It is very muddy but I don't care.

When we get home he waits for me to dry and then Adam and his dad brush me, I like being brushed because it tickles and I am very ticklish. It makes me feel nice.

He plays ball with me and he tries to throw it as far as he can. He can throw it a long way and it is hard to chase it. After this, he takes me inside and I go and lie down in my basket. The basket is red with green padding in it and is very comfortable, and ideal for a long nights sleep.

Adam Stephens (11)
Crossgates CP School

A Day In The Life Of Little Molly Carter

Little Molly Carter, that's what people called her. She was no ordinary girl like you or me. For little Molly Carter was only three foot one inch tall and at eleven years old she certainly was short.

Things in life were hard for Molly, she was teased almost every day at school and even holding a pencil was hard. She tried her best at everything she did, but nothing was like the rest of the class.

Little Molly Carter couldn't even ride a proper bike like all her friends because she was so short. Most of the time she wasn't at school, she read books and watched TV.

One morning Molly woke up as normal and got ready for school, she walked down the stairs and scampered up to the table. She had her breakfast and left for school. When Molly was walking down the street she saw an article lying in the road, although it was wet from the frosty morning's dew, Molly picked it up and tried to make out the words which said *'Think big to be big!'*

Molly wished she could be big like all her friends so she thought big thoughts all day and when it was time for Molly to go to bed she said 'I wish I was big' once more and then she fell straight to sleep.

When Molly woke up she felt very strange then she realised that she was a whopping five foot! She was shocked but happy.

Amy Louise Howell (10)
Crossgates CP School

A Day In The Life Of A Sheep

One sunny bright morning I woke up in a bed of straw. The farmer came on a motorbike and one of his children ran me and my sheep friends into the back of the very uncomfortable motorbike trailer. The farmer called Mr Jacko and his child called Samantha, drove to one of the greenest fields on the farm. We stopped at an iron gate. The farmer opened the gate and we were unloaded into the field.

That day we had an excellent play, jumping, rolling and hopping around. The farmer came to the field and took us to the shed. That afternoon there was a tray of disinfectant. All the sheep were walking through it, even my friend. So I thought I should follow.

We got our long toes and fingernails chopped off and our tails shortened to a reasonable size. We walked into a lorry which drove past many houses and farms. At last we stopped outside a tent and we were put into a pen with a huge tent over us. Our fur was pulled out and our faces were cleaned with boiling water. Some of us had halters put over our heads, but I didn't. Sheep after sheep after sheep!

They carried on until there was only myself left in the pen, the gate was slightly open and I pushed at it with my nose and it opened wider and wider until I could fit through it. I crept past all the other farmers and their sheep and I crept and I crept until I was out of the market.
Yes! I was free at last!

Gemma Davies (10)
Crossgates CP School

A Day In The Life Of A Pig

One rainy day a massive lorry pulled up outside my sty. I thought it was bringing me some new turnips. Somebody jumped out of the lorry with a thump, the man who was driving the lorry started walking slowly. The man was wearing black clod-hopping wellies. When he came out from behind the lorry, I saw that he was in a white suit and I started to panic.

I watched him walk up to the house, he rang the doorbell once or twice. When the farmer came, the man in the white suit went into the farmer's house. I went into my sty for about half an hour and then the farmer took the man in the white suit around the farm.

I looked in the corner of my sty, I was getting low on turnips and I started to panic again. I thought I was going to die. By that time it was starting to get dark, the farmer had let the man in the white suit go into the house.

The farmer had gone out with the Ford and tipper trailer. When the farmer came back in the trailer there was a load of turnips. The man in the white suit came up to me with an electric gun and before he had time to pull the trigger, the farmer jumped on top of the man 'Why did you try to kill my pig?'

'I thought it had foot and mouth.'

'No, it hasn't got foot and mouth. Now get your lorry and go!'

Daniel Drew (10)
Crossgates CP School

A DAY IN THE LIFE LASSEY THE SHEEP DOG

Lassey woke up and went for a walk. She went to see her mum Bessie in her kennel then the owner came to the shed door and loaded up some sheep and lambs into the trailer. Then he hooked the trailer to the quad and drove down into the field. Lassie went with him and barked and barked all the way.

When he was gone his child Amy went up to the farm and gave all the sheep some food and then she heard a noise, it was a squeaking sound. Amy thought it was somebody trying to open the door, she went outside, Lassey was squeaking, Bessie had got loose had somehow tied Lassey up, the owner had come back and Lassey was sitting in the feeder squeaking. She loosened herself and the owner tied Bessie up.

Lassey had her dinner in peace, of course Bessie had her food as well. Lassey felt sick and they took her to the vet. They gave her some pills which she had to take every day and they took her home and they played with her. She seemed to get better and she only had one pill. They took her to the vet and said 'She's only had one pill and she's getting better.'

The vet examined her and said 'She's pregnant.'

Amy Jane Powell (9)
Crossgates CP School

A DAY IN THE LIFE OF A DOG

I woke up this morning in my dog kennel
'Hello Mac!' Called out Glyn, who was my owner.
'The big competition is today, so let's go!'

We walked to the van and I jumped in. He was driving really fast and I couldn't even stand on my own four feet. We got to the Dog Trials, he opened the door and there were loads of people looking at me.

An hour later and it's our turn. Glyn and Mac are called over the tannoy.
I walked up towards the stand, I had seen my dad do this loads of times so I should be good at doing it. 'Dog *comeby!'* (That means left) so I ran left.

'Mac, that's the wrong way. *Comeby.'* he shouted again.
Whoops! I was so embarrassed so I quickly turned my tail and ran the other way.
'Woof, woof!' I barked. The sheep slowly went into the pen and Glyn shut the gate. It was finished.

Later on everybody had finished.
'The winner is . . .' we all waited patiently 'Glyn with Mac!' said the Judge. We must have had the quickest time.

'Nice one Mac!' Glyn said.

Glyn held the gold trophy with his two hands and we went home in the van.

'Who won?' shouted Glyn's wife when we got home.
'We did!' Was the reply.
He patted me on the head and gave me a treat and said
'Goodnight Mac and well done.'

David Owen (11)
Crossgates CP School

A Day In The Life Of . . . My Sister

She wakes up with the sun
On an early Saturday morning
She walks downstairs
Hungry for her breakfast.

Her hair is black as a raven's wing
She dances to Elvis the king
As she dances, it's like she's conducting
A never-ending choir.

The day is darkening
The sun goes down
But night never comes
When she's around.

She comes down
To watch TV
'Good morning, goodnight'
She says to me.

Once again
The sun goes down
She gives me a smile
And not a frown

Some people think
That she is a horror
But now you know
About my sister Laura.

Kassie Foden (10)
Felinfoel Junior School

A Day In The Life Of A Goldfish

I swim all day
What can you say
I don't get tired
I just get admired

I eat from the floor
But I want more
I'm an orange fish
And I don't have a dish

Watch out, watch out
I'm swimming about
I am watching the ground
Which I have found

I suck the stones
I'm skin and bones
I'm living with a friend
But he's driving me round the bend

Around, around I swim all day
Dreaming of Camarthen Bay.

Rhys Jones (11)
Felinfoel Junior School

A Day In The Life Of A Spider

This morning I ate my breakfast
As fast as I could eat
I ate it ever so quickly,
I just flopped down in my seat.

Before long it got very sunny,
I got out and spun my web
But instead of doing it properly
I got tangled up instead.

As soon as I got untangled,
I saw a snake as long as a pole
He chased me for a while, so I jumped up in style
And it chased me back down to my hole.

I love my very smart, long legs,
They move so fast when I want them to.
Especially when that snake tried to kill me.
Oh no, I've got a cold . . . atchoo!

Now I'm in bed
All snug and fed,
I loved this adventure,
But it's so nice in bed.

I'm so happy to get rid of that snake,
By pushing it into the lake
I did it with all my might
Goodnight!

Lowri Williams (9)
Felinfoel Junior School

A Day In The Life Of . . .

A day in the life of my sister
Going to school is hard
So she says.
I think
Waking up is hard for her
Not going to school
So I say.
I'm not pretty
She moans.
She may not be pretty
But she's fussy.
She doesn't wake up for a long time
But when she does
She's grumpy.
She hates loads of things
But she loves her bed,
As she sleeps
Dreams float into
Her head.

Victoria Griffiths (9)
Felinfoel Junior School

A Day In The Life Of The Archaeologist Howard Carter

I trample through the gritty sand
With a sieve and shovel in my hand.

I see some buildings up ahead,
But I turn the other way instead.

I stand on something hard and cold,
It may be treasure, it may be gold.

It could be ancient, it could be new,
Or in the world there could be few.

I start to dig I'm getting closer
I may just find a cup and saucer.

But to my amazement that's all I found,
Was a secret chamber underground.

I saw a lot of steps below,
I thought I'd better take it slow.

And there inside I found a tomb,
Containing the corpse of Tutankhamun.

I've worked really hard for today,
So please will you now give me my pay!

Gemma Gibbs (10)
Felinfoel Junior School

A Day In The Life Of A Car

Speeding down the M4 in the hustle and bustle, the noise and fumes, was a little blue car called Sammy.

Sammy lived at 37 Crimson Road Cardiff, with his family. Laura who was seven, her parents Jane and Paul and Will, her older extremely annoying brother, who kept thumping and bumping poor Sammy.

One day in July the family decided to go on a trip to the seaside at Pendine. Sammy was very excited as he had never been there before. Actually, he'd never been to the seaside before.

As they drove through the countryside, Sammy saw some strange black and white animals, they were Fresian cows, but Sammy was puzzled by these animals, there wasn't anything like this in Cardiff.

They reached Pendine and Sammy got another shock, he saw the one and only, extremely famous Babs. He *had* to introduce himself. He shouted,

'Hi Babs.' (It was safe to do this as humans can't hear car language).
Babs replied 'Shwd mai, er who are you?'
'I'm Sammy.'
'Hi Sammy, would you like me to show you around?'
'Yes, I'd love you to.'

They set off around the beach but there was one problem - Babs was too fast. He sped away and left poor Sammy chugging behind. He went back to the parking lot, very sad, and on top of it all, Will returned and all his ice cream melted over Sammy.

He never wanted to come here again! But it certainly had been an experience he'd never forget.

Gwenllian Young (11)
Llanboidy Community School

A Day In The Life Of J K Rowling

The alarm went off again. I had been staring up at the ceiling for about ten minutes. I jumped out of bed and called my daughter as I passed her room. I trotted down the stairs and popped some bread into the toaster, my daughter came bounding down the stairs and gave me a hug.

As my daughter chatted away happily, I buttered the toast.
'Mummy what's the new book about?' she asked, chewing on her toast.
'It's a secret' I replied.

After I had taken my daughter to school I decided to go shopping for a new dress for the 'Blue Peter Book Award' tonight.

I drove to Marks and Spencers, where I chose a light blue dress, marked with a darker blue around the edges. It only cost a tenner (a bargain!).

I went for lunch and suddenly had an idea, I pulled out my notepad and started to write. By the time I had finished writing I realised it was time to pick my daughter up from school.

When we got home I made my daughter some chips, which she wolfed down and I told her to go and play in the garden. By the time the baby-sitter had arrived it was five o'clock and my limo was waiting outside.

When I got to the Hall, everyone was asking me for my autograph. I saw Connie and Matt and waved to them both.

Finally, when the awards were being given out, everyone clapped when I was announced Britain's most adventurous writer.

After the ceremony, I was really pleased with myself because I had won four awards - two for my book 'Harry Potter and the Goblet of Fire' and the other two for the books I wrote for Comic Relief.

Cassie Longford (11)
Llandeilo Primary School

David Beckham

Saturday morning, I've just got up and I need to travel to Manchester for a training session. We are practising our free kicks and corners. During the training I have to take these various moves so that Solkjear can head them in. We were told that the line-up would be - Fabien in goal, Gary, Mikeall, Phil and Joap in defence. I was in midfield, with Paul, Roy, Sherringham and Solkjaer are attack.

I rang Victoria and told her I was in the team for today's game. Alex told me to hurry up as it was almost time for kick-off.

It was great being on the pitch. Phil passed the ball to me and I passed it to Solkjaer, who passed it back to me. I took a shot and it flew into the back of the net.

Forty-five minutes gone and I couldn't wait to hear what Alex had to say. I went into the changing rooms and Alex said to me 'Great game. Keep it up!'

It was the second half and I passed the ball to Vorke. He then passed it back, giving me a chance to take the ball past two defenders and I took a second shot. The ball hit the crossbar and came back to me, I hit it on the volley and again it flew into the net.

Eighty-nine minutes gone and I thought we were going to win the match. But the other teams goalkeeper came out and hit the ball really hard. It went off the post and the referee blew his whistle. We had won the match.

I got home dog tired, but pleased as punch!

Dan Woodhouse (11)
Llandeilo Primary School

A Day In The Life Of My Dad

The day starts when the alarm goes off at half-past six in the morning. Ten minutes later I get up and make a cup of tea for myself and take a cup and a biscuit up to Mum. I drink tea, shave and shower, get dressed and go down and have breakfast.

After breakfast I check that Robert and Andrew are up. Try and enter into a conversation to find out what they are doing today - usually without success.

I check that I have my papers from the previous night, pick up my lunch and leave home to drive to work, usually at 7.30am. I arrive at the office in Swansea at 8.15am.

First job is switch on computer then make a cup of coffee. I then read my e-mails and the Internet and respond where necessary. Next job is to check my diary to see what appointments I have and then talk to my PA and my secretary to see that I have all the necessary papers.

Another coffee, read the newspapers and speak to the rest of the team. Review post and printouts.

Normal day would involve two customer site visits/interviews. One in the morning, one in the afternoon.

Return to office, read messages, e-mails and Internet.

Collect papers to read for tomorrow and leave office, hopefully at 6.00pm. Arrive home at 6.45pm, catch up on the family's day.

Robert Tipton (11)
Llandeilo Primary School

The Terrorists

'Bring! . . . Bring!'
'Hello James. We have a new assignment for you.' said Q
'Okay, I'll be there in an hour,' said James.

James jumped into his car and arrived at HQ twenty minutes later. He was told that his assignment was in Russia and that terrorists had stolen a nuclear weapon. He was to fly into Berlin where he would be met by Boris who would brief him on the mission, give him any guns and gadgets that he would need.

James filled his boot up with guns and drove all through the night, he arrived in Moscow at five o'clock and he checked into his hotel and started to make plans for his raid on the terrorists base.

He decided to arrive as early as possible to try to catch them before they started moving anything. James was sure this was the day that they would try to smuggle the weapon out of the country.

When he got there he opened his sunroof and fired a rocket at the big wooden door, he ran to the boot of his car and got out a machine gun and started shooting the men as they came closer. When he was sure he had killed all the terrorists, he looked around to see where they had hidden the weapon. He saw a helicopter with a nuclear weapon already loaded on board ready for take off. He got in and flew back to HQ.

Good work James!

Matthew Davies (11)
Llandeilo Primary School

THE EXCITED HORSE

Yesterday morning I was grazing in the field in the warm sunshine when Susan, my owner appeared.

'Come on Chestnut!' she shouted to me.

I went up to her and she grabbed my collar and attached the lead to it and led me to my stable.

There Susan tied me to the stable door and started to give me a thorough grooming, even though I didn't need one.

Susan went to lunch and when she came back out she loaded my saddle and bridle into the horse box.

I did not know where or why I was going.

'Come on Chestnut, you're going to London to the horse jumping show,' Susan said as she led me into the horse box.

When we arrived at the grounds I was very nervous, because it was a competition.

'First up is Susan Rees with her horse Chestnut!' the Judge announced. I cleared the jumps and I was in the lead.

After the final jump, the Judge announced the winners in ascending order.

' . . . And the winner of the Champion of Champions is -
Susan Rees with her horse Chestnut!'

The applause was incredible and it was all for Susan and I.
I felt very proud.

Nikki Rees (11)
Llandeilo Primary School

A Day In The Life Of A Magic Book

There was a flash of lightning, I woke up to find myself in the library. It was a bit too quiet for me. I started to wriggle about and fell on the floor.

This boy came over to see what had happened, I saw that it was my rival. He had spiky hair and lots of body piercing. His name is Spike.

'Hiss
Go away!' I hissed.

Spike freaked out then and ran for it. I started giggling but the enormous librarian came over
'You keep falling don't you?' She talks to books.
'If you fall again then you will be put with the baby books,' she said.
She is so annoying!

About an hour later this girl came in. She was half-mortal, half witch. I overheard her speaking to her friends. She suddenly saw me and she hurried over to me.

'I never knew this book was out. I've been waiting for a long time for it to come out. Oh, I've forgotten my library card.'

'Don't worry . . .'
'But . . . But . . . How can you speak?' she asked.
'Secret! If you leave me alone then I can be naughty. The librarian will take me to the back. But before she does you can suggest that you will take me home to stop all the naughtiness.'
'Right!'

So we did that and it was a success. She took me home and up to her bedroom.
'I'm a half-mortal witch called Libby. I've been waiting for this to come out for ages,' she said in a hurry.
'Right!' I said.

The next day it was raining. Libby was moaning for food but her mum wouldn't give her any.
'Please mum, please!' Pleaded Libby.
'No!' her mum shouted.
So she looked in me and found a curse to put on her mum so that she would turn really hot. Libby sneaked some food upstairs so she could eat it.

'That wasn't very nice of you,' I said to he as she walked in.
'Oh, shut up, will you,' she said in a moody tone, 'I'm going to take you back to the library. I don't want a book that is Miss Goody Two-shoes.' So she did.

The library was closed and I didn't turn back into a human.

The next day somebody else took me out, but that's another story.

Sophie Williams (10)
Llangwm (VC) Primary School

A Day In The Life Of Hannah From Home Farm Twins

I woke up to find Spettle lying next to me and Helen snoring. I opened the curtains and called Spettle.
'Come on Spettle, downstairs,' I whispered
'Woof!' Spettle replied.
I crept downstairs with Spettle running behind me.
'What's on the calendar today?' I whispered.
'Oh no, it's Mum's birthday' I said in horror.
I ran upstairs as fast as I could.
'Helen, it's Mum's birthday' I whispered loudly.
I ran to the cupboard to get some clothes.
'Quick, we'll have to go to the Mall' I said.
Helen got dressed and ran downstairs.
'We'll have to give Solo some hay first' shouted Helen.
'Quick then!' I replied

After Helen had given Solo his hay net, we went to the Mall. We bought Mum a gold necklace which cost £70.00 and a huge birthday cake with the words '*We love you'* on it. At ten o'clock we got home, we hid the necklace upstairs and the cake at the back of the fridge.

'Let's muck Solo out' I said to Helen.

We mucked Solo out, did his hay net and water and put his bed down and of course his tea. After that we went inside and called Mum.

'Mum, come here' we both shouted.
Mum came downstairs.
'Happy Birthday!' we all shouted.
'Here's something which we all bought you.'
'Oh thank you, come and give me a hug,' said Mum.
'Are you going to wear it all the time?' I asked
'Yes, I will,' said Mum.
'Goodnight Mum and Dad,' we both said.

Sarah Llewellyn (10)
Llangwm (VC) Primary School

A Day In The Life Of An Ant

I woke up at nine o'clock and went out of my home, which is a box. I saw somebody running past so I bellowed as loud as I could and said 'Hey mister, do you know where I can find food?' But he just ran straight past me and I nearly broke a leg.

So I went to find food, I found five crumbs, I ate them and went back home. But on the way I thought I saw my friend Abigail the borrower, but she went out of sight. I went back and walked across the wall wondering what to do. Then I thought I could get loads of food ready for the winter. On my way I thought I could find a better place as well. I saw someone speaking on something called a telephone so I hopped onto his bag and went into his house with his friend. I saw another ant in a cage and she looked very sad but pretty. I went over to the cage and said to her
'What's the matter?'
'Oh nothing.'

I didn't care about the food or my new home at the moment as long as I was with her I didn't care what happened. She had lightened up my life.

'I heard somebody talking about a party at number one Robinson Street. Do you want to come?'
'Sure I'd love to come,' she sneaked out of the cage and we danced under the moon, outside number one. We started to sing to the music even though it was sort of fast.

After the music had finished we found a crack in the wall and thought that could be our new home.

We lived happily ever after in that new house, we found loads of food and put it inside the crack in the wall. We went outside after the party had finished and watched the sunset. When we were going to sleep in our new home, we were planning what we should do
tomorrow.

Natalie Blyth (10)
Llangwm (VC) Primary School

A Day In The Life Of A Lion

Dossh! A small black bullet came very fast. It was as quick as light, I ducked, it skimmed my tail. I was very worried. A lot of men came with guns, I ran into my cave to hide.

A light shone into the dirty and damp cave. My friend crept to the back of the cave and put her paws over her puppy dog eyes. I thought back to all the good times that Sam and I had had when we were cubs. I wish Sam was here now but he was not quick enough!

'The men are coming. Run back here and keep your head down!'

Ales and I cuddled up together, the men went away and I crept to the front of the cave and popped my head out. I ran to the king lion and told him all about the men.
'There are men in the woods with guns,'
'Okay, go and get Ales and then come back here.'

I ran back to the cave and Ales came with me to the king. He said there is a safe cave on the side of the hill.

'Thank you, thank you. How are we going to repay you?'
'You just have to kill a rabbit and bring it back here.'

It took us two hours to catch the rabbit and I took the rabbit back to the king. It took us three hours to get to the cave and Ales was feeling unwell when we got to the cave. She had a small cub called Simber Sam. We were in the lion's cave and then we all had a lovely party for Simber.

Carwyn Morgan (10)
Llangwm (VC) Primary School

A Day In The Life Of A Dog

Hiya, I'm Ben, I'm a King Charles Spaniel. A dog if you didn't know.

'Hi Ben, do you want a bone?'
Woof, woof, woof.
'Here you go Ben.'
Crunch, crunch, crunch!
Yum, yum, time for a rest.
'Ben, time for a walk to the river.'

Time to stretch my legs for a change.
Ah ha! A cat to chase, you're all mine Mr Pussycat.
'Ben, come back here now!' the master shouted sharply.
There's the river
Splash, Oh ah it's cold.
'Come on Ben, time to go to work.'
There's that pesky cat again
Woof.
'Ben, dinner time.'

I suppose this means boring old gone-off meat and stinky old biscuits again. What do they take me for? Rotten old humans.
Hcy, hcy down hcrc!
Let me out to do my business quickly.
Ahhhh that's better, now let me back in it's freezing out here.
Woof, woof, woof, woof, woof.
Finally in the warm.
Hey now, it's nine o'dog (doggy language) time for bed. Goodnight.

Matthew Pritchard (10)
Llangwm (VC) Primary School

A Day In The Life Of Rolf Harris

Bang!
Ow! (I fall out of bed)
'What's that?' gasped Sheila, she rushed upstairs.
'Fell out of bed again? asked Sheila
'Yes!' I replied
'Well get dressed and I will make breakfast' groaned Sheila.
'Okay' I replied miserably.

I stretched and got dressed slowly . . .
I then had a gigantic breakfast cooked for me by Sheila but it was burned, so I called Pizza Hut!

Once I was ready, I set off to work with a bad back and a big cunning smile, although I didn't know why.

Meanwhile Sheila was racing in her car to see me perform. I raced along to work, however Sheila beat me there.

At work I was performing, I could see Sheila shouting at me to be an excellent performer. I couldn't stand it, she looked so funny . . . I burst out laughing, the camera man looked angry shouting 'Cut!'

We started again . . . 'Gooday! Welcome to Animal Hospital . . .'

I zoomed home in a limo with all my fans sprinting after me for my autograph!

Sheila was in for a surprise!

I'd brought home five dogs, two cats, six hamsters, four budgies and three chinchillas!

However you would think Sheila would leave me for this, but no, she was so happy. She threw the greatest party in the galaxy and a massive sanctuary for animals and you can guess what happened next!

We bought all the animals into the Animal Hospital to make them healthy and then they were all sold as quickly you could say *Alakazam!*

Arianwen Winfield (10)
Llangwm (VC) Primary School

A Day In The Life Of Nick Skelton

It was Saturday morning, I didn't want to wake up because I had to muck out my horses Smartie and Red Morauder.

At breakfast I dropped a dozen eggs I was going to have for my breakfast but I had to have some burnt toast.

Down at the stables Smartie had tipped up his water bucket and it had gone everywhere. All of his straw was dripping wet but I suppose it will be quite easy to muck out because all I had to do was to take all of the straw out.

As I was putting Smartie's head collar on Red Morauder started to rear up. I took Smartie out into the field but as I was opening the paddock gate he pulled back out of my hands and cantered off towards the gate. I ran and shut the gate and then ran to catch him. I managed somehow in the end and put him out in the paddock. The other horses were grazing out in the field one minute and then they started to buck and rear up. I went to put Red Morauder out in the field and he tried to pull back as well but I took a firm hold of the leading rein and opened the gate. I walked out into the field and he was very calm but then I took the leading rein off of him and he galloped off to join his friends.

Whilst I was mucking out Smartie's stable, Smartie was getting bullied, I left him out in the field just for today but if he is going to get bullied tomorrow I will move him into the jumping field. When I was mucking out Red Morauder's stable I noticed that the water from Smartie's stable had run through into Red Morauder's stable. After I'd mucked out, I went to the Co-op, the horse shop.

In the car I was thinking that the day was all going wrong. I went to get some cool mix, bran and oats. On the way home I had to stop and wait for a herd of cattle to cross the road.

Back at the farm some people took their horses out for a hack, I put the horse feed away and went to check if I had any post.

There was one letter that looked very important and I opened it and it said that I was invited to the biggest show in the world in two days time and sorry about the short notice, it will be held at Wembley at 12.00pm and I hope you can join us.

I threw the letter on the floor and as I was just about to run out of the door the phone rang, I answered it and it was Harvey Smith.

'Have you had a letter to go to Wembley in two days time!' he asked.
'Yes!' I replied.
He asked me if I would like to travel up with him and I answered him.
'Yes.'
We were on the phone for at least another hour.

Down at the yard I got the horses in first of all, then I groomed them.
I groomed Red Morauder and my friend Ian groomed Smartie. We cleaned their show saddles and show bridles and their head collars. They looked a dream, they stayed in their stables for the rest of the night.

Back at the house I cleaned my show riding boots, show jacket, show jodhpurs. Harvey and I are going to leave the house tomorrow at six in the morning and when we arrive we are going to practise some jumps first and then we are going to bath them and groom them and plait their manes and tails to make them look their best.

I went straight to bed that night and I slowly drifted off to sleep.

Leanne Murphy (11)
Llangwm (VC) Primary School

A DAY IN THE LIFE OF STEVE TYLER

I woke up trying to get up and open my eyes. Another day of writing songs and signing autographs (I thought). I went downstairs to have breakfast, I got some cereal and put the kettle on for a cup of coffee. Then I turned on the wide screen TV. Then I poured on the milk for my breakfast and my tea and I looked at the clock and it was half-past seven.

After my breakfast I got dressed and had a wash. Then at eight o'clock I went out into my car and started up the engine and went to work. When I got to work I got out of my car and a herd of people were running towards me shouting.

'Can I have your autograph?' So I gave out about 175 autographs. Then I went into work and the boys said 'This is the music of our new song.' So they played it.

'Now all we need are words,' they all said. So I went into my office to write the words. Then at eleven o'clock I had finished it and the song is called 'Jaded'. I played the music and sang the words to get them right, I finished it at a quarter to twelve. Then I had to go home for dinner. After dinner I went back to work and we started to write a new song called 'Just Push Play'. Then we finished it at ten-past four, now we need to write some songs I'd finished it at five past seven and it was time to go so I went out into my car. When I started up the engine a crowd of people came running towards me so I drove off. When I got home I had a lovely roast for tea.

James Davies (11)
Llangwm (VC) Primary School

A Day In The Life Of A Fly

Suddenly I woke up and I was starving hungry. I had to go down to the city dump to get some food. But first I went to get Billy and Bodge. They were twins who lived in an old baseball hat which they had found in the dump, but they couldn't come out because they had to go to the Fly and Ladybug Restaurant for dinner.

I went down to the city dump on my own and there were lots of other bugs there and lots of scraps of food. After I had my breakfast I went back home but on the way I saw a beautiful blue light. It distracted me so much I couldn't stop flying around it for about two hours. Then Thud came and snapped me out of it. Thud is a Ladybug (He's called Thud because he's an enormous Ladybug) I got home about five o'clock but I didn't know why. Then the door opened, it was Billy and Bodge.

'Do you want to come out?' They asked.
'Okay then,' I replied.
So I took them to the dump and after that I showed them the beautiful blue bright light.

Amy Hughes (11)
Llangwm (VC) Primary School

A Day In The Life Of Popstars

Ting-a-ling, ting-a-ling, ting!

'Oh there's the alarm clock going off' I said to myself as I got out of bed and switched the alarm clock off. It was a nice day as you could see its brightness of colour. Anyway let me introduce myself.

My name is Britney Spears and I'm a popstar. I have to go shopping to get new clothes for when I sing on stage in Wales. I made myself look smart and got in the car.

Brumm, brumm!

When I was in town I got out of my car and shut the car door gently. Here I was just outside the shop I wanted to go into. As I walked in there was a lovely pair of black leather boots which I really liked. As I went further down the aisle I walked upstairs and in front of me was a black cat suit. I thought to myself that it would go nicely with the black leather boots, so I decided to get them both. I was very pleased with them and I walked outside to get some fresh air. When I looked up into the sky it was very bright, it was even gleaming into my eyes. I walked to the car and drove quickly to my manager's home to show him my new clothes.

Knock, knock!
'Come in' the manager shouted.
'Hello!' I smiled.

I showed him my new clothes and he was impressed. He told me they would really suit me on stage. I was getting more nervous each hour. As I was leaving, I told him what my hair was going to be like tonight. I told him it would be as bushy as a cloud. Suddenly he jumped up and said 'That's great!' He was even more impressed.

Click! I opened my door which lead into my house and I tried the black leather boots on and the black leather cat suit too. They were beautiful! It was seven o'clock already and I'd had a very nice day shopping, but now I'm going on stage and I'm so excited.

I ran to the car as fast as I could and jumped into the seat. Brum, brum!! I got there just in time. I leapt out and tidied myself up as I was walking towards the door. Click! The door opened, I was behind the stage.

As I was peeping out on stage, there were hundreds of people. Everyone who was backstage opened the curtains for me to sing. My cheeks were as red as a rose and I sang great songs and the most important bit, I would like to say, is I had a great time during my first day as Miss Britney Spears.

Kimberley Waller (10)
Llangwm (VC) Primary School

A Day In The Life Of A Caterpillar

The big day had come. It was time to find out where the biggest, crunchiest, juiciest leaf was. I packed some blankets and a torch in a bag, all ready to go. Almost forgot to go and tell Papa where I was going, the hardest part of the journey as he never stops talking! I think I'll just leave a note, or I'll never get going. So I got some paper and a pen and wrote a little note saying where I was going.

Time to set off, so I crawled along the floor as happy as a May flower. Oh no, mud - yuk! I could just reach some daffodils, so I held onto the necks of the daffodils, swung myself across the mud and landed on the other side of the grass.
'My neck! Hey, what were you doing?' the daffodils yelled.
'Sorry,' I replied and carried on crawling along the ground, greeting all the poppies and the dandelions.
I saw it! I saw the best tasting leaf in the world! Licking my lips, I quickly scurried across the floor heading towards the scrummy leaf.
Suddenly there was a terrible noise. It was getting louder and I saw a human being walking back and forth with something in his hands. The human was pushing it along the grass. I also noticed that wherever the thing was pushed, all of the grass and the weeds got shorter. The human's pushing monster was very close to the crunchiest leaf in the world.
'Oh no, stop, please stop.' But it was too late. The monster had gobbled up the leaf and it was heading my way. I dropped my bag and ran as fast as I could back home. I could hear the monstrous noise becoming gradually quieter and then it stopped. I stopped too. I turned around and saw that the human was putting the monster back into the house.

I looked down and saw that I was in the mud. I had to lift all my feet out and take enormous steps until I was on the other side. I lumbered back home to see Papa looking very worried.
'Where have you been? I've been worried sick. Now you should know never to leave without telling me. Anyway . . . '
'Papa,' I interrupted 'I left a note. Oh look, it's still in exactly the same place as when I left.'

Papa sighed with relief. I looked at my calendar and saw written in bold 'Time to go inside the cocoon'. I told Papa so we got our cocoons and dragged them out and went inside them.

Two months later I tore the cocoon open and Papa and me flew away into the sky together.

Kate McLoughlin (10)
Llangwm (VC) Primary School

A Day In The Life Of Scott Gibbs

I was woken by the sound of my limousine driver pulling up in the drive and he called:
'Scotty, are you up? You've got a big day today.'
'Yah, I'm getting up now. Come in.'
I got my kit ready with my boots, shoulder pads and towel, and set off.

We got to the Millennium Stadium. I put my bag in the locker and headed for the gym. I went on the pedal pushers for an hour.
After the gym I went to the changing rooms to get changed for the game. I was nervous. The manager, Graham Henry, talked to us very seriously.
He said: 'This is a serious game for us.'
We went out and he had confidence in us. We worked up steam and won the game. Our captain was very happy.

Mathew Kiff (11)
Llangwm (VC) Primary School

A Day In The Life Of A Dog

I went to the fair last night and there was a magician. He said:
'A day in a life - which would you be?'
I said, 'It will not work.'
'Come and see for yourself,' he said.
'I would like to be a dog tomorrow.'
'You will be a dog,' he said.
'Really?'
'Yes.'

Next morning I woke up, looked at my legs and they were all furry. I tried to say 'oh my God' but it sounded like 'woof'. I tried to speak but couldn't, so I got out of bed and thought, let's go and be a dog. I'm going to walk like a dog, talk and eat like a dog. First thing, bark at Dad. *Woof! Woof!* Looking good. Now, let's run! Phew, that was good. He is running after me!
Oh no, I am naked in the street. Run! Wow, that was a close one.
I am in bed now. That was fun, I cannot wait until the next fair.

Jamie Smith (10)
Llangwm (VC) Primary School

A Day In The Life Of A Mermaid

I woke up.
'Aaaah,' I took a deep yawn. 'Oh, good morning Anne,' I said.
'Good morning Cherrie,' Anne replied.
Anne swam over to the table with her long brown hair trailing behind her. She picked up a brush and came over to me. She started to brush my blue, waist-long hair. Anne then tied it back with some red seaweed in two plaits.
'I'm going to see my friend today, so please can you try to stop Father looking for me?' I pleaded to Anne.
'Well,' Anne said suspiciously.
'Come on, you're supposed to be my sister,' I added.
'OK, but if you're gone too long, you will get us both into trouble,' Anne agreed.
I swam out of the window with a brown bag and set off to Jade's home.

She met me round the side of her house.
'Come on, my mum doesn't know I've come out,' Jade explained.
We quickly swam to a rock that was halfway out of the water. We looked up at the sky.
'It looks like it's stormy over the ship,' Jade warned.
'Nah, it can't be,' I said.
I quickly dived into the water and held onto Pesky, the dolphin. He was quicker than me and Jade, so I got there in no time. I had to send Pesky back to get her.
When she got here I was already in a sunken ship. I was picking things up, like forks as humans call them. I put them all in my bag and showed them to Jade. She said:
'They look nice, but mine look better,' she boasted.
'Are not,' I corrected her.
'Are too,' she argued.
'Are not, are not, are not.'
'Are too, are too, are too.'
'Are not, are not, are not.'
'Ummm, Jade there is a whirlpool behind you.'
'Oh right, as if,' she joked.

I swam away as quickly as I could. I looked back and Jade was getting further away from me, but closer to this whirlpool. I looked forward, then back. It wasn't far to the nearest sea village but I couldn't leave Jade behind. I went back to her. I tied a strong piece of seaweed round a rock and then round my waist. I let go of the rock and went flying into the whirlpool. Jade was near enough at the top of the whirlpool and I was at the bottom. Jade started to swim down to me when I couldn't go up any further in case the seaweed snapped. She grabbed my hand. I pulled her out and we got back to our village in no time. When we told our parents what had happened to us they were very angry with us, but happy we were still alive. After this lucky break I don't think we will ever go out to the ships on our own again.

Gemma Phillips (11)
Llangwm (VC) Primary School

A Day In The Life Of Suzanne From Hear'Say

I woke up and slowly walked down the stairs and into the kitchen.
'Morning everyone,' I said.
'Morning Suzanne,' said Noel.
I sat down at the table and nibbled on the toast Noel had made for me.
'Kym, Myleene, what do you think I should wear today?' I asked.
'Well, your flared jeans with the rips in would be good,' replied Myleene.
'And your ripped sleeveless top,' exclaimed Kym.
I quickly ran upstairs to get ready for the big, long day ahead of us!

I came back downstairs with all my make-up and everything on and looked like a real *groovy chick!* We all ran outside and stumbled into the limo and slammed the door shut.
We finally arrived at the recording studio and got started. We recorded 'Monday, Monday' first:

'Monday, Monday,
da, da, da, da, da, da,
so good to me,
da, da, da, da, da, da . . . '

then 'Bridge Over Troubled Water':

Like a bridge over troubled water,
I will lay me down . . . '

then last, but not least, our favourite 'Pure and Simple':

'You've been saying I'm driving you crazy,
and I haven't been around for you lately,
'cause I've had a few things on my mind . . .
you know I've been walking around in a daze,
baby, baby,
you gotta believe me when I say,
a oooh, oooh,
wherever you go,
I'm gonna be there,
whatever you do,
you know I'm gonna be there,
it's pure and simple,
yeah, yeah,
I'll be there for you,
pure and simple gonna be there . . . '

We finally finished recording but, it was down to the dance class for us. We danced to 'Pure and Simple' and 'One'. We did all kinds of stuff, from high kicks to caterpillars. We bundled back into the limo after all that hard work. We stopped at the Chinese on the way back home. Three boxes of egg fried rice, two large boxes of chow mein, two bags of prawn balls, four bags of chips and twelve poppadoms.
'I'm stuffed,' said Danny.
'We all agree,' the rest of us exclaimed.
I slowly walked up the stairs and crept into bed. I fell asleep extremely quickly, tired with my new-found pop success.

Kate Bevan (10)
Llangwm (VC) Primary School

A Day In The Life Of The Black Tar Haunter

It was the night when the party began. The waves were gently overlapping each other, but that was just about to change. I gently climbed out of the river and leapt into the swaying bushes.

'That should keep them puzzled for a while,' I giggled to myself.

The fun had only just begun when a mysterious looking man walked into the bushes. Oh no, what was going to happen?

I had a plan. 'Come here man,' I whispered. 'Over here stupid,' I said again. 'Right then, let's get things straight. You do not speak or move unless I say.'

'OK,' he said looking very worried.

'I want you to do this. Walk down to the river and wait for me.'

Splish! Splash! Splosh!

'Right. Go out deeper, as deep as the top of your head.'

'But . . . '

'No buts, just do it,' I demanded. 'Stay there.'

Ahh! Splish! Bubbles were drifting to the surface. Bye bye! And do you know what? They never knew he was gone.

I wonder what I shall do next. I shall finish what I started. OK, let's think. Ah, seaweed. I will throw seaweed at them. *Splat! Splat! Splat!* Ahh! Ahh! Ahh!

And from then on, no one knew who it was . . .

Zoë Studley (10)
Llangwm (VC) Primary School

A Day In The Life Of A Celt

The noise of the war horns echoed through the land. The Romans were getting near but we were much better warriors than they were. We were prepared and anyway we knew this land inside out. The Romans just knew they had to fight. We had our plans, we would all spread out then charge. The horn blew again. They were getting closer. We all got on our horses ready to ride to the huts. I've got my spear. I'm behind a hut. We blew our war horn.

Suddenly a massive ball of fire came over the wall, then our door started to break - they were in. I threw my spear but it missed. I couldn't go to get it because it was too close to a soldier. I had no weapon, I was vulnerable. What should I do? I stayed as still as possible. I remembered the trap door. I ran but I saw a sword come flying towards me. I dashed out the way. I picked up a shield and I ran. I made it through the trap door. Yes, no one was there. I lay down and closed my eyes. When I awoke there were two soldiers with knives either side.

I awoke in a cold sweat. I had had a dream, well not a dream, a nightmare!

Amy-Jayne Nevins (10)
Llangynidr Primary School

A Day In The Life Of An Astronaut

The engine rumbled as we speedily set off into space. Fiery, tongued flames shot from the rocket's exhaust as we stared through our capsule at the wonders of the stars. Gigantic meteorites and comets whizzed past in a blur and we passed bright halos of cloud suspended in the surroundings. Spiralling circles of gas twisted in the supernatural atmosphere like wispy whirlpools.

I was so excited. We were heading for Pluto and we were going to be the first humans ever to land on the planet. My feet tingled in my metal boots and I was sweating vigorously with anticipation.

Then my heart seemed to stop beating as I sighted our destination sparkling in the sky. The rocket shook and rumbled making a deafening noise as we landed. The exhaust gave one last vibrating rattle then everything was quiet.

My foot crunched on the icy, barren plain of Pluto as I stepped out. Three other astronauts jumped out and started taking samples of the frozen rocks, which lay scattered. I set off exploring the silent planet my suit rippling in the icy wind.

My oxygen was running low so I headed back towards the rocket. Suddenly I realised the other astronauts were taking off. They were going to leave me behind. I grabbed a loose pipe hanging underneath the ship and started to climb. Suddenly I slipped. My oxygen pipe burst and my suit was ripped to shreds. Then as if a giant hand had grabbed me I was sucked up into the enveloping blackness.

Ioan Manson (11)
Llangynidr Primary School

A Day In The Life Of The Loch Ness Monster

One morning while I was eating fish in the deep, dark lake, I heard a noise on the surface. It was a line of boats scanning the lake trying to find me. I quickly found a cave and hid. One hour later the boats came back. As soon as they had gone I came out of the cave to finish my breakfast. I knew they wouldn't come back for days, but I was wrong.

Later that day they came back, there was no cave around to hide in. I swam as fast as I could but they caught me. They put a net in front and behind me. I had nowhere to go. Eventually I had to give up, I was gasping for air so I surfaced. As I surfaced they threw a net over me, I was trapped. They brought a huge ship out and reeled me in and put me in a cramped cage. When they got back to the shore they left me on the ship and then went for lunch. Now was my chance. I swung my tail and broke the bars, I then quickly slithered over the edge of the ship and I was free. I quickly swam out to the deep, dark lake never to be seen again.

Nicholas Thomas (10)
Llangynidr Primary School

The Day In The Life Of An Ant

One morning I woke up and found myself outside down on the ground and I was very small. I found out that I was an ant.

The first thing I did was collect food. I had to walk quite far. I wasn't going very fast and everything was huge compared to me. I got up a tree and bit a part of a leaf. Then a huge colony of ants came charging at me. I ran to my home as fast as my legs could carry me.

When I was at my house I turned around and the colony of ants had gone. I said 'That was close.' I ate the food that I had got.

Late midday I went out for a walk. Then a giant foot came down. There was bubble gum on the bottom of my shoe. I was trodden on and got stuck in the bubble gum. It seemed like I was flying through the air. Then I got out of the bubble gum. The gum was getting dry but it was wet enough to stick to me again. This time when I was away from the bubble gum, I ran home even faster than before.

Three hours later a huge bug came after me. The bug caught up with me and swallowed me whole - I was still alive. Then I bit the bug inside and he spat me out as far as possible.

Two hours later I found I was only a five-legged ant. I grew another leg and one hour later I turned back into a normal human being.

Richard Hansford (9)
Llangynidr Primary School

A Day In The Life Of A Mouse

I woke up to find I was lying on the bare, damp floor. I looked above me and saw a leaky, dripping pipe. There was a small crack in the wall where the only light came through. All was silent in the dark hole in the wall. My small hands touched my small furry body. I had become a mouse!

I crawled over to the crack to find a furry, gigantic creature towering above me - the cat! A great roar of the mammal frightened me to death. The cat opened its black mouth and sunk its teeth into my furry body. The cat put me in its mouth and closed it. I was trapped! I bit the cat's long, pink tongue. 'Miaow!' It screamed, opening its mouth. I jumped out while I had the chance and dashed upstairs, but something delayed me. Very much to my surprise I saw a piece of cheese on a small plank of wood with a metal attachment on the other side. Clumsily, I grabbed the cheese and the metal attachment flipped over. It was a trap! I struggled to get out of the wooden structure but it was useless. But then I had an idea! I started to nibble the trap away. It worked! Eventually I got out of the trap and went into my room. It was very difficult to get up onto my bed but at last I got there, tired and very sleepy. I dozed off to sleep. In the morning I was back to my old human self. What an adventure I had!

Sam Jobbins (10)
Llangynidr Primary School

A DAY IN THE LIFE OF AN ALIEN

Lugia picked up the engine and threw it in our evaporation bin.

'Why do astronauts always land on our planets?' I said.
'Dunno, replied Zetrogin (Lugia's girlfriend.) 'But why don't we have breakfast?'
'OK,' I replied.

After a breakfast of astronaut on toast we went to the 5-60 spaceship. It took us everywhere. Today we were heading for Venus to see our friends, the oucher-pouchers, who had just taken an astronaut captive.

When we arrived we had to put on our super-cool-down boots because the heat was too hot for us Binker-roos. The oucher-pouchers said to us 'Human called Neil Armstrong we put him in a ship and throw him to Earth.' The oucher-pouchers are really hard to understand. We had some coffee then went to Saturn to see the Swordtails, then we headed to Martian Waerseekerusa (a planet theme park.) At the park I went on space race and Human Killer (both roller coasters!) Then Lugia, Zetrogin and I headed home. On the way home we almost hit Earth and a comet nearly crashed into us.

At home Lugia and I played a game of hide and shriek with some banshees next door, then had fire shrimps for tea. After that we all went upstairs I shouted goodnight to everyone before I fell asleep. Another space day in over.

Daniel Langhorn (11)
Llangynidr Primary School

A Day In The Life Of A Celt

The huge battle between the Celts and the Romans is taking place tomorrow and I, Oriten, am getting ready for the battle.

As I put my war paint on my face, arms and chest I was thinking about how the battle would take place and if I would live or die. I sharpened my spear and fixed my armour - the thought of dying still in my head. I couldn't bear the thought of facing the strong and powerful Romans tomorrow out on the battle field. All my friends were mending the golden chariots, their golden, grand flags blowing in the wind. The captain called us in for a talk about where our positions were in the battle. I was up-front with the shields and spears. It was my job to change into the shield of Romans and break them down but also, that was the most dangerous job of all because there was a row of Roman archers behind them.

The captain told us all to go and get to sleep early. That night I couldn't get to sleep, I was so scared and yet so eager to battle now. The captain's eagle was howling in the dark night.

In the morning I woke up to hear the war horns howling. I gathered my weapons and armour, put on my shoes and walked out of my tent. We all had breakfast and set off. When we arrived at the huge field which would soon be filled with blood and dead bodies, we heard the evil sound of the tramping Romans feet moving across the field. Then we saw them! The battle would begin.

Daniel Wood (11)
Llangynidr Primary School

A Day In The Life Of Julia Roberts

9.00am - I eat my toast and low fat butter at my home in England. I am careful not to spill black coffee down my white dressing gown. Next is a hot bath and a face pack but I look at the clock and decide not to - my personal trainer will be here in ten minutes. Instead, I put on my lycra gear, get a towel from the airing cupboard and bounce down to the gym.

12.00pm - After a hard session with Mike, my trainer, I'm ready for a day's shoot in Hampstead. I grab my keys, coat and another piece of toast as I clip-clop out the door. My car, as always, is parked on the curb outside my Victorian mansion and my agent, Katie, is waiting by the bushes.

3.00pm - I'm halfway through a tiring shoot for my new film, Notting Hill. After a light lunch with Hugh Grant, I am back on set.

5.00pm - I head to The Ritz for tea. Katie is nattering away to me and I look at this genius who had made me famous. Thank you, I think as we draw up outside the hotel. I put on my dark glasses to protect me from the dreaded press and run up to the door.

7.00pm - I am now back at home, full of a delicious three course meal. I ring up my friend and we have a long talk - goodness knows what the phone bill will be! I eventually get to bed and close my eyes after a long but normal day.

Brodie Hayward (10)
Llangynidr Primary School

A Day In The Life Of My Hamster

I woke up in the morning, Lucy came to give me some breakfast. It was delicious and yummy - it was apples and a little carrot. After that I went to have a sleep.

When I woke up I went on my wheel. After this I went outside in my cage. It was lovely and warm outside. I had some nice cold and clean water. I was being silly and naughty - I got told off. I bit my owner's thumb. Lucy said that she wasn't going to give me any treats until tomorrow.

Today, Lucy put me in my plastic ball and I ran around the sitting room bumping into the furniture. Rover the cat tried to catch me and eat me. I was frightened. Lucy saw me, I was very happy. Lucy put me back in my cage to be safe. I went in my cage, it was night-time. I went on my wheel. After that I went upstairs to my house and I got some food from my bowl and in the morning I went to bed to go to sleep and rest.

Lucy Jackson (8)
Lyndon School

A Day In The Life Of My Pet Dog

Today I woke up, I could not believe that Mish was coming to give me some food. But no I forgot, I don't get food in the morning. Anyway, Mish is going to take me for a walk. Oh yes, we are going on the quad bike. Oh good, a hole to dig now. Yes, yes, I have found a rat. Oh no, it is not a rat it is a nettle. Ouch! That hurt. Mish, Mish can I have a doc leaf please?

Marisha Chelsey Robinson (9)
Lyndon School

A DAY IN THE LIFE OF NATALIE

I woke up at 9.00am (very early for me.) I went downstairs to have some toast and I asked Mum if I could go shopping today. Mum sad 'Yes, but hurry up Natalie.'

At 9.30am I got dressed into my DKNY dress that is blue because it's 28°c outside so why not? At 10.10am I had a drink of Danone Activ and said goodbye to Sid. I go in the car but Kristen came (my big sister.) Kristen decided to take me shopping so we left the house (at last!)

We got to Chester at 11.00am. We ran to Junior to get some clothes. We got a DKNY skirt and a DKNY shirt to go with the skirt, and a DKNY dress. We went to a shoe shop hoping to get ten inch shoes.

As soon as I finished shopping I fell asleep in the car. At 6.15pm I got home and watched TV until 11.00pm, then went to sleep.

Sarah Morris (11)
Lyndon School

A DAY IN THE LIFE OF ME

It was my 3rd birthday and I was not having a birthday party at home, I was having a party in Spain. I was really excited I was having family only and it was also my mum's birthday.

I woke up at 8.30 to find my mum, my dad, my grandma and my grandad all outside. They didn't notice I was awake because they were too busy preparing the party.

At about 9.00 I got out of my room and went to my mummy and asked her if I could watch TV. Mum said no, but I could go swimming with daddy. When I had my swimming costume, armbands, sun cream and a rubber ring on, I was allowed to go swimming with daddy.

At 9.30 we came back from swimming, got dried and dressed. My mum went shopping and I stayed behind with daddy and papa and watched TV. Dad said I could have an ice cream or lolly with him.

At about 12.30 Mum rang to tell them to put me to bed because of all the presents.

After two hours sleep mummy woke me up and said to come outside.

When I went outside there was a *big* cake, lots of presents and lots of food. When I had opened all my presents my mum said there was just one more present which was a cute, little teddy bear.

After clearing up at 6.30 we got ready to go for a proper meal to celebrate my mum's birthday.

Felicity Collins (10)
Lyndon School

A Day In The Life Of A Spider

I was out hunting all night last night and I am exhausted. I had a really good dinner. I had three flies and two wasps - it was really nice. Today I am going to weave my web. It will take two or three days to make, I will have to weave all night and all day tomorrow to get halfway through. No fly will be able to get through.

I will be stopping for lunch with my best friend Phil, we have such fun.

By the way I am called Eddie the black widow. I live in South America in a very big wood there.

When I got to Phil's web he was still weaving it. Phil and I have great fun pulling down distress flies. We hate flies, they sting our good friend the big lion, Linal the ruler. One day he was lying in the sun and I was sitting catching him. Suddenly a wasp flew up and stung him. I jumped up and saved him. He was very pleased that I had saved him.

When I have finished weaving my web I will rest for three days.

Samantha Bream (11)
Lyndon School

A Day In The Life Of Cleopatra

Hello, I'm Queen Cleopatra of the Nile. I am the daughter of King Ptolemy XII of Egypt. On the death of my father I have succeeded to share the throne with my brother Ptolemy XIII. Although I'm being driven into exile by supporters of my brother, Julius Caesar defeated my opponents and my brother, Ptolemy XIII, was killed. I was proclaimed Queen of Egypt but I had to share the crown with my other brother Ptolemy XIV. I then gave birth to my son, Caesarion. After that Ptolemy XV claimed Caesar as the father.

I lived in Rome as Caesar's mistress (for a while) then Caesar got assassinated. I moved back to Egypt but Ptolemy XIV did not like that so I decided that I was sick of sharing the throne and I poisoned him and made my son Caesarion my co-regent. Also Mark Antony succeeded Caesar as joint ruler of Rome, with Octavian and Lepidus.

I summoned to meet Mark Antony and lived with him in Alexandra. I gave birth to my lovely twins. I married Mark Antony and gave birth to my next child. After a while my dear husband announced the division of the former empire of Alexandra the Great and me and my children.

Later on, Octavian declared war against Antony and I. We defeated the battle of Actium, overjoyed about the news that I wanted to contact Antony but one of his soldiers said that he'd committed suicide. So my dear Anthony killed himself because he couldn't bare to live if it was without me. I'm feeling very depressed I'm not sure what to do but I feel that I must act quickly before Octavian tries to take the Egyptian throne but with my children I must think of their safety - that was the story of my life.

Natalie Jones (11)
Lyndon School

A Day In The Life Of Myself

On the 20th May 2001 I went to see my third cousin for the first time. John had travelled from New York to Wales to meet his family. Although he was born and brought up in New York he can still speak fluent Welsh. His mother had taught him to speak Welsh. My grandmother was named after his mother Barbara.

Barbara had emigrated to America when she was 23 years old and married an American. John had traced his family tree back to my mother's grandmother's parents and that's a long way!

We all met at Mum's cousin's house in Llanrwst on Sunday afternoon. It was a lovely day, I was in charge of the bar.

John had photos of a lot of our relatives and it was funny to see how the boys used to be dressed as girls when they were babies.

John has put all photographs into a big album with certificates. He had got his parents' birth certificates, wedding certificate and death certificate. It was very heavy and he had carried it from New York.

John is staying with a friend of his at Bethesda, who is also married to an American. When John met his family for the first time he got very upset because it made him think of his mother travelling so far on her own so many years ago. John has four children and seventeen grandchildren. He returns to New York with his wife next week.

Catryn Roberts (10)
Lyndon School

A Day In The Life Of Molly

I don't remember when I was a kitten. I don't remember the nasty people who dumped me outside and then went away. I do remember the cold, white snow one evening when I was digging for shelter after they left me. My paws' fur was frozen and I couldn't understand why anyone would do this to me. I had no food and felt cold, miserable, tired and unwanted. The snow was crisp and deep and I struggled to keep warm. Luckily someone had told the Cats Protection and I was taken to a nice old lady who looked after cats like me. She spoke to me and stroked me until my purr came back. She was small and grey with a soft voice. She called me Tabitha and gave me a snug bed to lie in for my first night. I felt better out of the snow, but still lonely.

I was in a house full of cats but I was the only tabby and white one. 'Rather common,' I heard someone say, even though I thought I was quite beautiful. People called all day, always looking for a cat, always wanting a certain colour and never much looking at me. Breakfast and lunch had both been interrupted by noisy people saying 'Puss, Puss, here kitty, kitty,' and I carried on eating, not wanting them to share me at all.

Then it happened - it was 3.55pm exactly. The door opened and a little girl in a royal blue uniform walked in with her mum and brother. She looked at me kindly and bent down and stroked me. It was a lovely stroke from head to tail and I just had to roll over to show them my tummy and how affectionate I really was, and how I liked the look of them. 'Please choose me,' I miaowed.

The little girl called Rebekka said 'Oh Mum, we have to have this one, she is beautiful.' I was now purring at the top of my voice. Could they hear me? To make sure I rubbed in and out of all their legs, in and out and round and round. *It worked!* I heard the magic words 'We'll take her.'

I was so excited, I had forgotten my cod and salmon tea. There was no need to worry because Rebekka took me home to her family and helped me settle in, fed me and stroked me and loved me (they even kissed me, which I don't remember happening before.)

It was the happiest day of my life and I snuggled into my new bed and still had eight lives left in a happy home, in cat heaven, and Molly is my lovely new name.

Rebekka Baddeley (11)
Lyndon School

A DAY IN THE LIFE OF MY MUM, KAREN SAUNDERS

I woke up this morning at 5.00 to hear a vigorous knocking on the downstairs windows. I went downstairs to see what it was. It was the crows again. I knew I had to get something done about it before they scratched all of the paint off the windowpane. All the windows were scratched. I better get back upstairs before I wake someone up. As I was walking out of the kitchen on the tiled, cold floor, I heard the floorboards creaking gently. I didn't think it was my husband or my oldest daughter, Indya, because it was a too softer movement. I walked out of the kitchen onto the furry green carpet. I looked out of the front door at the pinky-blue sky, then I heard a little voice saying 'Mummy, can I watch the Dalmatians in your bed with milky?' said my youngest daughter Clementine.
'Oh darling,' I said softly, 'did the naughty crows wake you up?'
'Yes they did and I can't get back to sleep.'

I decided to take her into the playroom and put her video on and got her some warm milk in a bottle. Since it was nearly 6.00 I went and got the video and slid it into the video player. Clemmie started to enjoy the first part of the story but when I gave her her milk she went to sleep halfway through. I picked her up gently, her long golden curls fell over my arms. I walked up the stairs with all her weight on me. I put her back in her bed and pulled the covers over her gently. I walked along the hall back to my bedroom. I got back into bed and tried to get back to sleep.

Suddenly I heard a beep, beep, beep, beep. I felt like I had only been asleep for two minutes but it must have been longer. I heard a groan and a bang of a hand on the alarm clock. I got out of bed and went to wake up the girls. I opened the curtains in their room and a piercing light shone through. Indya woke up twitching her eyes and Arabella turned around a bit and rubbed her eyes furiously. I shouted 'Come on, get up or you're going to be late for school.' I went and started to run my shower, the cold water trickled on my fingers. I went and got my towel and put it on the towel rack. I opened the door and stepped into the shower, the warm water pouring down my back. I picked up the bottle of shampoo and squeezed it into my hand. I rubbed it into my hair vigorously.

I washed the rest of my body with bodywash, then got out of the shower and dried myself with my towel, it was all soft and warm. I went into my room and got dressed. I dried my hair quickly with the hairdryer and then after it was dry I brushed it through with my hairbrush. I went into the girls' room to see if they were dressed yet. When I went in Arabella was just getting her socks on but Indya was dressed and had already put her hair up. I took Arabella into my room and grabbed the brush and bobble in a hurry because it was nearly 8.00 and they hadn't had their breakfast. I brushed Arabella's blonde streaked ginger hair. It was like rats' tails because she always turns around a lot in the night and it messes her hair up. Every time I went through a bunch of hair the hairbrush got caught in a knot and there was a scream from Arabella. Finally, after I'd brushed her hair thoroughly I put her silky hair into a firm ponytail tightly. I took them downstairs to have their breakfast. I got out the Weetabix and put two into two bowls. I went to the fridge and got out the milk. I poured it onto the Weetabix and went to the cupboard to get out the sugar. I sprinkled it on, got two spoons out and gave the girls their breakfast which they scoffed down.

When they had finished I told them to go upstairs and brush their teeth. I don't normally have breakfast so I just took an apple and put it in my handbag to eat on the way to work. 'Arabella, Indya, come down and get your shoes on, you're going to be late for school,' I bellowed. I heard a running of footsteps and in came my two daughters. They got their shoes on, I quickly went and got mine, I grabbed the car keys and rushed out the door to the car.

The morning was bright but the dew on the grass sparkled like diamonds in the sunlight. We got straight into the Range Rover. I started up the car, its engine crackling. I reversed and drove down the drive fast. The journey on the way to school was silent because they had got to sleep late and they were tired. When I arrived outside the school gates I dropped them off and said bye and hoped they had a good day. I drove off but those stupid traffic lights stopped me. I had to wait for ages. I pulled out when they turned green and started my journey to Chester.

Just as I went round a corner this old man pulled out in front of me and I nearly hit the bollard. I pipped him loudly and overtook him. When I arrived in the Chester car park I stopped and paid the man £3.50 for a day and told me where to park. I got into the space easily, probably because I was parked next to no one. I got out and walked into our Optician's Practice in the Chester Precinct. We have a selection of glasses and sunglasses. When I arrived at the shop it was 10.00. I met Jan and Debbie at the door - my two most newest staff. 'Hi!' I said pathetically. I put my bag behind the desk and looked at the orders for today. I re-did the window. I took out the Oakley sunglasses and put in the Chlóe hearts. I took out the Moschinos and put in the Gucci sunglasses.

It was 12.00 when I'd finished the window so I told Jan and Debbie to go and have lunch. I had forgotten to have my apple on the way to work so I had it for lunch. Just as I had finished it Mrs Sparrow walked in. 'So are my sunglasses here yet because I'm going on holiday tomorrow?

Great, yes they are here, I thought. 'Yes, they are here,' I said. 'I'll just go into the back and get them.' I routed them out and asked her to try them on.
'They feel a bit tight,' she said. 'Could you loosen them for me dear?'

I took them off gently. 'Oh yes, sure,' I said. I started to adjust them and fitted them on her.
'Thank you very much indeed,' she said and she walked out.

Debbie and Jan came back at 1.15. Mr Jones came in at 3.45 to pick up his glasses, he was pleased. He thanked me when I gave him the glasses and said he would recommend us. It was getting really stuffy in Chester so I went and got the fan. Miss Tucker didn't come in for ages, it was a good job too because her sunglasses hadn't arrived. Just as she came in the postman walked in at the same time. I took the sunglasses off him and thanked him. I opened the box and took them out carefully. I placed them on Miss Tucker's eyes. I checked they were okay and she paid the balance.

It was 5.45 so I thought I better start my journey home. I told Jan to lock up and Debbie to go home. When I arrived at the car park I got my keys out and unlocked the car. I started the engine and I was off. Chester looked very pretty as I drove through, the river gleamed in the moonlight. The lamp posts lit up making Chester look like Santa's grotto.

When I arrived at home I got everything out of the car and locked it. As I walked into the kitchen there was this lovely smell. It must have been my steak and kidney pie. I went and got it out of the oven. I got a knife and fork. I started tucking in, it was gorgeous. After I finished I put my plate and cutlery into the dishwasher. I got out a cup and poured myself some water, I gulped it down quickly and thirstily. I went into the lounge and asked my husband, Quentin, if he'd put the girls down. He said he had. I said I was going up to bed because I was tired. I took off my dirty clothes and got into my pyjamas. I took the covers off my bed, got in and fell fast asleep.

Indya Saunders (10)
Lyndon School

A Day In The Life Of My Kitten

I woke up this morning and I saw Fern walking down the stairs. I ran to her and lay on her shoulder. She gave me my breakfast and water, then she let me go outside but I didn't want to go out. I ran back in the house. Fern's uncle scared me and I ran to Fern. She lifted me, then Fern's uncle Shamus came to help her look after me.

My uncle came again and scared Snowflake. Fern took me to the vet because I wasn't feeling well. Fern wasn't feeling well either because she had just had her tonsils out and I had an operation so I wouldn't have kittens.

When I felt better, and Fern felt better, I played with my master and then went to sleep.

Fern Wickham (7)
Lyndon School

A Day In The Life Of Myself

The morning of May 18th 2001 - my mum called me down for breakfast 'Matthew!'

After breakfast Mum took me to Christian's house to rollerblade. As soon as I got to Christian's house he got on his skateboard and I got on my blades. Christian's brother, Ben who is 16, got on his BMX. We went on his ramps on the drive and I learnt how to do a proper grab. We skated until it was lunch time.

After lunch we came back out to skate and we learnt how to do some more tricks. We went down to the park and skated down the slopes.

When we got back we practised a few more tricks and then went into watch telly. At about 6 o'clock my mum arrived to pick me up. She was with Debbie, Alex and Sam. We all then went to 'The Nol' for our tea. We all fancied steak, chips and garlic bread, so that's what we had. We then took Alex, Sam and Debbie home and went home ourselves at 9 o'clock.

Matthew Cripps (9)
Lyndon School

A Day In The Life Of A Spider

As I crept along the ivy leaf a large sparrow had followed me every pitter-patter of the way. I turned around in a creepy turn just to see if I had not mistaken my gaze, its large, beady eyes staring down at me. Emerald and hazel, a look of confusion of why I hadn't scuttled away or of why I just stood there looking at it, but happiness shone in those big round balls as well a look of food and easy prey , but I was not going to be that easy. I started one way then the other, careful not to get too close. Easy does it, then *bam,* he went for me. I spun a piece of my silky thread which I was once amazed by, but now I take for granted. I spun the silk across the leaf but I dropped it so to succeed I tried again, but I did it this time. I crossed it over and over again, three more crosses then it would be complete. I did it and scuttled back.

I stayed at my new home for a day or so, then I was to move on to another part of the wood where I would build another home, get a wife and new children. It is not safe for a spider like me to stay in one place for too long. I will attract birds of many kinds who try and feed on me. I trotted across the web to another leaf where I spotted a green fly. I crept up and out my feelers came - lunch, easy lunch, that is one of my favourite things. I went back to my new web and spun some of my silk into it. I like to eat green fly but when the big animals come, like horse fly, they are extremely delicious and it is named 'catch of the day' by one of my friends I see once a month as she lives far away on the ground. She is very sneaky and sly and hasn't been trampled on yet. she has had over four near-death experiences! I manoeuvred back to my nest and sat there to eat the fly wrapped in tasty silk. Not only does it do the handiwork, you can even eat it.

Once I have mated, I will go and build a nest in a house in a nice, cosy corner because all the flies and mites make a lovely meal. All the houses have millions of corners to live in and furniture to hide behind when hunting. In houses though, people put you in water or down the water whirlpool if you go into the soap room.

I am now in the tough bark of a tree looking for caterpillar because if you can kill them the tails make tea. I need some liquid from the tree skin because the bug catching makes me thirsty, as I am little. I have seen caterpillar over there. If I'm quick I'll catch it. Yes, I've caught it. I cut the caterpillar's tail off and carry it home but there's a spider twice the size of me breaking my nest, so I drop the tail and run to safety. From now on I will make nests in bark so that's what I've done, and now I will go to sleep for the time being.

Victoria Still (11)
Lyndon School

A Day In The Life Of Hanna Jones

I woke up at 6.00am, got dressed into my jodhpurs and shirt, and put some old clothes on over the top. I went to see Kizzy my horse. Kizzy was lying down in her stable sleeping. She woke with a start when she saw me. She stood up when I went to get her for her breakfast. When she had eaten it I bathed her and scrubbed her stable stains off. I dried her bay coat shiny clean and sprayed her mane and tail with special spray so that the hairs didn't come out when I brushed it. Then I plaited her tail and put the tail bandage in. I plaited her mane and rolled it into balls and put her rug on. Then I led her into the trailer and gave her some hay to eat.

I went to have breakfast. I made some feed for Kizzy and some sandwiches and crisps for me for lunch at the horse show. I loaded up the car with jackets, a riding hat and our lunch. We were off to Birchenley Manor (horse show.) It took us one hour to get there.

It is the 24th July 1998. The class we were in was at 9.00am so we had lots of time. I saddled her up and worked her into a nice trot then a canter. I slowed her down and walked her around, and went in the class. There were thirty-two competitors including myself. I was pulled in 15th. It was my turn. There were ten fences to clear, all of them about 3ft 3 inches high. Kizzy cleared all of them but I lost my balance on the 5th, but stayed on. When everybody had done them I knew we hadn't won because I had lost my balance.

We were all walking round, the judge was looking at us then the others. To my amazement we were pulled in 1st - it was the greatest thrill of my life, we were actually pulled in 1st out of 32 starters. The judge gave us a bright red rosette. We cantered around the ring very happy. We both had lunch and then went home. You could see Kizzy was happy too. I put her in her nice clean stable and she went to sleep.

Luci Duncalf (10)
Lyndon School

A Day In The Life Of My Little Sister

Today I woke up and heard Sally downstairs, so I went down just to annoy her. I started to sing, I really don't know why. She really despairs of my singing. Sally went upstairs to get away from me, but I don't like being on my own so I went upstairs to Mum and Dad's room. Mum was in the hall ironing my school dress. I put it on and had my breakfast, then watched the Pocket Dragons ''til it was time to go to school.'

Today I was going to make gingerbread men with Mrs Millar. First we did some maths and I got a star for being the only one who got four plus four right. At playtime I got a graze on my knee. At lunch time I was really hungry, it was a good thing I liked this dinner the best because it was fish and chips. After dinner I went out to play but Sally was still eating, so I played with Hanna for a while and then we went inside for a little bit of free time. I played on the computer.

After I went to play scheme and watched the Tweenies. Mum came late. In bed I thought of my pleasant day I'd had.

Sally Cunliffe (9)
Lyndon School

A DAY IN THE LIFE OF . . .

When I woke up in the morning I went into the bathroom to look in the mirror. I saw that I had still got my suntan. I washed my face and hands and went back into my room to get dressed. I brushed my hair then I went downstairs to get my breakfast. I came down to discover my mum was up and dressed ready to go to work - I couldn't believe my eyes. She turned round and said 'Breakfast?' happily.
'Why are you up so early?'
'Nicholas started crying.'
'Did he? I didn't hear him.'
'That's because you were fast asleep.'
'Was I?'

Stop chatting.. Come on eat your breakfast, you don't want to be late for school do you? I ate my breakfast, put my coat and shoes on and got into the car, put my seat belt on and my mum came, so we went to school.

I was late for school. 'Oh no!'
'You're late!' shouted Mrs Cracker.
I said sorry and sat down next to my best friend Arabella. 'Hi!'
'She shouts at you for no reason.'
'Tell me about it?'
'Um you two, stop talking. All right. OK everyone, line up,' said Mrs Cracker. 'OK, English books out. Today everyone, we are going to learn about friendship, all choose a partner. Where's Arabella?'
'I'm here.'
'OK. As it's Friday I want you all to spend time with each other. You will have to spend Saturday with each other also if you can. Now you can write the day, date and title and put your pens down.

I told Arabella what had happened in Calidor.
'Wow! That must have been fun,' said Arabella.
'It was,' I said.
'OK, today I would like you to write a poem about your partner.
'OK,' said the class.

'Yes, Elise?'
'Um, does it have to rhyme?'
'Um, not necessarily.'
'Good,' I said.

'Break time,' said Miss Robinson. 'Who would like to get the drinks?'
'We would,' I said.
'But Elise,' said Arabella.
'Let's play tip outside.'
'OK,' said Arabella.
'Shall we ask other people to play?' I said.
'Yes,' said Arabella. So we got Fern and Tesni and play Tip. Tesni was on, then she tipped me. I couldn't catch anyone because I'm so slow, then it was time to go to lunch. We had curry for lunch and choc ice for pudding, it was lovely. After, we went to rounders - I would love to go in the rounders' team. It was boiling. My feet go slimy, it's disgusting. After we went home, I went to bed really early because I was so tired - I could sleep for a week.

My mum said 'Are you sure you want to go to bed now?'
'Yes. I'm so tired I could sleep a week.'

Arabella Saunders (7)
Lyndon School

A Day In The Life Of King Urien

I woke up this morning with a big yawn. To my surprise there were Picts marching up the field ready for battle. All my soldiers were ready so I sent them out. When I was ready, the battle had almost finished and only a few of my men survived - it was a terrible fight! They were saying they needed me to keep them in order. After the battle I rode around on my horse hunting for deer. I turned and headed back. When I got back I had my deer and soup with bread.

Later on we sat around the fire, planning our next battle and we were against the Anglos and the Saxons. We drank our wine whilst we discussed a wild plan that would win our battle. Our plan was to hide behind our walls and barriers until we were safe then creep out to attack.

It was a hard battle, though we managed to conquer them. We had to keep guard because we were going to get a lot more enemies.

We sharpened our weapons with a stone and grease. In the morning we were all prepared for the battle. All our weapons were sharpened and our shields were sturdy and strong. We had eaten a hearty meal, we needed good food in our stomachs because we knew we were fighting a strong team.

Then the battle had begun, there were men screaming everywhere. Luckily we survived. I went down to the river to wash my face but while I was doing so I felt someone breathing on my neck. I turned around and suddenly 'bymph' someone killed me!

Harry Pemberton (8)
Lyndon School

A Day In The Life Of My Brother

I woke up this morning and my sister made my breakfast. After that my sister and I went running on the racing track.

My mum bought me a car for my birthday and I paid her back. We went to take my driving test and I failed. The next day I took it again and passed then I went home to sleep.

Next morning I had breakfast in bed and had a relaxing day. In the evening we went to Brewsters and I went to take my sister to Charlie Chalks. I went to order our food. After that we went for a drive. I was the driver and on the way home we stopped at the Shell garage and then went home to sleep.

In the morning we went to a Little Chef for breakfast and then I took my sister to school. I dropped her off and went and got some petrol. At home I asked mum if I could go in my car for a ride. An hour later I went to get my sister and she wanted to go to McDonald's.

Sophia Bennett (8)
Lyndon School

A Day In The Life Of . . . My Pet Hamster

I woke up this morning and as usual, I'm stuck in the pet shop. The pet shop keeper came to give me some food and drink, the keeper is very nice to me but he won't give me a name, don't ask me why because I don't know. I really want to get out of this place, it's really boring.

Suddenly, the family of my dreams walked into the pet shop and funnily enough, bought me! I was so happy, I couldn't wait to get to their house. It was dark in the box but I didn't mind, it was nice to have a family.

When we got to their house, they took me out of the box and put me in a cage, gave me some food and drink and played with me and they gave me a name . . . Chip!

They put me in a ball and when I walked in it, it moved, I'm in it right now actually. (Looking up) - oh help, help, hhhhelp! I'm struck behind the TV. There are lots of wires here and electrical stuff.

Aaa help! I'm being electrocuted!

Oh no! Naughty chip! You shouldn't go round there, you'll be electrocuted screamed Cathryn.

Anyway I'm recovering now.

Samantha Campbell (9)
Lyndon School

A Day In The Life Of Me

On Friday at 12.00 p.m. I was looking forward to home time but not looking forward to the homework. When I get home I am going to climb the trees. Today has been boring so far, except for drum lessons which I think is fun. At the moment the food does not smell too good.

It is soggy chips and peas with fishcake. I don't think I'll eat any of it. I think the pudding is yoghurt. I am inside doing my work now instead of outside playing with my friends. Who would want to be me today?

Michael Mollis Sanders (11)
Lyndon School

A Day In The Life Of My Naini . . .

I woke up this morning and I got washed and dressed. I went down the stairs and had some breakfast. I had muffins with jam. Then Tesni woke up and said
'Good morning Naini, I am going to watch television, OK?'

Then Aron and Jill came downstairs.

Aron and Jill and Tesni had breakfast. After that they went to school. I saw a bit of Kasha, then I went to work. My boss had some interesting pieces of work for me.
'Oh no,' I don't know what this is? It is too difficult so I just left it. I have been on this for hours. Oops I didn't look at the time. It is half past 12. I should be leaving work 5 minutes ago.

I better go, Jill will be wondering where I am. I will go home and have my lunch with Jill, then I will come back and do my work.

'Hi Jill, I got us some sandwiches, they are tuna and salad. I hope you like it? Yet I love it. Yum, yum, I love tuna and salad! Well I better go or I will be late. Bye bye Mum.'

'Bye bye Jill, hi boss, I will get on with my work. There we go, finished! Now I will go to Safeways and get something for tea. I will need some chicken nuggets, chips, peas and cottage pie. Well that's it, I will go and pay.'

'Hello that will be £5.00 please.'

'There we go, thank you goodbye.'

We are home again,

'Hi Kasha, are you on your own?'

'Purr purr' I will take that to be a yes. Oh there's Jill's car, 'Hi Jill, hi Aron and Tesni. Have you had a nice day?

'Yes Naini, yes Naina. Do you have any homework Aron and Tesni.'

‘We have some homework. Why don’t you do it while I make tea?’
‘OK Naini’ Aron said, ‘can you help me with this question?
‘OK I am coming.’
‘I have done my homework.’ said Tesni.
‘So have I’ said Aron. Jill told them they could watch television for a bit. After Jill and I had our coffee, it was time for Aron and Tesni to go to bed.
‘Goodnight Naini.’
‘Goodnight mummy’
‘Goodnight Aron and Tesni.’
Jill and I watched some television and by 11 o’clock, we were both ready for bed.

Tesni Kujore (8)
Lyndon School

A Day In The Life Of One Of The Queen's Servants

One day I was walking along the road looking for any job signs but there were none. I started walking down another road and there was a house right in the middle of the road and it looked quite new and a bit on the posh side. Funny enough, there was a job sign up in the window. Without any thinking I went inside and had the job interview there and then. The job was being a servant for the king and queen. I was surprised at this but I said yes because it would be an interesting job. I would start the next day. I was really excited the next morning, even though I didn't have a clue what it would be like. When I arrived at the palace I was shown around by another servant named Sophie.

The tour took at least one hour because the palace was so big. After the tour I was introduced to the king, queen, prince and princess and then I set off for the kitchen where myself and four other servants prepared breakfast for the king and queen while five other servants prepared food for the prince and princess.

After I had cleaned up, I was cleaning for the rest of the day but it was still very hard work. It wasn't really my type of job. At the end of the day I went to the queen and said I can't take it and I quit.

She wasn't really bothered but she said I could come back whenever I wanted. Nineteen other servants said goodbye to me and then I went home and looked for a job once again.

Emily Harris (11)
Magor (VA) Primary School

A Day In The Life Of The Jungle

One day I went to call for Nathan. We had a play and were bored so we went to call for Owain, Mark and Stuart. We had a play at my home and were bored again. We decided to go and explore. We were walking along and we saw a flap on my home. We went to have a look at it and as we went close to it, it pulled us in. Suddenly the next thing we knew, we were in a jungle. We saw a tiger with its friend lion. They came up to us and said
'Hello, who are you?'
We were very surprised that they could speak English. I said
'Oh hello, I am Andrew and this is Nathan and this is Owain and this is Mark and this is Stuart.'

The tiger said 'What are you doing here?'

Mark said, 'We got pulled through a flap on the wall of Andrew's home.'

The lion said, 'Well this is our home and we are best friends,'

The tiger said, 'Some of our other friends are walking around somewhere,'

Stuart said, 'Well who are your friends?'

The lion said, 'Our friends are cheetah, leopard, cat and kitten.'

Nathan and Owain said 'Well we have got to go home now but we will come and visit you again some time.'

We went back through the flap and all went home.

Andrew Watson (10)
Magor (VA) Primary School

A Day In The Life Of Emile Heskey

I get up in the morning at 8.30am get changed into my swimming trunks and have a quick swim in my pool. I get changed into the red Liverpool home kit for today's match against Barcelona in the finals. It's going to be a good match.

9.45 a.m. I'm driving to the airport to get on the plane to France. The plane seat is first class. It has taken an hour.

As we approach the crowds are flooding in, as we get there, the stadium looked packed and people were still coming in. People were hanging off the security fence and off chairs. This doesn't look right. We trained for two hours and people were coming in at the very last moments.

It was now 5.00 p.m. and the match had started. The stadium can hold 85,000 people but there looked like 110,000. The fence was wobbling. The police were trying to hold everything . . . 'Heskey'

I looked down the ball was at my feet, I ran but lost it. They ran and scored. The crowd was huge, the rail was snapping. We scored the next goal and I scored. We scored again, the barrier snapped and the people fell. The ambulance came. We ran out but the police used tear gas and people were running over people, trying to get out. They were throwing chairs everywhere. We got out and ran to our helicopter and as we went, we heard people screaming.

When I got home, I turned the TV on and it said, '143 killed in stampede.'

Luke Boast (11)
Magor (VA) Primary School

A Day In The Life Of A Dog

Early in the morning, I was getting ready for school when my dog came into my bedroom. I bent down to stroke her but when I stroked her along the back, I started shaking and the next minute I had turned into my dog and my dog was me.

My mum called Jenny but instead of me running down the stairs, Sophie ran down the stairs, then she called Sophie so I ran down the stairs. Then I went into the kitchen to see if there was any food in my bowl, I ate the disgusting dog food. Soon I was in the house on my own. I lay in the sun at the front door.

All of a sudden the postman pushed the post through the letterbox but it landed on me. I got up and started looking at the postman. My mum and dad have just come in for their lunch.

Now they are going back to work. I lay in the sun until Mum comes home.

Jenny Ford (12)
Magor (VA) Primary School

A Day In The Life Of A Cat

One day when I was walking down the road, I saw this gold lamp on the floor. I picked it up and took it home to show my mum and dad. They said to rub it, so I did.

Instantly I shrunk and turned into a ginger tabby cat. I was so frightened that I ran and hid. After a while I heard my mum and dad call me.
'Dan, Dan where are you?' they called.

I came out of hiding and I suddenly had the urge for tuna.

I tried to speak but all that came out was 'miaow'. I ran towards my mum and dad and rubbed against their legs for food. My mum put some left over chicken down for me and I ate it.

My mum then put me out to go to the toilet. I didn't want to go out because I felt embarrassed to go to the loo in front of everybody.

It was getting dark now and I felt like catching a mouse. I sneaked around like an eagle in the sky and I spotted a mouse in the distance. I ran towards it but the mouse heard and ran away. After that I went home and miaowed at the door. My mum let me in and in the morning I was human again.

Daniel Hoffrock (10)
Magor (VA) Primary School

A DAY IN THE LIFE OF MY DOG

I have just woken up and I am looking for some food. I heard Paul and Kiran getting up and getting ready for school. They came downstairs and into the kitchen. They gave me some food and they had their food as well. Before the children went to school, they let me outside into the garden. Then they left for school.

When I am out in the garden, I find a hole in a fence. I then heard the children's mum Sue, calling me. I didn't want to go inside so I went out through the hole. I ran as fast as I could, as I was running towards the school, I saw children coming out of school so I ran even faster. As I got nearer the field, I began to slow down as I got tired.

Then as I reached the field, I began to roll about on the grass and in the mud. Then the sun came out and I began to get hot so I went and laid down in the shade of a tree. In the field I saw a stream so I walked over to the stream and had a drink. I began to get hungry and I could not find any food. I decided that I would go home so I could get some food. I ran all the way home. When I got home I went in through the gap in the fence.

Everybody was happy to see me back home again.

Sascha Spence (10)
Magor (VA) Primary School

A DAY IN THE LIFE OF A KING

A day in the life of a king starts like this, a servant knocks on the door to see if you are awake, if so, he comes in and gives you breakfast and a newspaper for that days news so far. Then after you have had breakfast, washed and dressed, you are escorted to the throne. You are escorted then to the car to visit places that have been on the news or to visit poor people and put a smile on their faces or you and other royalty could go to see the horse racing.

Lots of people can tell if the King or Queen are at the palace or not because if they are not there, the Union Jack is not there. If you were there, the Union Jack is flying.

When you are a King or Queen, every meal is done for you, you don't have to cook at all. Every time anyone speaks to you they always address you as 'Your Majesty' and by no other name.

Stuart Roach (10)
Magor (VA) Primary School

A Day In The Life Of Gary McAlister

I woke up this morning and I suddenly remembered it was the big match today. I went downstairs and made myself breakfast. After that I cleaned my kit and boots and got ready for the bus trip. Soon after the special bus came to take the team and I to the match. Within half an hour we were at Anfield. As we went in, fans were already packing in.

We changed into our kits and walked out onto the pitch. We had won the toss for kick-off which we took, Owen passed to me, I chipped the ball to Babel who was tackled by Giggs who passed to Cole who side rolled a shot at goal just missed.

After the goal kick, Hypia passed to Babel who passed to me. I ran fast to Gerrad who took a flying shot into the net. Only minutes after half-time came. When we went back out, they took kick off and made an attacking run at us.

Just then Beckham crossed and Cole scored the equaliser. Now the pressure was on but in the last minute, Owen crossed to me and I scored just before full time.

Rhys Waters (11)
Magor (VA) Primary School

A Day In The Life Of Mat Pini

My name is Mat Pini, I play for Newport Rugby team, I earn £15,000 per week. We have a big match on the 13th of May against Neath in Cardiff. There is going to be thousands there. The day has come for me and my teammates, we are ready to go on the pitch. The brass band plays, we walk on with our mascot and the crowd cheer Newport, the whistle blows, Neath give the ball a boot up the field and Pritchard catches the ball and runs and passes to Snow but Neath catch the ball and gets a drop goal and get three points for getting it through the H.

It is then we get a try back and a penalty, then we have eight points and Neath get a try and a penalty but missed, the player was so embarrassed.

Then it was the end of the match, 13-8 Newport won, we got our plaque and then held the cup.

David Sefton (10)
Magor (VA) Primary School

A Day In The Life Of Lennox Lewis

I got up about 8.00 a.m. ready to have a light breakfast, after I had eaten I started to train by lifting weights and skipping and a light job. As time went on, I was getting more and more worried. The closer I got to the fight, the more I prayed.

About 1 hour before I got my hands taped up and I got my shorts on and talked to my coach, the time seemed to fly by until I got on my robe and made my entrance with the belts.

As I got into the ring, I saw Hasem Rackman make his entrance, he was dancing and doing his back chat to me, then all of a sudden, the fight started, the first round went neither way and no man was winning, then it went to Round 2 where I worked on a cut in his face but in Round 3 he dominated me and I could only block with my arms, in Round 4 he knocked me down but I managed to get back up and fight but towards the end of Round 5, he knocked me out and that was it. I was out.

Sam Pupic (11)
Magor (VA) Primary School

A Day In The Life Of Gerri Halliwell

Today at nine, I had to go to the photographer's office and I had to go and change for my video shoot, 'It's Raining Men.' That took us an hour. Then at ten I had my video shoot, it was great although it took four hours to do! The producers were funny and great.

Then I went to dinner and I had to sigh loads and loads of autographs. After dinner we had to do it all over again because the producers weren't happy with any of the videos.

After that I went shopping, I spent thousands on a dress, shoes and to have my hair done. My dress is really long and is dragging on the floor. The colour is gold and silver, my shoes are gold and silver and the heels are 5 inches high. I had my hair done in Chop 'n Change. I got my outfit from Gap.

Then I went home and put my feet up but then I had a phone call, to go to a very important party, so I was a VIP to a VIP.

It was great because I met JJ72 and A1 and Steps and even Bon Jovi, although the Spice Girls were there and me and Mel B had an argument. It was an argument over nothing, she just came up to me and started on me. Then I went home. It was one great day!

Kaitlan Stanlake (11)
Pembrey CP School

A Day In The Life Of A Mother

In the morning, I get up very early, I get breakfast for the children and sit down and watch cartoons with them. After the cartoons have finished, I get the children dressed and play toys with them. Later on we go to the park and have lots of fun.

At dinner time we go home and make dinner for everyone. We have a rest from doing everything and then we go to grandma's house and say hello to everyone. While in grandma's house, I take the children into the garden to play with the slide and the swing. While the children are playing in the garden, me and my mum sit down and have a cup of tea and watch the children play.

We go home and watch some more cartoons on the television, the children watch television some more while I start making the tea for when they get hungry. After tea, we play with toys in the house and then get ready for bed.

When 8.00 o'clock arrives, I put the children to bed and then make my own tea so I can sit down and relax. In the evening, my friends come round and say hello and we have a long talk and watch some television.

At about 11 o'clock, I turn everything off and check all the doors and windows are shut, so I can go to bed.

Kelly Davis (11)
Pembrey CP School

A Day In The Life Of An Alien

I woke up quite late in the morning. I had some tasty space hoops for breakfast. I told Mother alien that I was going on a space ride around the universe and again like always she reminded me not to go near the planet Earth. She says weird creatures called humans live there. While flying through space in my spaceship, large asteroids flew towards me. I'd never been in a situation like this before so I panicked. I tried to dodge the asteroids but it was no use. An enormous asteroid smashed the front of the spaceship, I was alright but the spaceship wasn't. It sounded like father alien in a bad mood! The engine stood to a halt. Suddenly the spaceship circled through the air towards a certain planet. Planet Earth!

The spaceship crashed down with a bump! Luckily I was alright, no injuries. Large brown and green objects stood high above me. While looking around, I heard splashing noises. I walked towards the sound. There in front of me was a large area of liquid. I looked up at the sign, it said 'Loch Ness.' The famous lake of Scotland! I noticed a creature picking up some kind of object. I knew he must be a human. I asked him what he was doing. Without looking around to look at me he told me he was looking for the Loch Ness monster and was putting an underwater camera in the water. I didn't understand anything he said.

I tapped him on the shoulder. I thought I had startled him because he nearly fell into the large area of liquid. He looked at me with strange eyes. On his white coat there was a badge which said Professor Jones. Maybe he could help me. He kept saying that it must be a dream so he might as well!

I directed him to the spaceship while the human was helping me fix the spaceship, I heard voices. The human told me to hide because someone was coming. Quickly the human covered the spaceship with a blanket and acted natural while the couple left. He said to call him Alex. That was when I found out that humans aren't really as bad as you think they are.

After he had finished fixing my spaceship, he thanked me for giving him a nice dream. What a strange human!

As I flew up into the sky I waved to Alex. On the way I met some unexpected guests. Jezzy and Cozmo the bully aliens.

I hate them, they always tease me that they have a better spaceship than me. I got back on them though. When they were about to charge at me in their spaceship, I dodged them and they ended up crashing into their parents. Although Mother alien grounded me when I got home late, she also asked me what the humans were like and I told her that they were strange, very strange.

Catherine Tarbuck (11)
Pembrey CP School

HMS INVINCIBLE

I am Captain James Jewell-Edmonds in charge of the aircraft carrier.

Today HMS Invincible is travelling to Bosnia with the UN. As Captain of the ship, I have the responsibility to control the ship but today as we approached the Bosnian coast, some fighter jets shot down some crew and some crucial equipment, so some gunmen are missing.

As I heard about this, I thought maybe I could be a gunman as I was one in my younger days. I left the Second in Command to control the ship as I was on the guns.

In fifteen minutes time, one of our aircrafts had touched down and reported one of the Sea Kings missing after being shot down.

As Invincible sailed into a Bosnian Port we were under fire straight away, so I had to be quick. I grabbed the gun and fired at will. Soon I ran out of bullets so I had to go to the arms room but as I arrived, all the men's hearts, lungs, etc. were splatted against the wall because our own bomb had exploded but I could not figure out how the computer didn't detect the blaze.

I raised the fire alarm and soon the fire was out but there was no time to wait because the Bosnians were still firing at us, but instead of going back to the gun, I went to the bridge and ordered for the missiles to be fired. As the missile hit the port, a bomb was fired at us but it missed.

Not to risk any more lives, the Invincible headed off down the coast away from the firing.

James Jewell-Edmonds (11)
Pembrey CP School

A Day In The Life Of A Shire Horse

Neigh, I am a black shire horse named Duke, I am nine years old. I wake up at sunrise, then my owner unbolts the stable door and fills my trough with oats and wheat, when I have finished my breakfast, my owner and I go out for our morning ride down the country park.

After arriving back, I go to the stable where I get hosed down by my owner, while I eat from my nosebag. After that I am let out in the field where I like to canter around and eat the luscious green grass, until my blacksmith arrives to come and change my horse shoes, that takes about half an hour.

Then the three children from next door come to see me and give me carrots and apples, so I give each of them a ride in return around the field. When they have gone home, my owner gives me a grooming from head to toe, ready for my evening stroll down the lane. During this, Sarah my owner's cousin, cleans out my stable and when I come back from my evening stroll, Sarah brushes my mane and tail so it is nice and silky. Then I go to my stable that Sarah has cleaned out for me. I lay down and go to sleep in my lovely clean soft straw.

Laura Busst (10)
Pembrey CP School

A Day In The Life Of Tony Richardson

1999 - The first rays of the glittering sunlight shined through the sparkling white window blinds. A few moments later the alarm clock rings, 'ling, ling, ling,' through the cold and silent house. Tony angrily pushed it off the bedside table. He climbs out of bed, his wife rolls uncomfortably but falls back to sleep.

Tony has a quick bowl of Kellogg's cornflakes with a nice cup of coffee for his breakfast. After that he tiptoes silently out of the gloomy house closing the door slowly behind him. He gets into his shiny dark red four-wheel drive Shogun and drives down the roads towards Cardiff.

After a long and tiring one hour drive through Wales, Tony finally managed to reach the quarry where he worked and at the bottom of the road to the quarry was a sign saying Redland, next to it, was a dark, damp road leading to a quarry.

A man at the weighbridge waved at him as he entered the quarry. Just after he had parked his car, it started to rain. Hard. As usual on a damp miserable Wednesday, Tony had to check the machines. He checked the rock beakers, the wheel-loaders, the excavators and the greasy dump trucks. One dump truck had a leak but he fixed it with a few tools. As he passed an excavator he heard a rather strange dripping sound coming from underneath it. Tony looked underneath and saw a huge puddle of oil that was dripping from the engine. Quickly and carefully he went back to his cabin, that was a pile of huge boulders to get some spanners. In only a couple of minutes Tony had fixed the back-actor. After that he went to see what his friend, John was doing. He saw him driving a dirty dump truck along a narrow, slippery road to the loading dock. He was by a cliff. Every time he came to a corner, some rocks or something fell off the side, to the bottom where some wheel loaders were working.

Tony went up a rounded hill to an old house that was about to get knocked down in a couple of minutes. Tony went to check some other things before getting into his Shogun and driving home, all the way back to Brynammen to get some new clothes and have some dinner! At 9.30 p.m. Tony went to bed. Oh well! Tomorrow's another day!

Zak Richardson (10)
Pembrey CP School

A Day In The Life Of My Great Grandad

When my grandad was a little boy, his dad, my great grandad (who I am writing about) went to work in the army and was in the First World War. One morning, it was 0100 hours when he set off for Egypt in the army aeroplane. When he got there, I think it was 0700 hours they set off to fight. While he was far away from his friends, lots of people were getting killed by the Egyptians. He thought to himself, 'Should I do this?' He said, 'I will do it for my family, friends and country.'

He went off to fight the Egyptians and my grandad seemed stronger as my great grandad's friends were dying and he felt it was his fault because he was the only person he could see alive. Later on it was dinner time, 12.00 sharp and he and five friends were in a hide out tunnel eating their packed lunches and having a rest. Half an hour later, they went back to fight. They started to get frightened and suddenly a hand grenade blew up in front of them and a piece of shrapnel hit my great grandad in the leg and made a hole in it. It did not hurt him. At 1800 hours he left to come home and then he was safe and sound. My grandad and great gran were very pleased. They lived very happily for over a year but then my great grandad sadly died of cancer.

Kerryann Buttle (9)
Pembrey CP School

A Day In The Life Of Roald Dahl

It was ten o'clock, he got up from bed and then he went to wash his face. He looked in the mirror, he saw an image in the mirror of a tired, craggy, old man. He had his breakfast and then he thought he would take his writing equipment and go to the park, sit on the bench and try writing his next story.

It wasn't a long walk to the park, he was there in five minutes, he opened the gate and sat down on the wooden bench. He opened his leather bag and he took out his blue pen and started to write notes. He paused and looked around. He saw a child swinging on the swing and three children on the see-saw. He wrote more notes and after hours of writing he decided to go back and have lunch.

He walked to the house and made himself a light lunch, then because he had finished his writing he went to his room. His room had a lamp, a desk and a large window. He had no phone because he didn't want to be disturbed. He started writing his story out, pausing from time to time, thinking . . . Finally after a long time he'd finished his story.

He had supper and decided to go to bed ready for tomorrow's morning of writing.

Katy Morgan (9)
Pembrey CP School

A Day In The Life Of Michael Owen

Michael Owen is one of the best strikers in the world with a total of 27 goals in this season. Liverpool have played 64 games this season and Michael has scored about a quarter of their goals. Michael Owen has five houses with all his family in them. He lives in the biggest of all of the houses.

Michael and Maria, his girlfriend have decided to get married in a years time and to have a baby. If it is a boy, they will call it James, or if it is a girl, it will be called Beth. Michael Owen is very fast indeed and is fit.

As well as being fit, he is strong, he can lift up a person that is 20 stone in weight, that is very strong. He also works out on his back, arms, legs. To be good at football, you would have to practice all day and all the next morning and some of the afternoon.

Football is a good sport, Michael Owen is my favourite footballer, he is excellent and can play well.

Michael Owen leaves 3 days early to train for a match and to play well for the whole world, who are watching him play.

Liverpool have a stadium which is called Anfield and I hope you have enjoyed reading this.

Geraint Hammond (10)
Pembrey CP School

A Day In The Life Of My Best Friend Victoria

Saturday May 2001, I woke up and found myself in a king-size bed. I got up and got off the bed and I was thinking about the room. I had seen it before.

Then something came to my mind, it was my best friend's room, I was shocked, you see the other night, I wished I was Vicky because I just wanted to see what it would be like to be her. Then I went in my cupboard and got my bathers out and changed into them. Then I went downstairs and saw my mother Sarah and my brother and sister, Tiffany and Andrew. I said good morning and they all said it back to me, I was so happy. Then at ten o'clock, I went to swimming lessons. When I did swimming in the pool, I thought it was fun, I swam 4 lengths of the big pool and jumped in too. I was so pleased. After I changed I went out but before I did the teacher gave me a certificate and a badge. I went home and thought it was fun. Then I walked my dog and went out for dinner to the Sheesh Mahel and I had a prawn curry. Then, when I finished, I went home and my mother came in and gave me a kiss and said goodnight. In the morning, I woke up and said even if yesterday was a nice day, I prefer my house, my mother and me.

Sian Morgan (9)
Pembrey CP School

A DAY IN THE LIFE OF MY MOTHER SARAH JAMES

Sarah James is my mother. I choose her because she had a dream job and she gave it away for me and my brother when we were born. Also my mum has given blood to people who need it. Although she is my mother, we are like best mates. She does everything for me and my family. I hope some day her dream job comes back.

She also lets me keep my dog even though she's really naughty just because I love it so much. She now works in an old people's home. She's got lots of certificates for lots of things.

I really appreciate everything she does. My mum buys me food and clothes and she really loves me and I love her very much. She buys us things and does not buy things for herself. She puts us first and she is groovy and a cool thing, that's why I picked her. She's not boring, she's my mum, the best mum in the world.

Wait, there's more, my mum is polite and generous, she has respect for people too.

I am proud of her because of all the things she's achieved. Again, I am very proud of her because she is brainy and pretty. I hope all her dreams come true, she's special in every way. She's the best.

Victoria Middleton-James (10)
Pembrey CP School

Sir Alex Ferguson, Manchester United Manager

In 1986 Alex Ferguson was made manager of Man Utd, the most glamorous and richest football club in the world. Like Sir Matt Busby he is a legend in his lifetime and has been honoured with a knighthood for his achievement since 1990. Alex Ferguson has brought one trophy after another to the club under his leadership. Man Utd have won seven premier league titles four FA cups, the European Cup, the Cup Winners Cup, European Super Cup and in 1999 he completed a unique treble.

Alex was raised in the tough Govern districts of Glasgow, where his father was a shipyard worker. Ferguson started his own working life as an apprentice toolmark. He went on to play for Queen's Park Rangers and five other professional football clubs including the idols of his boyhood rangers. Needless to say he was known as a hard and awkward opponent on the field as well as off it.

As a manager proved himself to be a born leader, building up total loyalty from Utd fans and players. When necessary he takes care to shield his young superstars such as David Beckham and Ryan Giggs. He has never forgotten the lesson he learnt at Aberdeen in the early eighties, that money counts for less than finding and nurturing your own lads.

Daniel Leake (10)
Pembrey CP School

A Day In The Life Of Hooch, My Dog

Hooch is my pet dog. In dog years he is twenty-eight years old and in our years he is four years old. His fur is like a red and orange mixed together and he looks like a Red Setter, Cocker Spaniel and a Labrador. I guess that you know by now he is a boy dog.

In the morning for breakfast he has fresh water and dried complete food. He doesn't have his breakfast until he has been to sniff around the garden and been to the toilet. When I get up he always wags his tail and gives me a lick.

Next-door there are three dogs, Shandy, Meka and Bruce. Shandy used to play with Hooch when he was a puppy.

Hooch looks after my mum during the day by barking at everyone and everything, even black bags, especially the postman.

Sometimes he has a funny half hour where he will race around the garden. We take him for little walks during the week but my dad takes him down the beach on Saturday if he's lucky.

For tea Hooch has more biscuits with a tin of Pedigree Chum or Tripe Mix, which really smells bad, but Hooch loves it.

Hooch loves a game of football, catch and even cricket or any game with a ball, which he manages to puncture. He loves crisps, chicken and digestive biscuits and our cat.

And we all love him too.

Rebbeca Wheeler (10)
Pembrey CP School

A Day In The Life Of A Crab

I started walking around. It was hard because my feet kept sinking into the sand. I was getting hungry and saw a tasty looking shrimp coming. Quickly I burrowed into the sand to wait for the prey to come closer. I grabbed it and chewed it up.

I carried on walking, my feet still sinking into the ground, when something bit me. It was a crab seal. I fought back but it bit my left claw off. I ran but the seal was much faster and I kept getting stuck. Suddenly a shark swam down and in one go swallowed the seal and almost swallowed me in the process.

The day went on and I had found the Titanic and a few other shipwrecks and discovered I could swim slightly. Just when I thought I was safe from danger I floated into a harbour and got caught in some nets. With only one right claw it was difficult but I cut my way out and scuttled back to sea.

It started to get dark and fish were getting weary of predators. It seemed the day was almost over, I was safe from seals at last because I was snug under the sand with my fellow cockles and crabs.

Thomas Denman (11)
Pembrey CP School

A Day In The Life Of A Butterfly

One sunny morning I woke up to find that I was being soaked. The owners had put on the garden sprinkler and didn't care that I was getting wet. I was staying in this garden because I was lost and I couldn't find my home. The owners were planting a lovely row of beautifully smelling roses beneath me and I couldn't wait until I tasted some of that delicious nectar. I was feeling very tired and dizzy because of the water soaking me so I went and hid in the bushes. I couldn't get to the flowers because of the water. I could see the children playing with a ball in the middle of the garden. Suddenly, the ball came flying at me, but fortunately it missed me by an inch. I flew over the wall and into the next garden into the sun to dry off.

The next garden was huge. There was a very strange thing in the middle. It was quite tall and made out of china. There was water coming from the top of it which was falling into a pool of water below it. There weren't many flowers in the garden except a small group of tall flowers with large, bright petals. It looked like there was a lot of nectar in the flowers so I fluttered over to it. It didn't sound as if there was anyone home, so I had the big garden all to myself. Hmmm! The nectar was gorgeous! I stayed there for hours feeding on the nectar until I heard a car parking outside the house. The next moment I heard footsteps but they weren't human. And then I heard barking. Suddenly, a strange animal pounced on me and nearly squashed me but luckily I escaped. I flew into the next garden hoping for safety.

I had never, ever seen a garden like this next one. It was amazing! All you could see were big, bright, colourful flowers! The only other thing rather than flowers, were stones intermingling with each other to form a small, windy footpath in-between the flowers. I could smell the nectar from on top of the high hedge. As I slowly fluttered down to the flowers, I nearly got trapped in a spider's sticky web. It looked like a soft, silky snowflake glittering in the sun. I hated spiders. They would send shivers down my spine - if I had one of course! I dodged the web and landed on a beautiful yellow flower.

I fed on the nectar and I got covered in pollen. I was very itchy. I went to another flower to rub off the pollen and feed on some more nectar. When I landed on that flower I heard a strange buzzing noise. I didn't like that noise and I started to feel scared. When I looked up, I saw peculiar dots floating towards me in the distance. Then they became clear. They were bees! I tried to fly away as they came closer, but my wing had got caught in the flower! I struggled as hard as I could and at last I got free. Now the bees were chasing me out of the garden! I hid in a small tree in the next garden waiting there for a while to hear if they were gone.

I could see the sun setting in the distance and I knew that I had to find a place to stay for the night. I went over to a hedge, where there were beautiful flowers, and fed on the nectar. After a while some children came out with big nets! I flew to the opposite hedge but they still followed me. I fluttered frantically around the garden hoping they would leave me alone but he next thing I knew, I was trapped inside the dreadful children's net. As I struggled to get out, my wings ripped a little. I got out in the end after struggling for ages. When I flew into the next garden, I was extremely happy. I had found my home!

Jemima Emily Jones (9)
Pembrey CP School

A DAY IN THE LIFE OF A DOLPHIN

I am a bottlenose dolphin, and I live in Marineland in Magaluf. I have a distinctive beak and I am the most common dolphin. My day begins when my trainer comes to give food like fish, squid and cuttlefish. When I see him with food I give him a welcome splash and squirt him with water. Me and my friends practice before the people come to watch us. There are two shows every day at 2 o'clock and 4 o'clock. We make clucking noises to communicate with each other. When we hear the crowd coming we get excited and splash our tails. We jump through hoops and hear the audience applaud. The trainers give us some fish as a reward after every trick. So we are very willing to please. I give my trainer a ride on my back around the pool. My next trick is to give him a ride on my beak with my friend Buba. The crowd think we are clever. Paul my trainer, picks a boy from the audience and puts him in a small boat and me and my friends jump over and give him a good soaking. The people think this is really funny and after that we give him a ride around the pool. That brings our show to the end. They put us back in the big pool where we stay and wait until the next show and just relax.

We do the same tricks for the next show. I love my life in Marineland because we are well treated and fed. We like to please our trainers and the people that come to see us and after our working day we just play and laze about.

Angharad Evans (9)
Pembrey CP School

A Day In The Life Of A Butterfly

Just imagine being a brightly coloured butterfly, yellow with red and pink spots with antennae two centimetres tall. Just picture it flying with the cold breeze hitting your wing as you're gliding through the bright blue sky.

It's weird one minute you're a caterpillar crunching on brightly coloured leaves and the next you're a beautiful butterfly with brightly coloured wings. Oh don't you wish you were one?

In the trees you have leaves and more leaves, they're better when they're wet, I'm telling you that's for sure.

Don't go for the drinks because there might be fly-swatters around, but if there's not, drinks are on the house.

I bet it's great flying through the sky watching birds hover by and when you're looking straight down at the green glittering grass with insects going so fast by, it will make me air sick, don't know about you. Anyway wouldn't it be great?

When you go to sleep can't you get birds to sing you a lullaby song. Oh well I guess I better go anyway, tomorrow is a new day. Who knows even I could turn into a butterfly for a day in the life of a butterfly.

Holly Painter (10)
Pembroke Primary School

THE DAY IN THE LIFE OF A BOGEYMAN

I'm so bored. Stuck under this bed waiting for this kid to go to sleep. I'm hungry for haunting!

Finally! He's actually gone off to dream land. But we can't be having that. Can we? *Pop!* I'm travelling through is ear towards his brain. Now let me see, a little twang here and a little mix up there. Tonight is his lucky night. He's going to have a nightmare he'll never forget!

Now I'm out of his head and ready for haunting. Oh no! Trust my stomach to kick in. I'm starving! Guess it's time to visit Mikey Joe's American bogeybar.

I'm here, so let's check out the menu:
Spog balls - 60 worms
Jello bogs - 180 worms
Creepers jelly - 20 worms
Weed coated creepy panatelas - 200 worms
Now I'm stuffed! I'm going to do some haunting. First let's go to the bogeyman's haunting club. It's just the same old palaver. Don't be seen. Do your best and be back before daybreak. If you're a bogeyman you don't need a mother. The bogeyman club does all the wining instead!

Right, I'm definitely ready for haunting. Firstly I'm going off to get my mate. (Us bogeymen scare better with company) and then we're off haunting, so I'll see you later and don't wait up!

Katie Morgan (11)
Pembroke Primary School

A Day In The Life Of A Computer Bug

Hi, I'm Blip, the computer bug. My job is to destroy the memory and send myself to people in e-mails.

I woke up in Tokyo, Japan. For breakfast I had some memory, yummy! Just as I finished I was sent to Cardiff, Wales, just in time for the FA Cup Final. Up the pools! But I had work to do, a computer to ruin - I love my work.

Wow, off I go again to Chepstow. Nice, a new PC to wreck. This is the start of my world tour. The world will be mine, soon there will be no computers left, anywhere.

Soon I'll be more famous than 'The Millennium Bug', I'll be a household name. The fastest bug in the world. Now for lunch, this chip looks lovely to eat.

On the move, once more, to a mobile phone, A Nokia I think. I've never been in one of these before. This is cool, more food to eat, more things to explore, and best of all, more things to destroy.

Now to the land down under. Sun, sea and computers. Today Australia, tomorrow the world. I love this place, computers everywhere. All around the world, I'll be sent.

Now to the land of the free, the USA. The Army had better look out, Blip could ruin all of the computers in three hours flat.

I've got to rest my legs now, as I travelled half the way around the world today. Roll on tomorrow, more work to do.

Matthew Collins (11)
Pembroke Primary School

A Day In The Life Of A Whale

'What happened,' I said 'I feel like 1000kg of blubber. Why am I all wet? Oh my I'm a whale, cool.' I thought to myself. 'Let's go check out the ocean.'
As I was wandering around I saw a grey thing coming towards me, then I said 'Hey that looks like a shark, *shark!*'
Then I swam as fast as I could, 'Wow that was close,' I gasped.

'Let's go and see something safe,' I said.
Just a black shadow as I went to sea I saw a group of guys with guns. Whalers! I swam back under and saw a pool. I swam to see but they swam away, then some baby whales came to me. As we were playing nicely the shark found me, I swam for it. Just as I hit the surface I was a girl and a boat got me and I said to myself 'It was good being a whale for one day.'
Then I saw my little friends in the sunset. I said goodbye and I said 'Was it a dream?'

Gabriella Thomas (11)
Pembroke Primary School

A Day In The Life Of Sarah Michelle Gellar

'Sarah wake up.'
What who's calling me at 6.30! And my name's Naomi. I sat up. *Woow* David's (Angel) there in front of me. I walked towards the mirror. Who is that looking back at me. I touched my nose. she touched hers. Either my mind was playing a trick on me or if it wasn't, I was in the body of Sarah Michelle Gellar.

David Boreanaz told me to get dressed because they were shooting in an hour. He left the room. I looked around. Where was my wardrobe. There it was. I opened the electric door and picked out something to wear.

American Studios: I walked into the studio, people dragging me to the set.
'And action' yelled a cameraman.
Willow and Zander were talking to me. I just went along,
'Vampire!' Zander yelled.
I turned around. My first time to be on telly. I grabbed a stake, did a back flip, aimed at him, when all of a sudden 'Cut more power, come on act like it's your life. OK take 2 and go.'
Great, here I was and stab straight in the head, blood gushing everywhere. Beautiful.
'Well done you gave it life, you gave it love.'
Yes I was actually doing it. Entertaining people. It was so fun until . . .
It was too good to be true. I fainted. Back in my bed back to the old life but it was fun while it lasted.

But David Boreanaz still buzzed in my head. A dream come true.

Lucinda Diyaolu (11)
Pembroke Primary School

A Day In The Life Of A Piano

Ting, ting, tinkle I have to play everyday for an hour. It bores me rotten, but if I don't play my notes Lucie (the pianist) gets the piano doctor out! When that happens it isn't very nice and I can tell you that again for sure.

One day when I was really stubborn with Lucie she called the piano doctor out and that was all I needed, when I was too tired to play my notes. the piano doctor looked at me sympathetically and said to Lucie that I needed tuning up.

The doctor lifted the lid of the top of me and started fiddling around with my pegs and notes. 'This is so uncomfortable,' I thought to myself.

When this silly doctor finished tuning me up as he calls it, he started playing my notes. Of course I had to play my notes beautifully or the doctor would be making me even more uncomfortable, unfortunately. But the doctor still thought I wasn't playing the notes right so he gave me a big bang with his hammer on the side of my leg. When the doctor started playing my notes again I just blurted the sound out of the piano. It hurt so much.

Finally the piano doctor had gone and a very horrible day was over.

Carys Holder (11)
Pembroke Primary School

Day In The Life Of . . . A Saxophone

Bom bom 'That's what's going through my head all day, oh and by the way I'm an alto saxophone and as I was saying it drives me crazy, but you get used to it, but not when the person who's playing is messing about (I have not totally recovered from Thursday!)'

'Anyway my owner has a music exam soon so I'm practised on every day. Oh here comes my owner now!'
'OK time to practise.'
Bom bom bom!
'I think that's enough.'
'Oh that's a relief to tell you the truth I'm not feeling so well myself. I think it's all the practise or maybe it's the thought of someone taking you to be repaired. No instrument likes it, but it doesn't sound bad but it is. One of my old friends went to the music shop and nobody ever saw him again! Oh here she comes I guess it's off to the music shop. Her mum made the appointment yesterday because I've got a loose note. See you later!'

'Hi are you still here? It wasn't as bad as I thought, but I still did not enjoy it very much, but the man cleaned and shined me very well. Is that the time? Goodbye!'

Hannah Williams (11)
Pembroke Primary School

A Day In The Life Of A Hamster

'Put down the gun you're under arrest'
Beep beep.
'What, oh it was just a dream.'
'I wonder if my bud sour is awake.'
'Hey sour dude what you doing?'
'I'm just mowing the lawn.'
'Ace I'm going to do some exercise on my wheel. Oh yeh wonder what's for breakfast. I hope it's one of those biscuit things.'
Uh it's an earthquake! No it's not, it's just giant Steve.
'Steve Steve' he can't hear me. I want my breakfast, he's coming ohh he's just getting the milk. Oh look there's already food in my bowl. It's Steve's mum. She's got the food and bedding, *hey* put my cage back on. She's cleaning my home, get off, wait I've been put into a ball now I'm on the floor. This is fun. I'm rolling around *ahh* it's the dog. Run run run, he's chasing me.
'Get back here hamster, I'm the boss around here grrr.'
'Help' yes Steve's mum has picked me up. I'm back in the cage. What a day. I hope it's not going to be like it tomorrow. All I want to do is have a nice long sleep. See you in the morning!

Steve Gabica (11)
Pembroke Primary School

A Day In The Life Of A Dustbin

It is a normal week day, I'm filled with rubbish. There's a bit of everything inside (and it smells.) When Wednesday comes I get all excited inside, because I get emptied. Well at least I have got a friendly bin right next to me.

It's a girl; she is a really nice bin. In fact I'll let you into a secret of mine: I think she fancies me!

Anyway the class doesn't really put a lot of litter in me, but I wish they did, because I can't bear to see my friends suffer, as they're all quite nice to me.

Anyway, today's Tuesday so we're not in that good a mood, and that is a fact, because I have been broken by a child and I might be the rubbish soon.

However, me and my fellow dustbin do not want that to happen, so we are going to run away, to a land of paradise. But I am very wounded and I am in agony today because I am broken. Tomorrow I am going into the rubbish truck, but I'm actually excited about it because my friend bin I've told you about, is coming along with me, to a land of paradise where I'm told all dead rubbish goes.

Alex Kerr (11)
St Mary's Junior School, Caldicot

A Day In The Life Of A Dog

'Hi, I'm Sparky, and yes I'm a dog; what sort of dog you say? Well I'm a Yorkshire terrier; hey don't laugh what is wrong with a terrier telling a story? Anyway here it goes.'

I was lying in my basket waiting for breakfast, eventually my owner Jane came down to feed me. She gave me a big bone that tasted of chicken.

After breakfast I decided to go down town and window shop. My favourite shop is the butcher's because the butcher Pete gives me sausages to eat.
'Woof! Pete excuse me Pete!' I shouted 'I don't know he's never in when you need him' I moaned.
Next I went to see my friend Bow Wow the Jack Russell who is usually outside Sommerfield about now. Bow Wow and I sat and talked until Bow Wow's owners came out of Sommerfield and took him home. Now that Bow Wow had gone home I went and looked round the market.
'£1 for ten bananas,' bellowed a green grocer.
'Juicy bones for man's best friend,' announced a pet shop owner.

It was a bad idea but I just couldn't resist so I ran up to the pet stall, took the bone and ran.
'Stop dog; that's an unpaid bone you're running off with,' the pet shop owner shouted.
I ran to the park, ate the bone and went home. When I got in I walked up to my bed and went to sleep.

Heather Poole (11)
St Mary's Junior School, Caldicot

A Day In The Life Of The Sun

Three days before:

'I repeat in three days, the moon will attack. Sun, are you listening?' asked a young boy in a high-pitched voice.
'Yeah, yeah, I'm listening and by the way, the name's Su . . . nny. I hate it when people call me 'the sun'.'
'What! Did you, just . . . ! The moon's gonna attack, why! What have I ever done to the moon?

The dreadful day:

A few hours later the sun was talking to Mercury.
'I know I haven't done anything to you before, have I?'
'Actually, you have. All these years you have been burning my planet.'
'Sorry this was where I was put: I actually wanted to be put by Saturn.'

Venus and Uranus were talking about all the planets moving the sun, but they couldn't do that because it was too hot.

One hour later, after a lot of ideas from the planets, they couldn't come up with anything.

The sun was upset for hours because he knew the attack was going to happen now.

The attack:

The sun could see the moon coming forward from a far distance, until it was right before his eyes. The sun was afraid.
'Hello,' said the moon. 'Wow, you're boiling.'
The sun cried, 'Go away! Go away!'
So, the moon went and the sun realised that it was only an eclipse.

Nicolle Price (11)
St Mary's Junior School, Caldicot

A Day In The Life Of A Racehorse

'Faster, faster,' shouted Tim (my jockey).
'Hi. I'm Lighting, a racehorse. I'm on the training track with Treacle, my mate and Richard, her jockey. We're training for the WWNHRC (The Worldwide National Horse Racing Championship).
'Oh for goodness sake! I'm running and jumping as fast as I can Tim.' (I'm being pushed to the limit). My mane and tail are blowing wildly because of the speed I'm going, I'm galloping through the cool, misty morning but I'm sweating like mad.
'Whoa!' cried Tim.
Finally we've stopped.
I galloped to my horsebox (after he'd taken everything off me). I ran up the ramp into my horsebox and lapped what seemed to be a ton of water down my hot, dry throat. I greedily ate my oats then sneakily went to Tim and pinched his last Polo mint and laughed.

After I'd cooled down, Tim brushed my coat and said, 'Must get you looking good for the race tomorrow.'
Then I whinnied in agreement. I trotted over to see Treacle, my friend, who was also going to go to the big races. Her owner, Richard was cleaning out her horsebox when disaster struck: the horsebox rolled forward and ran over a stone. The tyre burst and unfortunately Richard didn't have a spare so Tim kindly said 'You can put Treacle in with Lighting.'
So he did.
Richard said 'Look at the time. Let's go.'
Treacle and I fell asleep in the horsebox.

Emma Pilot (12)
St Mary's Junior School, Caldicot

A Day In The Life Of A Pound Coin

From the mint, there it came the 100,000 £1 coin! As it was a special day they decided to add a chemical to the £1 coin. It was called 'Junior coin acid'. They added it and it expanded to the size of a wheel nut.
'That's done it!' said Bill the manager: it went a normal gold colour, but in the middle it went a goldy-pink colour. They chucked it into the sack.

Meanwhile, in the sack, the coin came to life! It jumped up to the top of the sack and popped out. There it lay, in the lorry.
'Almost there!' announced the driver (to himself).
In the back, the pound was enlarging to a humongous size, squashing the sacks in the back.
'Here at last!' exclaimed the driver. *Aahhh!*
'T. . . h . . . a . . . n . . .k y . . . o . . . u,' grunted the coin, then jumped down and disappeared into the night.
The next day there were bins all over the road and cars upside down. In the street, the police were hanging around and it was blocked off.

Babies were crying, parents were shouting at children inside to be quiet in the house, whilst in the next village the pound coin was doing exactly the same thing.

Daniel Hughes (11)
St Mary's Junior School, Caldicot

A DAY IN THE LIFE OF . . .

'Millie you lazy cat!' says Heather.
'Come and have a look at this.'
'Get up you silly cat,' sighed Mum.
'Millie come on girl breakfast time!' shouted Rhys.
'Breakfast yum,' I said.
I ran downstairs, I ate breakfast and decided to go out and then go by the fish pond and hope I'm going to catch something.
'This is getting boring.'
I decided to catch a bird. I attempted and I caught one.
'Come trouble,' I growled.
I had a fight and I had a few scratches here and there but I was fine.

I decided to go to the countryside but as I walked in a field I fell in a ditch.
'Miaow, miaow,' I called. I heard some footsteps and a farmer came along and bellowed.
'What have we got 'ere then, ay?'
He helped me out and I ran away. It was getting darker.
'What was that?' I cried.
'It's a badger and it's after me!' I said panicking.
It chased me up a tree and it got bored and went away.
'Heck, I'm stuck, I wept.
I heard cries.
'Millie, where are you?' it cried. It was Heather.
'Miaow,' I yelled.
Heather was running towards me then picked me up, took me home. Everyone fussed me, my brother was jealous.
'That was a great adventure,' I thought.

Heather Mathews (11)
St Mary's Junior School, Caldicot

A Day In The Life Of A Hamster

'Hello, I'm Jocky the hamster and I am going to take you through a day of my life.'

It was Christmas Eve at the Hudsons; they're all about to wake up and open their presents.
'I would like to know what presents I got but I've probably got nothing. What's Tom got I wonder?'

Meanwhile outside in the snow next to the back door there stood a frozen black and white cat.
'Look!' shouted Tom.
'What is it?' shouted Tom's mother.
'A new bike from Gran.'
'So much for me, I don't get one present, this definitely shows that they don't love me.

The minute Tom takes me out of my cage he plays with me and my ball. It's nice to know I'm Tom's pet and not anybody else's.

Great, it's feeding time: my favourite time of the day. Later that day Tom lets his cat, Spice in.
'Great' said Spice.
'I must keep inside my safe cage so that I will not get eaten by the stupid cat of Tom's. Look it's Tom mum. I wonder what she wants. Probably coming to cook Tom some chips and fish fingers.
'It's time for bed Tom,' shouts his mother.
'OK,' replies Tom 'goodnight Jocky.'

Stephen Hudson (11)
St Mary's Junior School, Caldicot

A Day In The Life Of A Bottle Top

In the year 9999, a man picked me up in a factory (well, I think it was a factory). I could tell he was old because he had wrinkles on his hand.

He put me in a box with other bottle tops. They were very noisy and were very annoying.

When the vehicle moved I thought we were going to Saturn and back, because I was moving back and the box was moving.

The noise of the engine was louder than the noise of the other bottle tops. The other bottle tops were older than me and knew we were going to a shop so I just went along with them.

Then it went black: my face was squashed. I would have bitten the thing that was holding me but I said to myself 'Na,' because the man would drop me (or at least I think it was a man's hand, because it smelled like it).

He went to the park, (I think). He sat on a chair (I think). I rolled off the chair and dropped some fifty metres (I think).

I slid off a slippery surface and onto something furry. It smelled foul. It ran and ran. It stopped and jumped onto the chair and I fell off and the man picked me up: he had just won fifty pounds.

Carl Morris (11)
St Mary's Junior School, Caldicot

A Day In The Life Of My Dog Winnie

One ordinary day something strange happened: Winnie, my dog, was inside my body and I was in hers. How strange can that be? Anyway, things were going great: everybody was patting my head and throwing the ball for me, but after ten minutes they didn't want to play with me. So I decided to watch television for a bit. I jumped up onto the sofa.
'Winnie, down!' my mum said.
I just lay on my bed and washed myself Yack! How sick can this be? I don't know how Winnie can do this. God I'm starving and no way am I eating dog food. I wonder if I can stare at Mum and ask for a slice of cheese. Oh goody she's getting me a slice *mmm* yuck what kind of cheese is this? Dog cheese to help keep their teeth clean! disgusting.

Oh good, at 1.00pm Winnie and I will change places. What's the time now? 12.30pm. Oh there's still thirty minutes left. What shall I do? *rrr* there's a cat: I know I'll chase it.
'Woof woof' ha ha, here I come. Oh he's gone. Yes it's 1.00pm. Yes I'm changing back.
'Emily why are you licking yourself?' asked Mum
'No reason.'
Boy I am glad to be back.

Emily Hughes (11)
St Mary's Junior School, Caldicot

A Day In The Life Of The Undertaker

In the morning Mark Callaway (The Undertaker), a wrestler, gets up and gets dressed in a hotel somewhere. He goes down for breakfast, which would be fruit and cereal.

He then gets his motorbike and zooms down to the gym to lift some weights and he goes to the swimming pool and swims ten lengths before getting a drink and some fruit salad for a snack. Then he drives his motorbike to an arena and practises running rope to rope.

Later on he meets up with the security guards and they show him to his dressing room where he puts his bag on a shelf. Then he sits down on a couch and watches the telly.

He waits till 11.30 then waits his turn for a wrestling match. After the match he goes back and puts his normal clothes on, then gets his motorbike in the WWF lorry. He is then transported by limousine to another place in America.

He then gets out and sleeps in a hotel for the night. He gets very tired and goes straight to sleep. Until it all begins again tomorrow.

Matthew Trawford (10)
St Mary's Junior School, Caldicot

A Day In The Life Of Skull Legs

Once upon a time in a damp and dark cave there was a monster called Skull Legs. He was horrible and would hunt anything. His cave had skulls of anything or anyone he had decapitated and he could not die.

One day Skull Legs was walking along and a half man half horse monster called Centoro came up. These two were old foes and hated each other and then as soon as they saw each other Centoro spat out a fire bomb and Skull Legs used his acid bomb attack. Then the acid bomb hit Centoro, and Centoro rotted away.

Then Skull Legs picked up Centoro's skull and went to the village and killed two humans and ate their corpses, and then ten of his hardest foes came. He used twenty acid bombs on each of his foes and they finally died, so Skull Legs quickly ate their corpses and went back to his cave, sat down and went to sleep for a million years.

Thomas Karpinski (9)
St Mary's Junior School, Caldicot

A Day In The Life Of The HH Club

The HH club were sitting down at breakfast when the post came, but Hannah's brother Percy ran to get it. Hannah was eleven and Percy was thirteen. Hannah had had her friend Harry over to sleep.
'Morning Percy,' said Mrs Bloom to Percy.
Percy dropped a letter in front of Hannah. She opened it and read it aloud,
'Dear Miss Hannah Bloom, you have a place at Frogtoads School for young wizards and witches, Yours faithfully Dormeines Herones, Headmaster. Wow' shouted Hannah.

Harry was disappointed, but when he got home he had a surprise. When he got home he had the same letter. Harry ran upstairs and packed. His parents didn't care if he was gone. They were never there. They were out at a hotel tonight. Harry had another letter on the table and it said,
Dear Harry, meet me tonight at your nearest bus stop. Midnight. Bring Hannah with you. Dormeines Herones, Headmaster.

At midnight Harry and Hannah crept outside with things packed and waited for their headmaster. Then she saw a big black thing park in front of them. It was a big bus with children on it and it flew from the moon. Harry and Hannah got on and found a seat then they flew up.

The bus turned upside down and Harry fell out. Hannah jumped out of the window. Soon they realised they were lost and they built a tree house and lived in it for ever after.

Katherine Taylor (9)
St Mary's Junior School, Caldicot

A Day In The Life Of Spaceman Bob

One day spaceman Bob and his crew were ready to set off on another mission in outer space. 10, 9, 8, 7, 6, 5, 4, 3, 2, 1 blast off! From NASA. Bob and the crew set off in their super large thirty deck space cruiser. Their mission is to discover a secret outer space planet. The leader is Bob. He's got lots of quality.

'We have flown 3000,000 miles.' said vice-leader Gordon. 'Bob to control room do you read me.'

'Yes Sir.'

'Try and scan the distance to the planet.'

'Yes Sir.'

The crew had flown another 1000,000 miles.'

Captain Bob do you read me? I have scanned the distance to the planet. It's fifty miles to the right.

'Tell all control deck members to control the ship to the right.'

'Yes Sir.'

They had made it the four million and fifty mile journey was over.

'Everyone off the ship please.'

'I think I just heard something,' said Bob, 'Arnold check the scanner.'

'Captain I've spotted something.'

'What is it Arnold.'

'There's some funny green things like aliens coming towards us with heavy weapons.'

'Crew bring all weapons, doctors and medical equipment and Arnold tell all the vehicle drivers to get their vehicles ready for attack.'

'Who are you'

'I'm spaceman Bob and crew.'

Bang! Bang! Bang!

'Yes we did look at that we must have found the centre of the planet. We must take the gold back home to NASA.'

Off we go! On the way back it all went well. And when they got back they won 10000,000 dollars.

Daniel Williams (9)
St Mary's Junior School, Caldicot

A DAY IN THE LIFE OF MY DAD

6.30am My dad goes to church where an early morning prayer meeting is held. He meets people like Tom and other men and some women. Dad starts it off and then other people can pray as well.

Then Dad comes in and sometimes goes back to bed, or makes breakfast for me and my brothers. When Mum gets up and says 'Oh look at the time!' We know we are going to be late for school. We get washed, do our teeth, get dressed and then we set off for school. When Mum and Dad are alone Dad watches some TV for a while.

12.00pm Mum and Dad have lunch together and then after lunch Dad does some visiting. He visits some old people, people who are ill and people who want to come to the church but can't.

15.10pm Dad is waiting for my brothers to come out of school, and then Dad comes to pick me up from school. When all of us come home from school Dad helps to do the drinks for all of us.

18.15pm Dad goes on the PC and finds a holiday for us to go to and says 'This holiday would really suit us.'
My dad always has a lot of expression.
18.45pm Dad would do our milk and pray with us before we go to sleep. Good night.

Samuel Hall (8)
St Mary's Junior School, Caldicot

A Day In The Life Of Stacy And Marc

Stacy and Marc find themselves on the same boat to Hawaii to see James and Stevie's wedding, but when they saw each other they screamed with horror. When it got dark they could not get to sleep, so they kept each other company. But when they got to Hawaii they stormed off the boat because Stevie and James had been trying to get Stacy and Marc together for years. When they got in the car and went to the place they were staying, the room had a double bed, so Marc had to sleep on the hard floor.

The next day Stacy gave Marc a massage because he had a bad back. Marc of course was having the time of his life but poor Stacy was not. Afterwards they went to the pool for a swim. Marc was splashing about as Stacy was sunbathing. Marc got her all wet. Then Marc picked her up and dropped her into the pool and took her sunbed.

Stacy had to put up with this for a week but at the end of the week they fell in love with each other and had another month in Hawaii. After three weeks they got married and bought a house in Hawaii. They lived a happy life.

Stephanie Baker (10)
St Mary's Junior School, Caldicot

A Day In The Life Of A Secret Agent

'OK Joel, Scott, Leighton it's your turn. Your weapons are shotguns, assault rifles, combat knives and grenades. I'm expecting a good show. Don't let me down!'

It was scary stepping into the combat simulator for the first time in a month. We stepped in.

'Activate the radars and get out the assault rifles,' said Joel. We patrolled every room but there was no one around.

'Where are they?' shouted Joel 'they're not on the radar either!' said Scott.

'Look out!' said Leighton and jumped in front of Joel and an assault rifle fired, an assassin appeared out of thin air.

'Run!; shouted Scott. Joel and Scott dragged a half dead Leighton back to their base.

It was a small base you had to climb up a tiny passageway to get there. There were two windows anyway. They were in the base when suddenly the window smashed and a grenade came through. They ran out but they forgot Leighton. Bang!

'Uh oh' said Scott 'there goes Leight.'

'Oh you've had your turn' said the boss

'Deactivating.'

'Oh well that was fun,' said Leight.

'Yep' said Scott.

'OK next is . . .'

Callum Griffiths (10)
St Mary's Junior School, Caldicot

THE DAY IN THE LIFE OF THOMAS MOORE

The enemies were in our base. We got ready for battle stations. The war began. They came to attack. Craig got posted in the same battle station as me. Craig had a sub-machine gun and I had a sub-machine gun as well.

We shot a load of Chinese enemies. Then the Chinese people brought in their tanks. James blew it up. Then Koran stabbed the truck driver. I blew a man's head off with a bazooka. Craig killed their machine gunner.

We kept shooting until there were too many of them. We fell back because they were too strong for us. The planes flew off. There was a leaking oil tank and a fire nearby. Then it spread. It was bad I said. Just then Koran got killed. We turned around and shot the enemy. Then said 'That's the end of him.' We were losing. The base was lit in flames. A plane went by. James blew it up. James nearly got killed. Craig blew somebody's head off. One of our planes blew up. We blew up another one of the enemies' planes.

We were winning. Now there was one person left on their side. I sneaked up behind him and shot him. Our planes came back. We had won the war. We celebrated all night and sung the National Anthem.

Craig Bates (9)
St Mary's Junior School, Caldicot

A Day In The Life Of Stevie, Amy, Sion And Lloyd

It rose in the east and set in the west. What could it be?

It started when me (Amy), Stevie, Sion and Lloyd booked a holiday in Paris. We got to our hotel after a long flight, and found that our room was 250 floors up in the sky which was haunted by aliens!

'Let's flip a coin to see if girls share a room or if it's mixed. Heads - shared, tails - mixed. Right, here we go,' said Stevie.

As Stevie walked up the stairs, she said to herself 'I'm too scared to walk up the stairs all alone,' but then a scream came from upstairs. I ran up the stairs shouting, 'Stevie, Stevie, where are you? There was no answer. She saw a big light shining down on her. It was so bright she fainted and fell down the stairs but the light which was following her broke her fall so she didn't hurt herself. I ran up to her but then the light stopped me for a minute and then carried Stevie and I to a big UFO.

The next day the same thing happened to Sion and Lloyd but Sion turned into a little invention called 'Mini Me' and then Lloyd turned into . . . Dr Evil! When Dr Evil came to Stevie he turned her into a rock but I escaped and found a little robot called 'Mini Me' I switched it on and then I noticed a little sign which said 'Sion, if smashed, spell ended'. So I smashed it and Sion popped up. As we carried along the spaceship we saw Stevie turning into a rock which was so smooth it looked like crystal so we threw water over her and a with a puff of smoke she became alive again.

When we found that Dr Evil was Lloyd we had to come up with a plan. We got to the control panel, pressed the button that made him stop then said the magic words, 'crackle and pop'. We jumped out of the UFO and enjoyed Paris.

Amy Rooke (10)
St Mary's Junior School, Caldicot

A Day In The Life Of Ebony

A tornado almost killed me and my mates. We were so lucky it didn't hit us. It came through our town. We lived in America in the smallest city, at least everyone said so.

The tornado hit Stevie, she hurt her leg but she was coping with it. We found a nurse then, Stevie didn't want a nurse and she was shouting about it. The nurse said it might be broken. She ended up in a little tattered house with the nurse in the end.

It was just me, Stacy, Amy, Mel and Steph left. We then journeyed on.
'Oh no!' shouted Amy, 'we've forgotten the food and drinks!'
'No we haven't,' butted in Steph. 'I've got them in my bag.'

Then we heard a bang. It sounded like a gun to me and we all jumped. We then heard Stevie's voice. We ran back and went to see what had happened. An army was there!

We spied on them for a while but then we chased after the army. We got one soldier and punched him down. We grabbed the gun and started shooting, we then shot three and got their guns. We shot them all. We went to get Stevie and the nurse but they had died. We were silent for a while, then we walked on. Amy fainted and didn't wake up. They had been best friends.

We walked and walked and then had a picnic but we didn't have a drink. Steph said 'I can't go on without water' and a few minutes later she died.

We were quite sad but carried on and arrived at our Nan's house.

Ebony Hussey (9)
St Mary's Junior School, Caldicot

A Day In The Life Of Nick

'Look out!' said Nick, the boat's sinking, ahhh!
'Where are we?' asked Kieran.
'It looks like an island,' replied Josh.
Nick, Josh, Kieran and Lavitar went to explore the island but suddenly Josh found a map in a bottle.
'It looks like a map of the island,' whispered Josh.
'It probably is,' replied Nick.
'It's getting dark and cold,' said Kieran.
'Woosy!' yelled Nick.
'Let's set up camp,' said Josh.

The next day Nick woke up and felt something.
'Wake up,' uttered Nick. Kieran and Josh woke up.
'Can you feel it?' asked Nick.
'Can I feel what?' replied Kieran.
'The rumbling.' said Nick.
'I think it's an earthquake!' said Josh.

'Look,' said Josh, 'there are rocks coming straight at us! Ahh!'
'Help!' said Kieran, 'I'm stuck in the rocks.'
'I'll save you,' said Nick, but suddenly a massive rock came crashing into Kieran, killing him. Some other rocks crashed onto his dead body trapping Josh, Nick and Lavitar.
'Turn the torch on,' said Josh.
'OK' said Nick. A flash of light blinded the area.
'Look,' said Nick, 'there's a hole we could squeeze through.'
'Let's go,' said Josh.
Nick, Josh and Lavitar crawled through the hole until they reached the lair of the blood-sucking killer spiders.
'Oh no!' said Nick, 'what shall we do? 'I know, let's use our flame throwers.'

Four years later . . .
'Look up there, Nick' said Josh, 'a helicopter.'
Nick and Josh waved their hands in the air. The helicopter landed, it picked them up and flew away. Nick and Josh sat down and clicked their seatbelts together. Suddenly Josh felt a gun at his head.
'What are you doing?' said Josh.
'Killing you,' said the pilot.
Bang! The pilot shot Josh and he fell out of the door.
'I hate you' said Nick and punched the pilot out of the helicopter and into the sea. Nick took the controls and flew back to Japan.

Nick Bright (10)
St Mary's Junior School, Caldicot

A Day In The Life Of Myself

It was in the year 1992 when Ebony, James, Rhys and I went to a football match. On the way there we all stopped at McDonald's.

Ebony and I had chicken nuggets, Rhys and James had a cheeseburger. All of us were lucky because we didn't have to pay, because I spotted Chantele and she paid for us.

When we got to the football match, it hadn't started so we were lucky.

As James went to sit down, he had discovered Pikachu, Oddish and a Squirtle. Together they said to us, 'Can you follow us?' We got up and followed them. When they stopped walking, we saw some football players. The players were Alan Shearer, Michael Owen and David Beckham.

The football match was about to start, Alan Shearer grabbed Ebony and I, Beckham grabbed Chantele and Michael Owen grabbed James and Rhys. They changed us into some football clothes. We were really happy because we got to play a football match. Ebony and I were in the Newcastle team and Rhys, James and Chantele were in Liverpool's team.

We went onto the football pitch and started playing. I scored two goals, Ebony scored two goals, Rhys, James and Chantele scored one goal each. In the end Ebony and my team won the match.

We got a £100 cash prize. Chantele, James and Rhys got a £50 cash prize.

We all got a gold medal. We went home and they all ended up staying over at my house for the rest of the day, and we got out the mattresses and some bedclothes and watched a scary movie.

Melissa McConn (10)
St Mary's Junior School, Caldicot

A Day In The Life Of The Super Hamsters

Hi, I'm Sparkeline. I live in Hamsterville. Oh, I can't wait. I'm moving house. I'm going to live in Pellet Lane but I'm still also going to live in Hamsterville and I'm going to go to St Hamster School with my friends and my *best friend* Jacqueline Williams.

Guess what . . .? We are the *Super Hamsters!* It's ace, we can kick, punch, fly and do this laser thingamy-jig with our eyes!

'Knock, knock.' It must be the removal van. 'Mum, Mum, the removal van's here!'
'OK coming.'
Right, where was I? Oh yeah, I'm going to be living next door to Jacqueline! Oh well . . . 'Come on Sparkeline, get in the car.'
'OK.'
Wow! Look at this house, it's . . . it's like a mansion . . . *not!*
'Mum, it's only me and you but why a bungalow?'
'It's the only house I could afford.'
'Oh . . . sorry.'

Boom! Boom! Oh no, it's the Powerfluff girls.

'Laser those girls. Jacqueline fire at the Flufferpant girls.'
'Oh no, zoom, we'll be back, I promise.'

Hooray, they are gone, hooray, three cheers for the Super Hamsters, hip, hip hooray! Hip, hip hooray! Hip, hip hooray!

Sarah Driscoll (10)
St Mary's Junior School, Caldicot

A Day In The Life Of A Cat

I woke up in the morning one day and gave a big yawn. I heard a very loud noise. Then I remembered what it was, my horrible new owners.

My name is Cookie. Last night they made me sleep in the cupboard! I heard someone coming. They opened the cupboard door, it was my horrible owner Adam. I ran out of the cupboard, but I was trapped in Adam's bedroom! Then I saw Adam come up behind me with a big pet carrier!

Crash!

Adam threw the carrier over my head and laughed! Then Adam threw me out of the window and shouted. 'There it goes!'

I finally got out and ran into my den. But Adam's dog was there growling at me. I ran out but only to find Adam's horrible wife, Amy, looking at me. She said 'It's not fair to keep a cat if we're not going to look after it.'

'Well, being cruel to an animal is fun' said Adam.
'I know, but once it's dead, it's no fun anymore is it? Let's give it to an animal sanctuary!' So the next day they took me to an animal sanctuary. A really nice owner called Emma adopted me the next week. This is the best home I have ever had.

Emma Bryant (10)
St Mary's Junior School, Caldicot

A Day In The Life Of My Brother

'Du, du du, du du' went my alarm clock, 'du du, du du' - yawn - I got out of bed and took off my pjs, I went to put my knickers on, when I pulled out a pair of boxer shorts instead! But I just thought my mum had mixed up the laundry bags again. I put on the rest of my clothes and went to brush my hair, when I realised I was a boy! But not just any boy, my brother!

I rushed downstairs and ran in the kitchen and had a drink to calm me down. I then went outside to see my brother in my blue dress, with my long blonde hair.

I told him what I thought had happened and asked him 'What do you think we can do about it?' but all he said was,
'How about lunch?'
Aaarrrhhh! I screamed!

I ran back in the house and tried to think what had happened. All I could remember was drinking my green lemonade! My *green lemonade,* that was it! There must have been some sort of potion put in it! Well, it was getting late so I drank my blue squash and went to bed, 'Du du, du du, du du,' my alarm clock went, 'du du,' I ran to my mirror to see that I was a girl again!

Seren Thomas (10)
St Mary's Junior School, Caldicot

A Day In The Life Of A Long-Lost Dinosaur

Seren, Gemma, Bethan and Emily were walking home from school when Gemma saw a wood. 'That wasn't there before,' she said. The wood looked dark and dead.

'Come on, let's explore,' said Emily, for Emily was one for an adventure. Suddenly Bethan heard a noise

'What was that?' she said quietly.

'Oh stop being a baby,' said Seren.

'Didn't you hear it Seren?' said Gemma.

'No,' said Seren.

As they continued they spotted something. It was a baby dinosaur.

'Aaarrggh' they all screamed.

'Don't hurt me,' it said.

'I won't hurt you, I need help, I'm lost.'

'W w why?' said Emily.

'Don't be stupid, it just said he's lost.'

So they decided to help him. They walked through the woods and all of a sudden they came to a cliff with a stream running down below.

'How are we going to get across?'

'I'll get you across on my neck and then you find my mum and she'll help me over' said the dinosaur.

They all climbed over then ran to where the dinosaurs were eating leaves.

'Come on quickly;' they shouted.

All the dinosaurs came over and saw the little dinosaur. His mum leaned and got him.

'We'd better get back now,' said the girls, so Seren, Emily, Gemma and Bethan all went home.

Emily Davies (10)
St Mary's Junior School, Caldicot

A Day In The Life Of Living Under The Sea

I went into school and I was very tired so I put my head down and fell asleep. I found myself living in the sea with all my family and my pets. I went into my new bedroom and turned my radio on, it was quite late so my mum came in and told me to go to bed.

Early the next day I went to explore what it was like living under the sea. I saw a school, other houses, a park, everything fun, I knew I was going to like living under the sea. I met some new friends and we started playing with turtles and dolphins.

There are all sorts under the sea. One of the baby turtles followed me home so he was my pet. I called him Speedy. He liked his name.

The next morning I had my first day at school, it was great.

We all lived very happily together, we all loved living under the sea. Then I woke up. I remembered I was in school. Everyone had left. I just saw Miss marking books. I looked at the clock, it said 6 o'clock. I crept out of the classroom, got my bag and coat and ran home.

Jodie Cochrane (9)
St Mary's Junior School, Caldicot

A Day In The Life Of A Hockey Player

'Oh no,' I cried, 'beaten again!' Oh, by the way, our team's called Caldicot Cobras. At last it's the Easter holidays! We're not winning anymore because my brother's got heart disease and he gets puffed out really easily. He's really ill now, he can't play hockey anymore. Oh well, it's bedtime for me, goodnight. . . .

Ding-a-ling-a-ling! I hit my alarm clock really hard and put my head under my pillows, my mum pushed me out of my bed and I landed with a 'thud' on the floor!

I put all my hockey kit in a bag and phoned up all the players and rented a hall to train in. I ran as fast as I could to the sports hall (the ice rink). When I got there, Luke Williams, me, Siôn, Ellie, Katie Painter (our goalie), Sam Fok, and Thomas Davies. were there. 'Next week,' I said, we're going to play 'Australia Alligators'! There was a huge silence . . .

'Come on, let's get training.' We all skated 20 laps in total, we did that until our hearts were thundering! We started doing skills with the puck. Then that was the end of our training match! Phew, when I got home, my poor brother was even worse, I had to do something about it, then my phone rang, *ring, ring, ring, ring*. I picked it up,
'Hello, yes, okay, bye.'
'That was the ref of Australia Alligators, he said that whoever wins the match gets £100,000 pounds, then my brother will have enough money to go for an operation in America!'

Two weeks later . . . we've just had the match. We won! 3-1, yes!
Now my brother can have his heart transplant. 'Fantastic, now he'll live! I'm so happy now!

Joshua Williams (10)
St Mary's Junior School, Caldicot

A Day In The Life Of The Tudors

I wake up at 6 in the morning. I go down the stairs of my castle. My breakfast is ready on the table. I've got bread and a drink of ale. After breakfast I go upstairs and get changed. I wear a corset, long dress and a hat.

I go back downstairs and walk around my garden and play on the bilbouquet I go back into my castle, I go into the dining room, my dinner is ready.

I have rabbit with a refreshing drink of wine. After, I go outside and have another walk round the garden.

At 2pm I go to feed my ducks. After I have fed the ducks I go to the bench in my garden and read my book, 'The Tudor Criminal'.

Then I go into my house and sit by the fire.

After sitting by the fire, it is teatime. For tea I have peacocks' brains and beer for my drink. After dinner I go upstairs to get my dressing gown on then go to the bathroom. My pjs are pink with blue spots on.

Then I go back downstairs and have a drink of beer. After that I go upstairs to bed.

Elizabeth Gange (10)
St Mary's Junior School, Caldicot

A Day In The Life Of A Five-Headed Monkey

Swinging faster and faster through the trees that crawly thing goes. Where did it come from? Nobody knows. How was it made? Nobody knows. Swinging from branch to branch, with his big five heads.

Crash!

Bang!

There was a loud noise, slowly the weird animal peered around the corner. There was a family called the Thomas family who were unpacking their bags for a jolly little holiday. One of the little girl called Seren saw this little creature.
'Come on Seren, it is time for bed.' said her dad.
'Okay,' said Seren. *The next day . . .*
The next day Seren went to look for this creature and she found him suddenly, 'Hello little thing' she said and the thing said
'What are you doing here?'
'Aaaaaaaaahhhhhhhh' screamed Seren and ran home very quickly and screamed very loudly for her dad. 'Dad! Dad! Dad!' shouted Seren. 'Help me.'
'What?' Dad asked.
'I . . . I . . . saw . . . a . . . monster . . . speak!'
'What are you talking about?' said Dad. 'There can't be anything like that around here.'
'Yes, yes,' said Seren, 'come and look.'
'Okay' said Dad.
'It's this way Dad.'
'Where then, Seren?'
'Here, here, there it is!'
'It's not a five-headed monster.'
'Yes, yes it is.'
'Run, Seren, run,' said Dad.

Bethan Scott (10)
St Mary's Junior School, Caldicot

A Day In The Life Of The Ghost Motel

'Look, behind you Ebony!' said Lauren. He rose from the dead and grabbed James' leg and tried to pull him under, but luckily he got away from the zombie. They ran away to an old motel and rushed inside so they were away from all the zombies (but little did they know, they were in the Ghost Motel!).

'It is late, we should get some rest. So we'll rest here for the night,' said Rhys. It was midnight.
'Woaaaaoooah! Woaaaoooah' said a spooky voice. Tap, tap, tap, knock, knock, knock.
'Someone's playing tricks on us,' said Lauren.
'Don't say that, it could be something' said James who was half-asleep.
'Lauren, Lauren, Lauren, Lauuureenn, stop getting so mushy and in love with James, it's not time for that because . . . look, look, there's a monster and millions more running towards us,' said Ebony.

'Aaarghhh! Aaarrrggghhh! Aaaarrrgh! Arrrgghh!' the girls screamed. James and Rhys were screaming and were frightened. (If you would like to know these are all the monsters' names, Frankenstein, Mr Dracula, Mrs Dracula, Baby Dracula, Mr Zombie, Mrs Zombie, Mr Wolf, Mrs Wolf, Werewolf.

A few years later, the kids moved in and went to parties and did you know? The kids were ghosts too.

Stacy Marshall (9)
St Mary's Junior School, Caldicot

Day In The Life Of Josh

I was playing in the street. Zoe came out. We called for James. Emily came outside too. Mel and Cameron came back from a bike ride. So the street became full. I said 'What can we play?'
'I don't know' shouted Zoe.
'I think we shall play, um, that game when we are in water,' I said.
'Yes!' shouted everyone.
So we argued and argued what sea creatures we should be. In the end we decided what sea creatures we wanted to be. Emily was an octopus so was Zoe. Cameron and Mel were starfish. James and I were normal fishes. We played for hours and hours.

James said 'Why don't we go underwater in the sea?'
'Yes, that will make it real' shouted Mel. So we did. We made our oxygen tanks look like fish.

We went on an adventure. We split up into two. We went to different places. When we got out of the water, we talked about what we did in the water. It was excellent.

Zoe Arthur (9)
St Mary's Junior School, Caldicot

A Day In The Life Of A Head Louse

I wake up. I remember where I am. I'm in Lucy's hair. It's 8.30am. We're on our way to school. I sit in the tangled mass of hair. We'll be soon at school where there's lots of heads.

We walk into the classroom and sit down. Freedom! I crawl across her head and onto the next one. Oh dear, it's Ian's head. Ian's head is so dirty. I quickly move on. I come across Emily's head, having moved quickly across Emma's, Kymberly's, David's and Bryan's heads. I think I deserve a break. Suddenly we're moving. I try to grip on but I do not succeed. Next second I know I'm on Danny's head. This is not a good place to be as Danny has no hair. I move onto Hannah's head. Oh dear, this head already has inhabitants and they don't look very friendly. They crawl towards me. Where can I go? Where can I hide? They look really angry. I crawl onto the next available head for safety. I'm on Rachel's hair. It's so long. Like a slide. I slide down and crawl onto Grace's head.

The bell goes. It's 3.30pm. Grace walks out and walks home. When she gets home she quickly gets in the bath. Suddenly I'm dunked under water. Then, if this isn't bad enough, she pours shampoo on me. Then I see it, the nit comb! It comes right at me. I can see it coming. *Pop!*

Amy Wilsher (11)
St Mary's Junior School, Caldicot

A Day In The Life Of A Football

I sit in the games cupboard propped up against the cricket bats, waiting for those terrible boys from Year Six to come and collect me and take me out, as they call it, for a kick around.

They finally come to take me away, no, I'm wrong, it's the girls coming for the skipping ropes. They barge me out of the way as they all scramble for the multicoloured one, finally they flee away giggling merrily. As the Year Six boys run down the hall I hear the clip-clop of football boots getting nearer. Then the captain of the football team picks me up and carries me outside until we get onto the pitch. Then he drops me onto the newly-cut grass and starts to kick me around. About five minutes into the game, my soft leather coat is ripped and torn by the metal studs on their football boots.

Eventually, the bell rings for the end of break and I'm kicked down the slippery banks of the field into the school and then I get chucked into the usual space by the cricket bats, and I will stay in the dark gloomy games cupboard until next Wednesday.

Lauren Taylor (10)
St Mary's Junior School, Caldicot

A Day In The Life Of Thomas

Luke, Marc and I were in a dark, dangerous jungle. We were lost and scared but we didn't know what to do. We walked around in circles but we couldn't find a way out.

Luke said he saw something move in the green tatty bush. Marc was the bravest and he looked in there. A big bushy lion roared angrily. We ran as fast as we could and we jumped in the long, wet grass and camouflaged ourselves. The lion was looking around and he couldn't find us. The lion kept on looking and he was getting closer to us and all of a sudden, another lion came and we didn't know what to do. The nasty lions stamped away because they couldn't find us.

We crawled along the grass and I was wet. We still couldn't find a way out. Marc said, 'I'm getting scared.'

We rambled through the hot wet jungle. Luke saw an end to the jungle and we all ran out and we never went in the jungle again.

Thomas Davies (10)
St Mary's Junior School, Caldicot

A Day In The Life Of A Rubber

I never imagined that I could be held by so many people in a day. Let me tell you what happened. It all started on 27th May when Sam, my owner, had me squashed in his school drawer as usual. His friend needed me to rub out a word he'd spelt incorrectly, so over the classroom I went, soaring through the air. I landed with a bump on his desk. He picked me up and started rubbing me violently on his work.

'Oooh, that tickles,' I giggled. Just when I thought I was going to die laughing, he stopped and, to my disgust, he started drawing on me! He drew a face, a squiggly line and some other rubbish on me.
'Oi, get off me!' I screamed, but he just ignored me, I couldn't believe it.

The next thing I knew, I was zooming to another desk.
Please don't write on me, I thought to myself. Luckily he didn't, all he did was pass me on again to some girl. She used me to rub out twenty words and then tried juggling with me. This made me awfully dizzy! The girl whispered to Sam and then threw me back to him.

As I was flying through the air again, Mrs Brown noticed me and took me away and put me in her desk. It was cold and boring in there. No one to rub me and no one to hold me. I was stuck in there until home time when Sam rescued me and back home to his drawer I went until my next adventure.

John Beaver (10)
St Mary's Junior School, Caldicot

THE DAY IN THE LIFE OF A FIVE-POUND NOTE

It all started when the Royal Mint delivered some money to a bank in California. The manager collected the money from the delivery van and placed it in the cash till.

Susan came to collect some money from her bank account to do her weekly shopping. She finished her shopping and the total came to £25.63. She paid the cashier the money, which included the five-pound note. She then left the shop and went home.

The person queuing behind her in the shop (whose name was Claire) paid for her shopping and had five pounds change. The five-pound note was the one Susan had given to the cashier.

Claire went home and gave her daughter Tessa five pounds pocket money, the five-pound note she had collected from the cashier in her change.

Tessa went to the newsagent's and spent the five-pound note on a fountain pen she had seen in the shop yesterday. Tessa then went home to try out her new pen.

Bill, who called daily at the newsagent's for his newspaper, bought it and paid with a ten-pound note. He had nine pounds change including the five-pound note that Tessa had given the newsagent.

The five-pound note is as busy as a bee as it travelled from the Royal Mint, to the bank, to the supermarket, to Claire's house, to the newsagent's and into Bill's pocket.

Stacey Vincent (11)
St Mary's Junior School, Caldicot

A Day In The Life Of A Helicopter

0900 hours

Fred, Tim's owner opens up the hangar and gets him started up.

0930 hours

Tim is flying over the Cambrian Mountains from his base in Llandudno to Bristol.

1030 hours

Tim arrives in Bristol for first passenger. It's a bride going to a wedding.

1100 hours

It's off to London for Tim's next passenger.

1215 hours

It's S Club 7. They need to be taken to Portsmouth for their concert.

1300 hours

Tim arrives in Portsmouth. He drops S Club 7 off, then Fred goes to get his lunch.

1330 hours

He comes back. He's been to McDonald's.

1350 hours

It's time for Tim's lunch at Southampton Airport. It's his favourite, diesel fuel.

1420 hours

Tim picks up the Prime Minister, Tony Blair, to take him to the party conference, Birmingham. it takes a while to get there and Fred asks him some questions.

1530 hours

Tim arrives in Birmingham. The Prime Minister gets out to go to his conference. Fred goes to a pub while the Prime Minister is in his meeting.

1750 hours

The Prime Minister comes out and Tim takes him back to London.

1900 hours

The Prime Minister is back in London.

2100 hours

Tim is home in his hangar and Fred has gone to the pub. It has been a busy day.

That was a day in the life of a helicopter.

Tim Shuttleworth (11)
St Mary's Junior School, Caldicot

A Day In The Life Of My Rabbit Sooty

'Huh, what's all that racket about?' I said half asleep. Then I realised what had woken me, it was the human's getting ready for school. I watched them eating and oh how I wished he had already fed me. They're in a hurry this morning, I can tell because they're rushing around like mad.

'He's coming to feed me, oh no, he's forgotten something. Now he's coming, he's got the food, he's putting it in the bowl.'

'Out of the way, hungry rabbit coming through!'

The other human came over to me and starting stroking me.

'Ooooh that's nice, just a bit over to the right, yes that's it.'
Then off they went, no more love and pampering.

'My most favourite human, the one they call 'Dad' is a nice kind man. He always lets me out and strokes me, also he never tries to pick me up unless I'm in danger. He's walking towards me, yes he's going to let me out.

'Hooray!' I shouted. I was so happy with him that I kept circling his feet to show how much I appreciated him. I looked around me, it was a lovely day, I saw the drops of dew on the flowers and grass glinting in the sun. I spent about six hours just eating and exploring until the boy humans came home.

This is the time when I'm meant to go back inside my cage but I will give them a bit of hassle first by running away from them.

'Try harder, I'm not going to go in that easily' I shouted. He's cornered me, games up, I'd better go in now. I'm feeling really tired, good thing the cage is so nice and comfy.

Brian Beaver (10)
St Mary's Junior School, Caldicot

A Day In The Life Of My Bed

Monday 13th May, 10.00am. Bump, bump. 'Hello, hello, anybody there, put the light back on please,' whispered Miss Singer Bed.
'Yes, who are you? I am Mr King Size and you?' whispered back.
'I am Miss Singer Bed but just call me Singer,' said Singer.

10.30am - We came to a place which I have not seen before but I made a friend called Mr King Size. He is dead cool. I saw something very strange! They had two white things with a black dot in the middle and four long things with wriggly things on the end. They lifted me and Mr King Size and turned me upside down. I do not like those strange things. We were put on the floor with some other beds.

11.00am - I was having a nice sleep when suddenly I got cold. I had another one of those strange things came and took all of my covers off and left me cold, right by the open door - I couldn't believe it. Suddenly, I saw a big, big strange thing came over and sat on me. It made me scream, it was so bad. I quickly put one of my springs into the thing - ha, ha, ha.

12.00am - Do you remember the strange one who pulled all my covers off? He came back and put them back on and straightened me up. Suddenly I saw some more strange things pointing at me. They are taking me to a new place. I wonder what will happen?

Zahra Taleifeh (11)
St Peter's Primary School, Wrexham

A Day In The Life Of A Puppy

Rosie the puppy gradually woke up and got out of her basket. When she usually wakes up, she gets a treat from her owner (Sarah) but there wasn't one there. Rosie went out onto the landing and saw two men with red crosses on their backs carrying Sarah out of her bedroom. She was ill! Rosie went into the garden to stop them. She couldn't, they had already gone. Rosie ran back into the house, out into the back garden and dug a hole to escape. Rosie got under the fence and into Redwood Park.

On her adventure she noticed a big dog. 'What's your name?' Rosie asked.
'My name is Buster,' he replied in a croaky voice, 'I am lost and I'm trying to get back home, can you help me?'
'Yes, where do you live?'
'I live at 32 West Crescent,' replied Buster. So off they went to find Buster's home.
'Here it is,' Buster told Rosie.
'Bye.'

Rosie set off again back to the park and on she went until she saw Holly. She liked Holly even though she didn't know her very well. They made a promise that they would come each day and play together. So they did.

One day they went down to the pond and they both fell in, there was no one there to help them.

Thankfully, Buster came along and got them out of the pond and they decided that they would never go near to the pond again.

Sarah Benfield (10)
St Peter's Primary School, Wrexham

A Day In The Life Of A Tennis Ball

It all started a long time ago in 1996 when I was made in a factory in London, England. They put green rubbery skin on me, sewed it together and they printed 'Slazenger - Extra Light' on me. I was put in a box, sent up to Wimbledon and I have never been played with , until now . . .

One day I heard some people talking to each other about the final of the 'Davis Cup' and that they would need the one and only 'Slazenger - Extra Light' tennis ball. Then it clicked! I was the only 'Slazenger - Extra Light' tennis ball.

The hour came - it was 9 o'clock. They opened the box I was in, picked me out, bounced me about 10 times on the floor and took me away. The crowd was roaring, it was so loud and I was so scared. Tim Henman and Andre Agassi walked out of the tunnel. Tim and Andre had a little rally with each other (Tim served me, 'Ow!' Andre hit me back. 'Ow! Stop it!')

The match went on for ages. I was smashed, returned, aced and I was getting bruised and battered. Andre stepped up, bounced me a couple of times, through me up then *bang!* He hit me but a string on his racket snapped and I fell on the floor. He got me a new racket, served me again and I bounced into the box at 90mph. When Tim went to hit me an egg hit him. Andre had won.

I came off the court *black and blue.*

Daniel Jones (11)
St Peter's Primary School, Wrexham

A Day In The Life Of A Football

It was FA Cup final at Cardiff. The ref handed Robbie Fowler and Tony Adams a football for the match. The bell rang.

'Time to go lads,' shouted Fowler. Tony Adams brought Arsenal out. Robbie bounced me on the ground.
'Ah, ooh, ah.'

We stepped out on the grass, the fans cheered.
'Come on Liverpool.'
'Come on Arsenal.'

I was shocked to see the crowd all packed up in the stadium. The captains shook hands and the whistle blew. Henry kicked me so high I was almost sick. Fowler was on the attack. Wiltord kicked me up to Henry who took on two players and slotted it past Westerveld.
'Yeah goal!' shouted the crowd. They kicked off again, Fowler was running, Owen passed, Tony Adams slid.
'Penalty.'
'Yeah.'

Bang! Robbie Fowler hit the post and it went in.
'Ah, my head, I was almost unconscious.'
'Goal!'

Liverpool tied just before extra time straight onto penalties. Fowler stepped up.
'Bang, yes!'
'Ah, ah, ah, my head, watch out.'
'Adams stepped up.'
'Bang, yes!'
'I told you, watch my head.'
'Ha, ha, you missed, you hit the post.'

1-0 Liverpool. Michael Owen stepped up, hit it so hard, I almost flew through the net.
'Goal!'

Henry stepped up.
'Bang, past Westerveld.'

Liverpool finally won, 5-4 on penalties.

Daniel Hughes (11)
St Peter's Primary School, Wrexham

A Day In The Life Of A Sofa

I got a shock this morning from some very rude children. They were bouncing up and down on my lovely blue arm rests. I had been taken to this house yesterday in a small van and now this family own me.

The room was all right I guess, but quite small. The walls were blue and there was a TV in one corner and chair in the other. The children had now decided I would introduce myself to the rest of the furniture.

'Hello,' I said to the armchair, 'I'm Simon.'
'Oh hello,' said the armchair in a friendly voice. 'I'm Albert, I hope you'll like it here, the family are great.
'How many are there in the family?' I asked.
'Well, there's a mum, a dad and two young children,' answered Albert.

After I had finished talking to Albert I took a nap but was woken by a damp patch on my cushion.

'Oh no,' I screamed, 'orange juice all over me.' Suddenly I heard Mum coming in so I stopped screaming. She wiped it all but afterwards put some itchy white cushions on me. Once she had gone I tried to talk to them but they just ignored me.

A couple of hours later the parents came in to watch a film. I watched for a while but had to stop because there was a pillow fight. The cushions' guts were flying everywhere, it was disgusting. I'm going to sleep now, goodnight!

Clare Millington (11)
St Peter's Primary School, Wrexham

A Day In The Life Of A Snail

Slowly, swirly, the snail slipped off his stone and slid to his supply of snacks.

Suddenly, Slippy the snail, Swirly's enemy, sprung from the shadows and headed for the supply of snacks.

'Swirly,' he said slowly, 'I suppose I'll see you at the Sunset race today?'
'What Sunset race, Slippy?' asked Swirly surprised.
'The Sunset race of the season,' Slippy answered.
'Oh! That Sunset race! I'll be there Slippy.'
'Good luck,' Slippy said slyly.

At sunset Swirly the snail slid off to the starting line of the Sunset race.
'Ready, steady, start!' the announcer shouted.

The snails sped to the slippery track - the first obstacle. Slippy and Swirly simply slid off it and continued the race. They came to the second obstacle, the spring track. Slippy and Swirly simply sprang through that. They carried on. They came to the stone track - the last task. Suddenly, Swirly the snail slipped and slid into Slippy the snail.

'Aaah!' Slippy screeched.

Swirly steadied himself and sped off leaving Slippy stuck to the stones, squashed by the other snails as they swerved and slithered around him.

Swirly the snail swiftly slid to the finish. He felt super. He'd come first! He'd beaten Slippy.

'Swirly, Swirly, Swirly,' the snails sang slowly.

Silently, Slippy slid past the finish line - last!

Stephanie Kynaston (10)
St Peter's Primary School, Wrexham

A Day In The Life Of A Dragon

A world like Earth but twice as big, owned by dragons and humans. There was a dragon that was the best football player, he was called Roberto, he was big enough to skate on cars. Roberto looked a bit like the dragon on the Welsh flag. Roberto played for Dragon United, the best team in the world. But he was a bad sport. When he got a red card he flamed it out so instead of getting a red card, he had a burnt card. He was suspended for his behaviour, so he found a wizard in a forest.

'Can you help me be a good sport?' Roberto pleaded.
'Sure, but you have to go to Earth and score three goals in the final of the World Cup,' the wizard said.

Roberto appeared in the Brazilian practice pitch. He was disguised as a human.

''Hey coach, I can go in the team,' Roberto shouted and did some tricks and shots.
'Yeah, you can take Ronaldo's position today in the final,' the coach said.

One hour later they kicked off. The crowd roared. They were against Italy. Roberto tackled Baggio. He took on seven players and scored 1-0 to Brazil. Roberto did the same type of goal, 2-0. Italy's coach swapped Baggio for Totti. Totti scored two goals, 2-2. Just before full-time Brazil had a penalty placed into the top corner, he scored three goals and Brazil won 3-2. Roberto learnt not to cheat.

Andrew Hunt (10)
St Peter's Primary School, Wrexham

THE DAY IN THE LIFE OF A WATER DROPLET

'Here we goooo!' Mike the water droplet shouted.
'Ow oh eh that hurt,' said Mike as he hit the bottom of the metal sink.

The giant hands of a boy dunked into the sink. Luckily for Mike he was not touched or washed onto the boy's hands. The boy pulled the plug.

He zoomed down the drain and into the sewers. The sewers stank! Mike looked around for his friend Mac. Mac was nowhere to be seen. Seeing as Mike was clean, he went straight into the reservoir. Mike made a new friend, his name was Tom. The next thing Mike knew Tom and him were sucked up a pipe.

'So it's happened again,' Mike said sadly remembering Mac.
'This is my first time,' Tom said in a worried voice.
'It's not that bad.'

This time Mike was on top of the water in the middle of the sink, which was the worst place to be in that sink.

It was the same boy as last time. The hands came down and Mike was rubbed onto the left hand and got caught in the hairs on his hand.

Mike was rubbed onto the towel. He met Mac, who had almost completely evaporated. Mike and Mac died peacefully together.

David Johns (11)
St Peter's Primary School, Wrexham

A DAY IN THE LIFE OF WRAPPING PAPER

Ding! went the bell as he walked into the shop. I heard him say 'Have you got any wrapping paper?'
'I've got two more rolls left,' replied the shopkeeper.

The man took Timmy wrapping paper down off the shelf.
'Um,' he muttered, 'I think I'll take the other one.'

Before I knew it I was being snatched off the shelf, put in a bag and being walked out of the shop.

At first I felt nervous with the sounds of traffic. The sun was dazzling but soon I got used to it. Then I was moving again. There was a sound of a key turning and a lock opening. We walked inside, he put me in the hall and went upstairs. He came back down with another bag. He took it and me into the lounge and started to cut me. He wrapped me around a present.

One hour later we were in the car driving to Mega Bowl. There I saw kids bowling. I was given to a kid who put me on the seat. I could watch the bowling from there. Suddenly the birthday boy slipped. He had a bowling ball in his hand. He let go of it and it went sailing through the air, landing right on top of me. The PlayStation 2 broke and the ball was slowly crushing me and then I was gone.

James Ellingford (10)
St Peter's Primary School, Wrexham

The Day In The Life Of A Pencil Case

I woke up on a sunny day - it was a fine day, the sun was bright. I would have liked to go outside, but I couldn't because I was a pencil case.

Then it happened, a scruffy dressed boy walked into the shop and spoke in a loud voice to the shopkeeper.

'Can I buy a pencil case?'
'Yes, here you go,' said the shopkeeper. 'Goodbye.'

So there I was. I had been bought by a scruffy boy.

When we arrived at his school I was slammed down on a table as if I wasn't important. I was flung into a tray. A few hours later I was grabbed out and put back on the table and the scruffy boy started to push and pull things out of me, then he ripped me, it hurt me so much. Then I was put in a bin and just left there.

At the end of the day the caretaker looked at me and said to himself 'That is a worthless piece of junk.'

Suddenly it all went black and the next thing I knew I was stuck in a dump never to be seen again.

David Roberts (11)
St Peter's Primary School, Wrexham

A Day In The Life Of A Milk Bottle

Clink, clink, was the sound as all of the milk bottles made their way around the production line. I was lucky to be a gold top today.

After I was filled with lovely creamy milk. I was placed into one of the large crates along with my friends, who today were also gold tops. We were now ready to be loaded onto the milk float.

Fred our milkman is a happy chap who whistles a tune we have heard so often. The milk float doesn't travel very fast but we still manage to create a noise when we touch.

Finally we come to a halt and Fred the milkman climbs out of the float and carefully lifts me out of the crate. As it was a cold, frosty morning, he was wearing big, woolly gloves which made me feel warm. He then carefully placed me on the doorstep of number 39 Darland Lane.

I sat in the cold winter air for at least two hours before Mr Redmond opened the front door and picked me up and carried me into his lovely, warm kitchen where all the family were sitting at the breakfast table ready to eat and drink. Victoria carefully poured me onto her Sugar Puffs and her mummy into her coffee cup.

When breakfast was over I was placed in the fridge next to the Pepsi.

After school Victoria opened the fridge door and poured a glass of cold milk, I was now empty.

Her mum then carefully washed me and then placed me outside ready for collection the next morning by Fred the milkman.

Victoria Louise Redmond (9)
St Peter's Primary School, Wrexham

A Day In The Life Of A Feather

So elegant and streamline, the magpie looks with its soft black and white feathers. The feather lies beneath the rest, weaved as though it were a single stitch in a newly knitted sweater, 'or a soldier in an army parade', so perfect, so preciously needed as the magpie swiftly flies amongst the clouds. The feather loosens. The magpie expertly lands on a wild willowing tree beside the river to preen and clean. The feather loosens and is held tightly in the beak. With a slight tug it is pulled and discarded. The magpie flies away and the feather falls so softly, swaying from side to side like a dry, crisp leaf on a typical autumn day. It lies on the ground so far beneath the world, so lonely, not needed now for flight, but maybe the feather can be part of a whole new life . . . as important as it once was.

A swooping wood pigeon lands on the soft grass, grasping the feather in its beak, then it takes off so effortlessly, far above the trees, high into the sky she flies . . . now what will become of this feather? Maybe it will provide essential warmth to nurse her eggs. Maybe it will make her hatchlings feel secure and safe. Maybe this feather has become part of *the great circle of life.*

Corby Rodda (10)
St Peter's Primary School, Wrexham

A Day In The Life Of My Cat

A cat is a creature of habit. My cat, Fluffy, though she's quite an elderly lady by now, likes to do the same things in the same order every day.

Early in the morning, she leaves her bed under the hawthorn hedge, jumps onto my bedroom window sill, stands upright on her back legs and pats the windowpane with her front paws until I get up and let her in. That's her way of telling me, 'It's time for my breakfast!' I make a fuss of her by stroking behind her ears and under her chin. Then I take her to the kitchen and open a tin of Felix whilst she weaves herself in and out between my legs, purring like a traction engine.

When she's eaten her fill, she sits in front of the Aga and washes herself from head to tail with a busy pink tongue as the humans in the family get themselves ready for work and school. By the time we leave the house, she's already settling for a long siesta, which often lasts way beyond lunch time! She always twitches when she's asleep. I think she must be deep in playful kitten dreams. My mum says she wishes Fluffy could talk because she'd be a world authority on relaxation techniques!

After lunch, Fluffy takes some outdoor exercise. Sometimes she uses the cherry tree as a scratching post. Her favourite game is hunting in the field behind our house. She'll chase butterflies, birds, mice, voles - anything really. She likes to leave the odd catch on the back doorstep as a sort of gift token to us. Ughh! I would rather she didn't.

When I get home from school, she's sitting on the gatepost, waiting for me. She rolls over on the path so I can tickle her tummy. Then there's a lot more purring. When I'm indoors, having my tea, she climbs the elm tree, sits on a branch and looks down on the world like the Queen of England! My dad works some distance from home so we often don't hear his car pull into the driveway until 7pm. Once he's in the house, the car is irresistible to Fluffy. She's down from her tree-perch in a flash and sprawling on the bonnet, enjoying the warmth rising from the car's hard worked engine.

Just before I get ready for bed, Fluffy has her last meal of the day, some cat biscuits and a drink of nice, cool milk. Then she disappears quietly into the shadows of the night to meet up with all the other cats in the neighbourhood and who knows what they get up to when we humans aren't looking?

Todd Carter (10)
St Peter's Primary School, Wrexham

A Day In The Life Of A Coin

You can get different coins like 5p, 10p, 20p, 2p, 50p but this coin was a 1p coin. It was lying on the floor a bit dirty, but still round and smooth. It was a lovely day, the sun was shining and lots of people were looking at toys in the toy shop. Tom wanted the new car that spun round and went very fast. He had saved £9.99 but it was ten pounds! He walked out of the shop and then saw a dirty 1p coin. He ran to it, hooray! He could now buy the car. The coin was put in the cash register. The 1p coin stayed in there for a long time but later that morning the drawer was opened and he was picked up by the shopkeeper to be given as change to a customer. He was then put safely into a wallet, squashed next to all the notes and credit cards. When the man arrived home he emptied his wallet onto his kitchen table. The coin rolled onto the floor and under a dusty cupboard. The man's son was allowed to find it and put it in his penny jar. When the jar was full, the coin was taken by the boy with all the other coins and spent in another shop. The coin's life carried on like this and he got to see lots of cash registers and wallets and was held in many hands.

David Bayliss (10)
St Peter's Primary School, Wrexham

King Of The Air

Another day dawns - grey and dismal. My solitary life continues with the hungry screeches of my brood. I must find my helpless chicks some food.

I take to the sky soaring, gliding my strong powerful wings beating the cold Scottish air continually. My prey is insight. I swoop for the kill - direct hit! Successful again. I rise to the sky and return my prey to the open mouths of my children. They eat hungrily but they still 'Kaa.'

The two-legged enemy approaches trying to steal the precious eggs. I must protect my nest. I dive towards him, he runs away in terror but he may return some day!

The heavens open and the rain beats down upon my brown plumage as I protect my young from the downpour. I move them further under the jagged ledge above my huge cliff top nest. I sleep for a short time as I will need more energy to hunt again.

As I awake I notice that my nest is heavily damaged by the storm and I return to the air for branches to repair my home.

The end of the day is nigh. It has been a hard day and my wings ache. This is one tired, golden eagle.

Daniel McNulty (9)
St Peter's Primary School, Wrexham

The Day Of The Life Of A Window

Hello, I'm a window. My name of course is 'Window'. I'm a window who overlooks a park. It's so exciting looking over a park. Lots of things happen. I'll tell you about my day.

First of all the sun comes up and wakes me up. After that the milkman comes and puts bottles by our door. In the morning people walk to school. I like seeing all the bright colours on their lunch boxes and uniforms. Also, different dogs come past - fat ones, thin ones, anything you could imagine, they are there. Then the dustman comes. He blocks my view but when he goes to the landfill site my view comes back.

At midday people eat their lunch. In the afternoon people play on the swings and slides. People walk babies in prams and people play football and cricket. Hang on, what's that thing coming towards me? It's . . . it's a *cricket ball! Help!* Oh no, I've been smashed by the cricket ball. I'm glad the glazier was coming round the corner.

Right now, I'm fixed, I'll carry on. The afternoon is my favourite time of the day. Anyway, now it's evening. People are going for nice walks and the park keeper comes to shut the park up.

Well now you know what the life of a window is like. As the moon rises in the dark sky, above the quiet, deserted park, it's time for me to go to sleep. Bye-bye.

Robert Pugh (10)
St Peter's Primary School, Wrexham

My Day Out

One day, when my cousin was round, I went to Chester with my uncle, but my cousin did not want to come, so I was the only one who went.

My uncle was dropping off my auntie at work, she works in a mobile phone shop in Chester. After my uncle dropped her off he went and got some money. We then went to McDonald's drive-in and ordered the food we wanted, but it wasn't ready so my uncle took me to the toy shop called Toys 'R' Us. We looked around. I had a go on the PCs and I wanted a link cable for my Gameboy (so you can play together on a game.) I found one and my uncle asked if I'd like anything else. I said could I have a water pistol and he asked which one. I said a big one. We got one for my cousin as well.

After that we went back for our food from McDonald's. I had chicken nuggets. When we arrived at my nan's house I gave the water pistol to my cousin and I filled mine with water, and so did he. His friends came and we all had a giant water fight and everyone got wet.

James Rogers (10)
St Peter's Primary School, Wrexham

THE DAY I WENT TO PORTUGAL

I was getting really excited as I travelled to the airport with my family. We got to the airport, checked-in and went up the stairs to the departure lounge. It seemed like ages before we were finally called to 'gate two'. An air steward took us to our plane - it was huge. We clambered the steep stairs, found our seats and fastened our seat belts. The plane slowly began its journey down the runway, into the sky we flew. Before we knew it Portugal was in sight. The captain spoke and said 'The weather in Portugal is hot and sunny.' We fastened our seat belts and slowly began our journey down.

We eventually landed - it was very hot! We collected our luggage and went to find our car. Dad had to drive, Mum wouldn't. Then following the map we made our way to our villa. It was funny seeing Dad drive on the opposite side of the road and Mum yelling at him to 'Watch out!' After some time we came to a track. We drove up the bumpy, twisty dirt track until we came to the top of the hill, there it was, our villa.

Hooray! we all shouted. Jumping out we could smell the sweet scent of the flowers and the orange and lemon trees. We ran to the door, got changed, jumped into the pool and with a big splash, started our holiday in Portugal.

Beccy Roberts (10)
St Peter's Primary School, Wrexham

A Day In My Life Year 1600

Hello, my name is Mary and I am 10 years old. I am a dairy maid.

I was really lucky today. I got to get up at 5.00am to clean out the chicken shed, instead of 4.00am to light the fire and make breakfast - Amy is doing it today. After cleaning out the chickens I had to milk five cows which is not fun, it takes ages and makes your hands hurt. The cows names are Henrietta, Daisy, Rosie, Beth and Meg. Daisy is my favourite, she's a baby and Rosie is her mum.

I feed the cows twice a day on apples, carrots and hay, except Daisy who is too young to eat food, she has milk from her mother. After I had milked the cows my mistress gave me three coins to buy two goats. On the way to market I saw a man in the stocks.

At market I got the goats and found some rotten tomatoes. I kept them to throw at the man in the stocks on the way back.

When I got back to the farm I had some bread and cheese. I am tired but I have to churn the butter. After churning the butter I went up to bed and fell fast asleep.

Elisabeth Thomas (10)
St Peter's Primary School, Wrexham

A Day In The Life Of Isaac Newton

Woke up at 7.00am and had some burnt toast. Went outside and sat under a tree. Suddenly an apple fell on my head. 'Oww!' I wonder why it fell down, not up? I think I'll call this force 'gravity'.

It was a sunny day so I thought I'd do some experiments with light. I shone some through a piece of glass prism. The white light was split up into red, orange, yellow, green, blue, indigo and violet. I will call this the 'spectrum'.

Suddenly my mother's voice rang out saying 'Isaac, lunch will be ready in half an hour.' Went outside and ate one of the tree's apples. I had a bruise from where the last one hit me. Heard my mother saying lunch was ready. I trudged back into the house. Spent all afternoon inventing a new form of mathematics, I called 'calculus'.

Later in the afternoon had tea with my friends, but not Robert Hooke because he's my enemy. My friend, Charles Montague, offered me the job of Master of the Mint. I eagerly accepted it.

After tea disaster struck, a great plague followed by a great fire. After supper I decided to write my books called The Principia 1, 2 and 3, Optics and Fluxions. Worked late into the night on my hobby alchemy before I went to bed.

No success on this one yet.

Christopher Packer (10)
St Peter's Primary School, Wrexham

A Day In The Life Of An Ancient Greek

Hello. My name is Janus. This is just another normal day.

'Mother, I am awake.'
'That's nice dear,' came my mother's reply. 'Get ready for school. I have heard you are to do your lyre practise today.'
'Yes mother,' I replied.

Yes, I do play the lyre and I'm quite good. It is a tortoise shell with cow gut strings.

I went down the hard, white steps and I took a plate of olives for my breakfast. My sister and I always help ourselves to food because our parents have slaves to get them things like bread and wine.

I picked up my bag and walked to my school. It was a fine day with a light breeze. My friends were waiting for me as usual.

We didn't start until lunchtime so we went to eat our snack under an olive tree. The olives were ripe and we picked some and put them in our bags. At that moment our teacher called us and we went into class.

Mr Miletus told us to play one by one and he would tell us if we would be in the choir. At the end of the lesson I had made it into the choir. I was very happy.

At 4 o'clock we left school exhausted and flopped down on the grass before we went home. I was so tired I laid down on my bed and fell asleep at once, zzzz.

Matthew McFarland (10)
St Peter's Primary School, Wrexham

BINKY AND SNUFFLES BAD DAY

As soon as Mum had gone round the corner, Binky and Snuffles heard noises. Someone else had been watching Mum go shopping too. Curiously, Binky and Snuffles peeped out of the window and to their horror saw a fox in a gleaming, red coat staring back at them. The two helpless rabbits clung to each other shivering. The fox licked his lips and started breaking the glass!

They looked around the kitchen and Snuffles grabbed a bowl of yesterday's soup from the table and flung it at the fox through the broken window!

The fox disappeared from the window and next moment there were noises at the door. Binky and Snuffles ran down the passage way and saw the fox trying to break down the door! 'I have an idea! squeaked Binky, and led her brother upstairs. 'Look!' she said, showing him Mum's make-up box. Then, she opened the upstairs window and threw the 'whiskers powder' out of the window all over the fox.

Enraged and covered in cold soup and white powder, the fox started to climb the house, but Snuffles was ready and dropped Mum's stool on the fox. He fell and hit the ground with a thud. 'We did it!' sang Binky,. 'We did it!' as the fox limped away with his head hung.

Binky and Snuffles had a super quick tidy up and when Mum came home she didn't believe a word of their story and, of course, they did *not* mention the powder and the stool!

Katie Smith (9)
St Peter's Primary School, Wrexham

MY CAT PIPPIN

I have a cat called Pippin. She is sweet because she's ginger and white. In the morning she miaows to say hello.

Pippin has an enemy, my horse called Hedges. When Hedges sees Pippin he puts his ears forward so then Pippin goes into the hedges.

During the day Pippin goes looking for mice and I know she has been because she has a small grin on her face and she sometimes leaves the mouse by the front door.

I have a favourite tree and if Pippin sees me up there she will come up with me but if she doesn't she is probably sleeping in the greenhouse or on my bed or she might be catching mice.

During the day Pippin gets tired after catching mice so she goes into my nan's greenhouse because it's nice and warm in there.

During the night we don't know where Pippin goes, but I think she might be scurrying around in the grass.

Every night I give Pippin her tea. She has cat meat with biscuits and she really enjoys it and that's Pippin's life. After all that we all go to bed and Pippin only says to me 'Goodnight!'

Claire Samuel (10)
St Peter's Primary School, Wrexham

My Holiday In Turkey

At 5.15am, 16th October a taxi came to pick up Mum, Dad and I. It was taking us to Manchester Airport because we were going to Turkey. Our flight was at 7.30. We boarded the plane and took-off.

After four hours we were there at last. When we got to the hotel we went to our room and unpacked. Then we went to explore. I went down to the bar to get a drink but Mum had only given me 1,000 lira, when drinks were 1,000,000 lira. But a kind man paid for me just as I was about to run back. There was a pool and a games bar. The games bar had darts, a pool table and a TV. There was also a bar.

The hotel grounds were a great place to play blocky. My new friends and I played for a while then we went to the market. I bought a game for my PC, an infra-red laser and a marble chess set. The lady also gave me a block of marble shaped like an egg for free.

Later on in the day we went to a boat. We jumped off the side and swam in the sea. The sea was nice and calm. My dad and I went for a walk to Ichmeler and got a water taxi back to Marmaris.

And that was the first day of my holiday!

James Warwood (10)
St Peter's Primary School, Wrexham

A Day In The Life Of A Postman

'Ding, ding,' went the alarm clock. 'It's 5 o'clock, time to get up,' said Jim the postman. He makes himself a big mug of tea and three slices of toast and marmalade. He then gets himself dressed and washed ready for work. As he gets into his van he hears the birds singing. The roads are very quiet as he drives into the depot to pick up his letters and parcels to be delivered for the day. He shouts 'Good morning!' to his friends as he gets back into his van to start his day's work. It's a nice, sunny morning and Jim is feeling very happy.

He drives to his first set of houses. He sees that everyone is starting to get up.

As he delivers his letters he can hear children getting ready for school and mums and dads going to work. The roads are getting busy now. It is 8 o'clock now. Some of the letter boxes are low on the ground, so Jim has to crouch down to post his letters. Sometimes he catches his fingers in the letter boxes. He then gets into his van and drives home.

Stephen Bennett (9)
St Peter's Primary School, Wrexham

A DAY IN THE LIFE OF HELEN

I wake up and cry for attention. I know I shouldn't get out of bed on my own so I cry louder. I know that the louder I cry the quicker the grown-ups will come. It's a clever trick, I wonder if any other babies have figured it out yet? Anyway it worked, Mum lifted me out of bed and I yelled just to make sure George was awake. I got into Mum and Dad's bed, in the middle of course, where I always go. If I pull Mum's blue pillow from under her she'll have to get out of bed and get me a bottle. But wait, what's this I hear? It's Dad coming up the stairs with my bottle. My mouth is clamped on the teat before my hands grasp it. The hand over of bottles in our house is quicker than the hand over of the Olympic relay baton. Ah! That's better, down in one whole gulp and finished with a very satisfactory burp. What should I do now? I know, I'll destroy that pile of magazines while Mum's in the bathroom. I know she'll be mad at me but if I smile she'll forgive me. It works every time. I wonder if that's why us babies learn to smile so early in our careers as home destroyers.

Mum and I have just finished having the battle of getting dressed. My socks are crumpled and my nappy's on wonky but hey, I'm colour co-ordinated, that's what counts.

Frances Owen (9)
St Peter's Primary School, Wrexham

A Day In The Life Of Mum

At the beginning of the day your mum wakes you up. She goes downstairs, makes your favourite breakfast. She takes you to school, comes back and makes the beds. Then she goes shopping and buys you your favourite food and sweets. Then she comes home and puts the shopping away. She washes up and polishes the house and irons. Then Mum comes to pick you up from school. When you have changed from your school clothes Mum gives you your sweets and takes you to the park. She pushes you on the swings and pushes you on the roundabout. She takes you home and puts your dinner on and puts your pictures on the wall. She gets the plates out and knives and forks and she tells you to wash your hands. Then she gets the dinner out of the oven and eats with you. She cuts up some fruit for you and then she takes you to Brownies or Beavers and waits for you and then takes you home. Then she gives you a bath, she scrubs your hair and washes your body. She dries you with the warm towel. She tells you to brush your teeth then she gives you some hot chocolate. Then Mum puts you to bed and tucks you in, she picks a book and reads you a story and you fall asleep. She closes the curtains and switches the light off. Now Mum goes downstairs and makes herself a cup of tea and watches TV on the couch.

Sophia Piccou (9)
St Peter's Primary School, Wrexham

A Day In The Life Of A Goldfish

'Yo! I'm a great goldfish.' I got out of my underwater castle, and swam around the weeds. Then I saw the cat. It came towards the tank, then it dipped dangerous, dark claws in the water. I swam for cover in the castle. Then I heard shouting. It was Andrew, the cat ran away to the garden. Then Andrew got a box and tipped some of my food to the top of the water. I swam to the top and started my feast. It was delicious. I finished it in two minutes flat. Then I swam back to the bottom of the tank opening my mouth and closing it again.

I could see the cat watching me through the window. It was now midday. I could see Andrew's mum with the Hoover. Then she came over to the tank, she picked it up and took it to the kitchen. She took the castle out and tipped the rest into a bucket including me. She filled it up with new water and tipped some fresh stones in. She got the castle and weeds and placed them in the tank, then she reached for me, I tried to escape but she grabbed me. I was dying for water but then I was in my tank. I swam to my castle. She placed me in my normal spot. Then she gave me some food once again it had gone in two minutes flat. I swam back into my castle and shut my eyes. Goodnight.

Richard Andrew Parry (10)
Ysgol Caergeiliog

A Day In The Life Of A Newspaper

'Hello, good morning, I'm Nicholas the newspaper - (a Daily Mail to be exact), sitting in a shop in Tesco's. It's around ten o'clock in the morning and the shop's shelves are still being stocked. I was made and transported here around ten minutes ago. Oh look, the shop is opening and all the people are coming in. I hope they buy me. 'Hey Freddy.'

Freddy was a Financial Mail. 'Yeah,' said Freddy. Just as Nicholas hoped, a plump old lady around sixty bustled over to the newspaper rack. She picked me up and threw me in her basket and hurried off to the counter. It's very exciting being bought, for you see all these wonderful new sights.

When she had me at her house she gave me to her husband who opened me up and started to read me. After a while he was bored and got in the car to go for a drive. I was then lying in a box ready to be taken for recycling. Later I was taken back to Tesco and dumped in the recycling bin so I could be made into something handy, so trees wouldn't have to be cut down as much, to help global warming cease.

Peter Garrod (10)
Ysgol Caergeiliog

A Day In The Life Of A Maths Book

I'm a maths book. You have probably seen me before. I live in your tray. Anyway, this morning I was pulled out of Emma's tray. I knew what it meant, any minute she would be prodding and poking me with her pencil.

First came the date, Wednesday May 23rd. Then came the title, Circles. I nearly fainted. The title was Circles. That would mean she needed a compass. It was a nightmare!

It stung me as Emma plunged her compass into one of my pages. I heard her whisper, 'No that's not right,' to herself. Then she plunged it into me again. It tickled when she drew the circle.
'Let's see,' she said 'just nine left to do.'

My lines sank when I heard her, my pages curled and my cover turned red. I was so angry. I could have fallen off the table and hurt myself even more but I didn't. I stuck up to the dreaded compass. I'll shortly be known as the world-famous brave maths book. I bet it'll never happen though. I mean, all the maths books in here have to put up with ten or more circles, if they get corrections.

My nightmare started all over again when Emma had four corrections to do. Then she had a correction from her corrections.

I had a well-deserved rest after that. I was still exploding with pain. I just hope she won't need a compass again.

Robyn Seymour-Jones (11)
Ysgol Caergeiliog

A Day In The Life Of A Sunflower

Dung, dung, goes the water through my roots. Here I am stuck in the ground in the hot, summer week I have no family because people stood on them. Now all I have is one friend who is called Daisy. Next day, help, help, I need some water, I can't see, I'm going to faint, rain, rain come back. What is that noise, aghhhh, a human, no, no, no, squish, squash. That is the end of me.

Alana Davies (9)
Ysgol Caergeiliog

A Day In The Life Of My Dad

Hello, my name is Dad because everyone calls me Dad. I have two children and all I do all day is go and nag, nag, nag about mess, mess, mess.

I get treated like dirt I also get ignored. It's me who has to slave away. I'm the one who earns the money. I'm also the one who vacuums, washes the pans, cuts the grass and tidies up.

Can't I stop and have a rest, I know I shall pretend I'm sick that way they will give me sympathy. Here they come, watch it. They just went straight past and ignored me.

I will get them to notice me. I shall hide under the couch let them jump on me and boom-shanka-bob's your uncle it's done. Here she comes - ahh, oh I wondered who you were. I just vacuumed, washed the pans, cut the grass and tidied up. At last you noticed me.

Laura-Jayne Wesley (11)
Ysgol Caergeiliog

A Day In The Life Of A Sunflower

Today it's a nice, sunny day so I'm hoping Mr Williams will come and feed me some Miracle Grow because I'm thirsty. Mr Williams is a nice man except he keeps me indoors. But when I'm ill he puts me outside so I can have more sunlight. Hang on, what's that I hear, yes . . . it's water, my favourite!

Angharad Knight (9)
Ysgol Caergeiliog

A Day In The Life Of A Pencil Case

Hello, I'm Percy the pencil case and I'm going to tell you about a day in my life. I was sitting downstairs in the dark drawer when the drawer opened very quickly all my pencils and pens went flying and banged against me. A hand reached in and grabbed my friend Lucy the lunch box and put her in 'the bag'. Oh no, he was going to that awful place, school. Oh no, the hand emerged again, it grabbed me tightly and threw me into the bag. 'Ouch, a dent'! A big, painful dent right on the lid of me. He picked up the bag again and threw some smelly, dirty PE kit in. I couldn't breathe, I was caved in and suffocated, he started walking, with every step I bounced around with pain. When he finally stopped we were hung up. The large, bony hand reached in and grasped Betty the book and Derek the dinner money and then he clenched me tightly.

He arrived in a room full of other children and slammed me down on an empty table. I was left in peace till he started opening me and taking pens. My hinges started getting loose. Every time he opened me he let all the hot air out and I was freezing cold. After quite a while he threw me back into the bag and started the painful, smelly, bumpy ride back.

Jake Caffrey (11)
Ysgol Caergeiliog

A Day In The Life Of A Lizard

I live in a bit of countryside in a place which is known as France. I scuttle over each rock feeling vibrations of oncoming danger. Vast amounts of rocks and trees give me a safe habitat for me to live and hunt down my prey which is usually the smaller lizards living in my area and sometimes feasting on the odd locust or two. My area is made from a lot of rocks and trees, and many a tourist is attracted here.

I began my day by scuttling down the rocks and around the damp ground in search of food. I felt vibrations and focused on what was getting nearer. A rather small lizard was heading towards a pile of rocks behind me. The lizard was smaller than me and he was going to be the meal I was looking for. I sat on a pile of dead leaves camouflaging me. The smaller lizard was fast up the rocks and caught a locust which had injured itself. While it ate its meal I attacked and got the locust and the lizard.

One I had finished my lucky meal, two for the price of one, I scuttled into a bush and up a few rocks to a point that I could rest for a while. After a while it was night and I scuttled back to a rock that supplied shelter for me to sleep under. I ended the day after being chased by a group of people trying to catch me.

Michael Marchbanks (11)
Ysgol Caergeiliog

A Day In The Life Of An Ant

As I was crawling along the tunnel I stopped because right in front of me was a puddle of refreshing rain water and next to it was a small pile of food, so I thought I'd have a small dinner.

Later, I went for a crawl in the long grass where I met up with my friend Anthony. We played hide-and-seek until we got bored then we played charades but we got bored again.

As we went to get some more food and water to drink, a fox ran over us and as it did Anthony wished he was a fox so he could run free.

The sun went down and on our way back to the tunnel we both sighed and said . . . 'This is the funniest day ever!'

Ross Williams (10)
Ysgol Caergeiliog

A Day In The Life Of A Nail

I wonder if I am going to be used today or not. It is very boring being a nail. All you do is sit around until a human comes along and bashes you on your head, it hurts. Oh no, here comes a human, who is he or she going to pick? No, not my best friend! Phew, that must have hurt. Oh no, not me! At least I will be with my best friend. Oh well, aghhhhh that hurt!

Elin Parry (8)
Ysgol Caergeiliog

A Day In The Life Of A King Cobra

Slithering along the golden, hot sands of Africa in the desert, absorbing all the rays of sunlight into my body to warm my whole body up for the hunt in the moonlight. During the day I try to hide away from any man or rodent. If any of them come near me one day on my territory, I will rise my long body up and open up my hood so beware! If they come too close I will spit venomous poison, if that does not work then I will have no choice than to bite them.

The night has finally come, so I can go for the hunt in crystal clear darkness. I hid somewhere in the leaves to get ready to ambush my prey. Suddenly I felt the vibrations on the ground, it was a small mouse. Quickly I bite it, and it runs off to hide. I found it by seeing the heat on the ground and followed it till I found the mouse. I swallowed the mouse in one and then I went to hide for the very next day.

To find a new place to hide is very hard, I needed to find a nook where I can hide during the night and day. Finally, I found the perfect rock to stay in and rest for the day.

Jake Roberts (11)
Ysgol Caergeiliog

A Day In The Life Of A Snowflake

It's one of those boring old days when the snow comes down to the floor and falls on top of me. I'll just be lonely for the rest of my life. I sit here on the ground and nobody takes any notice when I'm about. When Jack Frost comes at night he treads on me without even knowing, he's so mean. It's so cold, I wish someone would throw a blanket over me, the snow just makes me cough and oh no, here comes another pile of snow! Bang, bang! Oh dear, oh dear, I hope it's not those big, clumsy kids again that came earlier. I'll just have a look, it is, it is, oh dear, oh dear, it is, bother, bother. I'll cover myself in snow. It was night-time, all the children had gone in, I finally melted in the snow.

Jenny Kay (8)
Ysgol Caergeiliog

A Day In The Life Of A Cloud

Today when I woke I seemed to be hovering in the sky. I floated over the Atlantic Ocean, I watched the fish go by. Oh no, a storm. Oops, I am a cloud, I think I will make it rain over my home town. Oh no, I am falling, help Mommy, help, help. help! Phew, it was only a dream. *Bang!* I hit the floor.

Richard Jefferies (10)
Ysgol Caergeiliog

A Day In The Life Of A Dream Ship

My life of a dream ship is like any other ordinary ship except for one thing. Every night I travel to a different country, and every night I appear in children's dreams. Every morning I go back to the Atlantic Ocean and think of other dreams. But one day there was a great, big storm while I was on the way to a different country and the lightning struck me and that was the end of me.

Angelique Le Page (9)
Ysgol Caergeiliog

Captain Hook

A day later Peter Pan had cut off my hand and thrown it to the crocodile and had eaten a clock. It was the rest of me that the crocodile was looking for. I was looking for Peter Pan's hideout so I sent for Mr Smee to get Tinkerbell for me. While I got ready for her it was a good idea for her to help me. She was sitting on the leaves with Mr Smee but she was in his hat when he got back so he let her out of his hat. I was good to her she showed me where Peter Pan lives.

Michael Bentley (8)
Ysgol Caergeiliog

A Day In The Life Of A Coin

Hello, I am a coin. I live in Tesco's counter. I have been in 96 different homes. I am a 50p coin. I have a friend called Matthew which is a 10p coin. Oh no, the Earth is moving. This is a story of what happened to me. One day I fell down a drain and ended up here.

Philip Jones (8)
Ysgol Caergeiliog

A Day In The Life Of An Orange

Two years ago there was an orange called Sean in the dusty, old shop. This orange was me, I'm called Sean and I'm a grown-up orange now. I'm now in a new, shiny shop. But when I was younger I was very poor. I will tell you the story when I was young.

Once upon a time there were six oranges. Six months later I was grown-up and so were the other five. All of them tried to escape but they got squashed by a car trying to cross the road. I was soon lonely and thirsty. I had decided to leave and cross the road and go to another shop! The road was very hard to cross indeed. But I managed to cross the road and found a shiny, new shop. There were drops of water and that's how I lived for the rest of my exciting life.

Stephen Yates (9)
Ysgol Caergeiliog

A DAY IN THE LIFE OF A LIMPET

As you know I am a limpet. I have a hard shell almost as hard as a rock! My body is soft, that's why I have a hard shell to protect it. I am an invertebrate creature. I belong to the mollusc family.

Now you know a bit about me. I'll tell you where I live. My home is on a great, big rock near the shore in Hell's Mouth. I love my home. It is quite craggy. The great thing about it is there's plenty of food there, I never run out.

I share my rock with loads of barnacles, a couple of winkles, about a handful of mussels and five sea anemones. But I share my rock with my family as well, my two daughters, my mum and my partner.

I eat seaweed and plants on the rock - they are delicious (especially the red seaweed). I drink water from the sea, it is very refreshing.

When the tide comes in I move. Once, when it was raining cats and dogs and the waves were as big as houses, I lost one of my daughters. It broke my heart. When the tide goes out I find my way back exactly to the same spot. Latin scholars call me *Patella Vulgata*.

Ffion Enlli (9)
Ysgol Crud Y Werin

A Day In The Life Of A Limpet

I am an invertebrate limpet. I've got a hard shell like a rock to protect my soft, slimy body. Some of us have got a hole in the top of their shell. They are called keyhole limpets. I've got a large, muscular foot so I can move when the tide is in. My shell is shaped like a flattened cone. I am about 7cm wide.

I live on a rock on Hell's Mouth beach. I share my home with barnacles, mussels, sea anemones and winkles. You will find me in cooler waters of the Atlantic Ocean and the Pacific Ocean. I cling tightly to rocks.

I eat seaweed and plants on the rocks. The seaweed is as slimy and as long as a ribbon but it is very nice. I am a herbivore sea animal. Many fish and birds like starfish, seagulls and people eat me. I chew with thousands of tiny teeth.

When the tide is in no one can see me because I am under the water. When the tide goes out they can all see me. I do not like the birds because this morning when I was sleeping a seagull came and pecked on my back. I was terrified. After it went I reluctantly came out. That was the most terrifying moment for me! bye-bye for now. Limpet.

Sera Williams (9)
Ysgol Crud Y Werin

A Day In The Life Of A Limpet

Suddenly I woke up and I saw a big, ugly seagull, she was right beside me. I tried to hide myself and she went looking for food in another place, what a relief.

I live on a black rock by the seashore, the name of the beach is Hell's Mouth! I live with lots of other animals like barnacles, mussels, sea anemones and winkles, they are very friendly. There's a human there, he's coming nearer and nearer and trying to remove me but I hold myself firmly and I made it!

I haven't got a backbone, I am an invertebrate, I look like a miniature volcano! My shape is like a cone. I want to tell you a secret now.
Are you listening? I am a female limpet, I lay my eggs in the water one at a time, don't tell anyone, OK!

I eat lovely, red seaweed. I eat it every day for breakfast and supper. When the tide comes in I move and when the tide goes out I move back to my cosy rock.

I have to be careful many fish could eat me. Starfish, birds and people are also enemies. Sorry, I've got to go. It has started to rain *cats and dogs* . . . Oh, yes do you know what my name is in Latin, I'll tell you it - *Patella Vulgata*!

Sioned Owen (10)
Ysgol Crud Y Werin

A Day In The Life Of A Limpet

As you know I am a limpet. My shell is shaped like a mini volcano and the colour of it is *brown, yellow* and *white.* I have two tentacles and a black eye at the base of each tentacle.

I live on a rock on Golden Beach in Port Meirion. It is called Golden Beach because the sand is golden. I share my rock with my friends - barnacles, mussels, sea anemones and winkles.

Peckish birds are my enemies. They are as white as fluffy clouds. I eat sea plants like *red, green* and *brown* seaweed, I drink sea water. It is a bit salty.

When the tide goes out I have a little wander around but when the tide comes in I stick to the rock like Superglue.

My Latin name is Patella Vulgata. In the night, otters, foxes and seals come to look for food on Golden Beach. Foxes look for crabs; otters look for molluscs like me and seals look for fish.

Sometimes humans come and try to remove me but I hold on tightly and I always win. But I'm still not happy because they hurt my friends. Anyway, that's me - an ordinary day in the life of a limpet.

Alex Annis (9)
Ysgol Crud Y Werin

A DAY IN THE LIFE OF A LIMPET

Reluctantly I woke up. It was raining cats and dogs. I felt a bit hungry so I decided to go and look for food. At last I found some seaweed. My favourite is green seaweed. Suddenly a seagull landed on my rock. It attacked my friend and his shell moved. I was terrified. In the end my friend got eaten by the seagull. It broke my heart.

My shell is as hard as a rock and the colour of it is brown, black and grey. I have two tentacles and a black eye at the base of each tentacle. I am an invertebrate animal and I cling tightly to rocks. I have enemies that eat me. The amazing starfish, peckish birds and some horrible humans sometimes pull me off.

When the tide comes in I've got to move or else the waves would carry me away. When the tide goes out I find my way to my spot. Sometimes some of us don't return to our rock.

At the end of the day as the sun goes down I settle down to sleep!

Caren Durant (10)
Ysgol Crud Y Werin

A Day In The Life Of A Limpet

I am a common limpet. I live on a rock on Tcasilian Beach, it's quite a big rock. When the blue sea comes in I search for food. My favourite food is red seaweed. It's the best. Last night my best friend Billy the limpet fell off the rock and we still haven't found him!

Suddenly a fish rushed by, I clung tightly to the rock. The fish nudged my shell and then went away. Thank goodness for that! Got to go now, the tide is coming in!

Dylan Rosa (11)
Ysgol Crud Y Werin

A Day In The Life Of A Limpet

I'm an invertebrate and I am a keyhole limpet. I've got a hard shell like a flattened cone and a head with a mouth, two long tentacles and a black eye at the base of each tentacle. I've got a large, muscular foot. When a seagull hovers above me I hide cautiously inside my shell. When the tide comes in, I pop my head out and I move around on a rock and when the tide goes out, I go back into my shell. I'm also a herbivore.

My home is on a rock in Hell's Mouth. I share my home with four other kinds of sea creatures. There are barnacles, mussels, sea anemones and winkles. I eat marine algae and other marine vegetation. I use a radula, a rough tongue-like organ that has thousands of tiny tentacles.

When I move slowly on the rock, I watch out for predators. My enemies are fish, starfish, birds and people. This morning some children came up to my friends and knocked them off the rock. Seagulls swooped down and ate them all. You have to be careful always.

Robin Hughes (11)
Ysgol Crud Y Werin

A Day In The Life Of A Limpet

Reluctantly I woke up, and it was raining cats and dogs. The tide was coming in. I was moving fast just in case the tide came in and caught me.

I'm a small animal living on a boulder on the beach. My name is Limpet. I've got a shell on my back to protect me. My shell is different colours, grey, brown and black. I'm living with other animals, small animals called barnacles.

When the tide goes out I move round the rock to find food. I like seaweed. There are different colours of seaweed like red, green and brown.

In the morning the seagulls come and try to peck and eat me and take me to their nest. In the evening some people come for a walk on the beach and they sit on the rock. When they sit in the middle they squeeze me but they cannot break my protecting shell because it is as hard as a rock. They cannot see me because I'm too small. I'm over the moon when there is plenty of food. Well, I have to go now because the seagulls are coming.

Sioned Mair Williams (10)
Ysgol Crud Y Werin

A Day In The Life Of A Limpet

I am a limpet. I'm shaped like a cone. My colour is *yellow* and *brown.* My shell is very hard like a rock and I have a big muscular foot.

I love on a rock by the seaside in Hell's Mouth. I share it with barnacles, mussels, sea anemones and winkles.

I eat plants on rocks like red seaweed and I drink sea water. When the tide comes in I move to search for food. When the tide goes out I return to the same place.

I have to be careful. I could be eaten by starfish, birds and even human beings.

Marc Williams (10)
Ysgol Crud Y Werin

A Day In The Life Of A Limpet

I am a common limpet. I have a cone-shaped shell and some people like to call me a mini volcano. I have two long tentacles on the top of my head. I am an invertebrate.

The name of the beach that I live in is Whistling Sands and in Whistling Sands there is a rock near the sea and that's where I live. I share the rock with mussels, sea anemones, winkles and hundreds of barnacles. You won't believe what I am going to say, they are like a white rash.

My favourite food is a mixture of red seaweed and green seaweed. Oh no! Here come the seagulls. I've got to camouflage myself.

Dafydd Jones (11)
Ysgol Crud Y Werin

A Day In The Life Of A Limpet

Reluctantly I wake up every day on my little rock in Hell's Mouth. It's a black, rough boulder. Sharing it with me are barnacles, mussels, sea anemones and winkles. Today there is a sharp, clear, blue sky.

I have a hard shell in yellow and brown. I am soft-bodied with a mouth, two long tentacles and a black eye at the end of each tentacle.

I eat plants on boulders. My favourite food is brown seaweed. I like the juice bubbling in my mouth.

When the sea comes in I go to find food and I move around. Sometimes a fish comes near. I get scared stiff. When the tide goes out people come. They are like giants. Yesterday one hit my friend down with a big instrument (I think it was a hammer), seagulls come and peck me on the shell but I always win. It is raining cats and dogs now and the waves are as big as houses. My Latin name is Patella Vulgata.

Sharon Roberts (9)
Ysgol Crud Y Werin

A Day In The Life Of A Limpet

Reluctantly I moved over the huge boulder on the beach. I am a sea animal. I am a limpet.

I have powerful enemies like seagulls that keep pecking my shell. Other enemies are people, they pull me off and might throw me away.

The boulder I live on is in Hell's Mouth beach. When the tide comes in I cling onto my rock just in case a fish comes and eats me.

My favourite food is green seaweed. I crawl over the rock to find my green seaweed and when I am full up I will return to where I came from. It's hard being a limpet.

Adrian Garner (10)
Ysgol Crud Y Werin

A Day In The Life Of A Limpet

I am a limpet and I have a very hard shell - it has orange, yellow and cream lines. It is exactly 3 cms wide. It is cone-shaped.

My home is on a rock in Porth Wisgi. It is a large, bumpy, grey rock. I eat and sleep all day long. I love red seaweed - it is delicious. I chew it all the time. When the tide comes in I have a bath and when the tide goes out I sunbathe. This morning a herring gull came on my rock and she was crying for food. I was feeling a bit down in the dumps so I clung tightly to the rock. Thank goodness she left. Last night an otter came out of the river and he tried to grab me. Finally a fox came and frightened the otter away - good for me!

Catrin Roberts (9)
Ysgol Crud Y Werin

A Day In The Life Of Rachel From S Club 7

Hi I am Rachel from S Club 7. I live in England. I have just got up, it is Monday and it is 7 o'clock and I have to go and record another song. I had a cup of tea and a slice of toast. Then it was 8 o'clock so I got in my car and drove off.

I got to the recording studio and met my friends Jo, Hanna, Tina, Paul, John and Bradley. We recorded our new song, sounds great! The girls and I went out shopping but after a while the others had to go.

Then I got my shopping and drove out of the shopping centre. I went to the gym because I have to keep in shape! Unfortunately I got there and it was closed, that made my day! So I decided to take a break so I went home to get my bikini on and went and sunbathed in the sun. I later went for a swim in the sea. Then after a while it started to get cold. Then I went to get dressed. Then my mobile rang, I had to go to the recording studio to rebase our new song. It is called 'Don't Stop Moving'. I got in the car and went to the studio, I got there then we started sing 'Don't Stop Moving'. Then someone went cut, you can all go and have a break while I am on the phone. Five minutes after we were told we have a gig at 8 o'clock. It was no 7 o'clock and we were told to go home and get ready for the gig.

Niccola Howard (10)
Ysgol Cystennin

A Day In The Life Of A Teacher

'Hi, I'm Miss Honey I am a teacher and I haven't got much time to talk right now because I'm late' I said as I struggled to get my skirt on! I rushed downstairs, put some toast on and poured myself a glass of milk. I went into the dining room, ate my breakfast, said goodbye to my husband and popped into my car. I struggled to get to school because of traffic jams. Finally when I got to school the class were reading quietly except for one boy who was messing out.

'Danny, stop messing! Well done the rest of the class! Any letters? Dinner money?' Five people stood up and formed a small line at my desk. There was dinner money and letters for our school trip. I went up to the hall to tell a story for assembly. It was lesson time and I told the pupils to carry on with yesterday's maths work. I went to the teachers lounge at dinner time and ate my packed lunch and thought of what the next lesson could be. Then I remembered I had had a letter for a competition to write a story. I gave the news to the rest of the class and they could not wait to get started. When they had all finished I sent them off and someone in my class won! At the end of the day I was exhausted, I got home, flung my shoes off and said 'See you tomorrow,' and jumped into bed!

Georgia Colman (10)
Ysgol Cystennin

A Day In The Life Of Mr Hind The Teacher

Hello, my name is Mr Hind. I'm a teacher, it is the first day of the school term and I'm just getting out of bed. I rolled around to see that the time was 8.35! I was late getting up, I had to be in the school to teach by 8.45. I was rushing to get dressed. As I was getting my trousers on while pouring a cup of coffee, I looked through the window to find I had missed the bus. I put my jacket on and ran quickly out the door. I had to walk, it took half an hour.

I finally got there at 9.15am! 'Sorry I'm late class, good morning,' I said.
My students all said, 'Good morning Mr Hind.' Well, all except one.
'Good morning Adam,' I said once again.
'Oh sorry sir, I didn't mean to get your knickers in a twist.' answered Adam.
'Adam Jones.'
'Yes, that's my name, don't wear it out!'
'I beg your pardon,' I said.
'Sorry, do you want me to say it again!' said Adam being obtuse as usual.
'To my office prompt. Oh there's a chair with your name on,' I shouted.
After dealing with him we got back to work, before we knew it was dinner time. After dinner I had to plan some work for Adam.

After much distress school was over. At home I plunged into bed and fell asleep.

Louise Owen (9)
Ysgol Cystennin

A Day In The Life Of A Baby

Hi, I am a baby and my name is Kayleigh and I am a very noisy baby! Every night till morning I cry and cry.

Today I woke up and I saw my mum and dad look over me and I started to cry again. They started to say 'There, there, don't cry,' so I stopped but I was very hungry. Then I started to cry again, so they made a bottle and gave it to me. Then they put my coat on and put me in the pram and took me to the park and put me in the baby swing and started to push me, but every time I went up I got cold so I started to scream, but then I calmed down because they stopped me and took me out and put me on the slide, I sat on my mum's knee and slid down. I was giggling.

Then I went home, I was tired so I fell asleep. On the way home I then had a biscuit but you know how hungry seagulls are, it swooped down and picked up my biscuit and flew off. I woke up and started to scream but luckily my mum had another one so I ate it so the seagull would not get my biscuit but this time I couldn't get to sleep. Soon we were home and it was 7.00 I had my nappy changed. Then I fell asleep but my mum sang my favourite song. Goo, goo (goodnight).

Catherine Williams (10)
Ysgol Cystennin

A Day In The Life Of Baby Arron

Hi my name is Arron. I am one year old and this is what I do in a day. I woke up and stretched my little arms. Then my mum came along and changed my nappy but I didn't need it changing and then I started crying really loud. After a while my mum put me in the bath. I started splashing the water, it was fun. After a while my mum invited some visitors but all they did was look over me. I wanted to go to sleep. I wish they would go away from me I thought to myself. Then when the people went I woke up as I was only pretending to be asleep! I started to cry so my mum got me changed and fed me. After she fed me she took me down town. My mum got me some new shoes, they were really wicked! Then after we got my shoes we went back home but I got really thirsty but my mum wouldn't feed me because I had already been fed. After a bit it came to my feed I had some more milk because I love milk. My mum had some more visitors I was on the sofa when they came in, they knocked something over, I started laughing but I fell asleep but the visitors woke me up because they were going 'Goo, goo.' So I couldn't get to sleep but in the end I did and I didn't wake up until the morning. That is my day!

Carly Bebbington (9)
Ysgol Cystennin

A Day In The Life Of My Dog

Hi my name is Wes I am a dog and I can do tricks and it is wicked man! Oh my mum feeds me some dog food at 7am then she takes me out after my breakfast for a walk in the park and she lets me off my lead so I can run about. Then I go home and have a sleep in my basket and it is dead nice and warm. Then I wake up and have some dinner. Then I play with my ball and I tear it open and my mum shouts at me and I say sorry by wagging the end of my tail. On every Sunday I go out in the garden and jump up on the gate and I watch the children on their bikes. I go back into the house and I have a sleep next to the fire. I wake up and have my tea, oh then I had a drink of milk. Then I went back to sleep until my owner whistled me to go out in the garden. Then I snuggled up in my bed next to the fire and I went back to sleep in my basket and my owners said 'Goodnight.'

Danny Russell (9)
Ysgol Cystennin

A Day In The Life Of A Nurse

Hi! I'm Jill, I'm one of the nurses on duty today. I went up to the staffroom to make myself a cup of coffee. In the hospital you meet different people every day. Today a young boy came in with a broken leg, he was really hurt. I had to help him, he had to have a plaster cast on his leg. Day in, day out, I always have to make the coffee, for all the staff. In the morning that's what I do!

Today I woke up late I was meant to be at the hospital at 7.30m it was now 8.15am. I phoned up the hospital to say that I wouldn't be able to come in till this afternoon. Lorna, she was the Special Doctor had just come round to see why I hadn't come in, I said I was sick. It was the afternoon, I went into the hospital. A little girl had cut her arm open I had to make the coffee as normal while the special doctor Lorna looked at the little girl's arm. After that the doctor said to the child's Mum Mrs Howard, she will be fine.

I was looking at the little girl I said she was brave. She said thank you. I went home, had my tea and went to bed.

Jodie Russell (10)
Ysgol Cystennin

A Day In The Life Of My Mum

Hello, my name is Eleanor. I am a mum, I have arthritis. This is a day in my life. I wake up and have a cup of tea in bed, then I do the housework. In ten minutes I will have a tea break. I am keen on tea but I am not keen on coffee. Then I will go to Tesco to do the shopping. I will then have some lunch, a very big lunch! Then I will put the washing out and leave it to dry. I will watch telly maybe EastEnders. Then make another cup of tea and get a biscuit of course, I will relax and enjoy. Later I will go for a shower then get changed into my work clothes and I'll get the washing in. I will go to work. I will stay there until 5.00 then I will go home and make the tea. After my tea I will watch telly. At 10.00 I will go to bed and read a magazine or a Malacy Macort book for about ten minutes or so. Then I will switch off the light and go to bed - goodnight!

Tom Williams (9)
Ysgol Cystennin

A Day In The Life Of A Baby

Hi, I am Bob the baby. I have my nappy changed every hour and when I have a pet I kick it down the bank if it is a cat just for the fun of it. Every Sunday my sister wants to go to the Barbie shop and we spend an hour in the shop. Instead of going to buy a bottle. We went home and I had a little nap. When I woke up my mum said 'Time to go to Nanny's.' When we got to Nanny's I played football with my cousin. When we got in we had dinner. I didn't want butties so I threw them at the wall. Then I went and watched the Tweenies. After that I felt like having a game of football so I went outside and I kicked the football and I got a goal. It got boring so I went in and my mum said, 'Time to go.'

When we got home the cat was near the front door, then my mum put me down and I chased after the cat but it got away. It went out of the cat flap to go to the garden. I wanted to chase it so I went through the cat flap. I looked in the paddling pool in the bird bath and in the tree. Then I heard the bench creak so I looked there and it was the cat. So I went 'Ga, ga!' I scared the cat away. After it was getting dark, so I went in.

Thomas Kirby (9)
Ysgol Cystennin

A DAY IN THE LIFE OF MUM

Hi my name is Paula Ryder I woke up at 6.00am and the first thing I do is get dressed and get Mark my son and then tell John to get up and to get dressed ready. Then I went down to have something to eat, then I said bye to John. Then I went to wake up my two kids Sarah and Hayley, they got dressed and then Sarah did her hair, I did Hayley's. Then I got Mark dressed and I went to take them to school. Then I went to my mum's house and then I went to the bank to pay my debts and bills, and then I went to do some shopping. When I came home I collapsed on the sofa, had dinner and put my shopping away and then started to do some housework. I sat down to watch Bob the Builder with my 3 year old son. Then at 3.15 I went to pick Sarah and Hayley up from school. When we got in I made sandwiches for tea. When they were playing outside in the garden John came so I made us a lovely salad (if I may say so myself!) Then at 8.30 I put Sarah and Hayley to bed and at 9.00pm John and I went to bed with a cuppa.

Sarah Ryder (10)
Ysgol Cystennin

A Day In The Life Of A Teacher

I am Mrs Campion.
It was Monday morning and I had just woken up, it was 7.15am I had to be in work by 8.30am I am teacher you see. I teach children English. I went downstairs and made myself a cup of coffee and some toast. When I had finished by breakfast I got dressed into my top and trousers and now it was 8.15am. I jumped in my car and made my way to school but there were traffic lights everywhere, typical! First it was on red then on green, I raced to school.

When I got there it was 8.40am, I went up to my classroom and the children were talking. I told them to turn to page 17 and do capital letters and full stops. Mark, a boy, was messing about, so I told him to go to the head teacher. At dinner I went to the teachers' lounge. I had to mark 25 people's work. Some were lazy and some were good. After lunch I did the same but with 3 year olds. They had to do a sentence with a capital letter and a full stop. At half-past three I was so tired I made my way home and made tea. I had pasta then my favourite TV programme Crossroads was on. I sat down and had my tea. It turned half-past 11 so I went upstairs waiting for a brand new day!

Charlotte Campion (10)
Ysgol Cystennin

A Day In The Life Of My Friend Danny

Hi, I'm Danny. My mum Jane said I'm going to Paris and I can't wait, it's going to be great. I love Paris but I'm only going for one day. But still I can't wait. I'm going to the airport right now. Yes, we're getting on the plane. I get my Action Man figure and Doctor X as well and pretend to destroy Doctor X before he blows up the plane. Then I put them away and got my Gameboy out and played Super Mario. I had to beat the Turtle Sword. I won so I shouted hooray. Then I got out. Oh we're here!

We were at the place where you get your luggage, then we went to the coach to go to the hotel and unpacked all our stuff. Then we went to see Mickey Mouse, Daffy Duck and Sylvester and Tweety Pie. Then we went to go and get some burgers and then we went to go back to our hotel, so I could play in the swimming pool. I swam under the water and it was wicked man. Then we got on the plane and I fell fast asleep. Then my mum woke me up and we were at the car and my mum drove me home and I fell fast asleep.

Wesley Earl (9)
Ysgol Cystennin

A Day In The Life Of A Horse

When I wake up in the morning I can hear the tractor and I can see the farmer coming with some hay and it is my breakfast time. Suddenly soon after I have eaten, Hannah (the girl) comes to get me out of my stable and she gets on my back and we go for a ride.

Hannah is 13 years old and she's got two sisters, Sarah and Cathryn. Sarah is 10 and Cathryn is 20. After we went for a walk I go jumping with Cathryn and then I go jumping with Hannah because I have to go to the show and I am in two races. I am in a team and our team is Trefeglwys. So I try to work hard. Sarah is too young to go jumping because she might hurt herself. After jumping I go to my stable to rest and to have lunch. Soon after lunch we are off to the show and we are busy getting ready for the race. The first race is under 12-14 so Hannah is riding me first. I am against Newtown. Ready, steady, go . . . and off I go. After that Cathryn is riding and this is the best race so I am extremely excited. Ready, steady, go . . . I'm off hooray. Trefeglwys have won. I am very pleased with myself today. And then I go home from the show with the family. After returning home the children groomed me and washed me and littered my stable. Before long it is my bedtime and the children are tucked up in bed.

'Night, night everyone,' I say.

Ffion Evans (9)
Ysgol Dyffryn Trannon

A Day In The Life Of A Butterfly

I am a butterfly and I am a beautiful flying insect, I have four colourful wings they are purple, red, yellow, orange with black dots. It is a lovely day and I like flying in the garden from one flower to the other. My favourite colours are pink, red, orange and purple. It is a lovely day and I like flying high when the sun is shining.

When I am hungry I suck all of the juices from the flowers and leaves with my long tongue. I meet my friends in the garden and we all go flying together.

I lay eggs on leaves and in a few days they hatch into caterpillars. The caterpillar eats and eats off the leaves and it loses its old skin many times as it grows into a butterfly like me.

A life of a butterfly is wonderful!

Lisa Jones (8)
Ysgol Dyffryn Trannon

A Day In The Life Of A Dog

'Woof,' I have a master called Huw who lives with his family. First thing in the morning Bryn lets me out of my kennel. He starts the four-wheeler and I get excited because I know we're going to see the sheep in Cae Bach. Bryn's black ewe was lambing, so Bryn blew his whistle that told me to send all the sheep to the bottom corner so Blackie could be caught. After Huw pulled the lamb, he goes to feed the cows. I go with him. After feeding the cows I go up the hill with my master to feed the sheep. I follow the bike and listen to his commands. The words 'Come by', means go to the right and 'Away', means go to the left. I look forward to when the children come home. At the end of the day the farmer feeds me and puts me in my kennel.

Bryn Jones (9)
Ysgol Dyffryn Trannon

A Day In The Life Of A Worm

My name is Wiggle. I live in the bare patch of ground behind Mr and Mrs Brown's house. One day I woke up with a fright and I saw a bird flying towards me, so I quickly hid behind a rock. When the bird had flown away I went to look for some breakfast. The soil was so hard and dry, so I squeezed under the fence into next door's garden. I couldn't believe my eyes it was like a jungle there were so many trees, plants and flowers that I did not know what to eat first. I started on the giant, juicy pears then the apples for pudding. I was so full I fell asleep in a big, warm greenhouse. I met some new friends and decided to live there forever.

Jonathan Evans (8)
Ysgol Dyffryn Trannon

A Day In The Life Of A Bug

A day as a bug isn't that bad. I spin a web from corner to corner to catch flies then rush to kill them and eat them.
What am I?
I have eight legs but no arms or tail and I can't fly. Sometimes you see me, sometimes you don't, but I can see you wherever I am.
What am I?
Sometimes I put the fear of God into people but I am completely harmless. I can run quite fast on the ground and on my web. Sometimes I'm waiting for a long time and other times I'm not. If I'm lucky I get more than one.
What am I?
Birds can eat me but nothing else so I'm quite safe but when females lay eggs they die but I am a male.
What am I?
It's getting dark and I'm on my way back to my corner. Now I'm home. Then I realise what I am and I'm a . . . spider!

Daniel Williams (9)
Ysgol Dyffryn Trannon

A Day In The Life Of A Bunny

There I was in my little house, in the pet shop. Then some people came in and started fighting over me. Then my owner came in and said 'Do you want to buy him?' And the two people said 'Yes.' When I got to my new owner's house I knew that I would like it there. They had two children, a girl named Josie she is 9 years old and a boy named John, he is 4 years old. I was their new pet. As soon as they got me out of the box the two children started to play with me. They chased me round the garden. I had a little hutch and a run to live in. Josie and John went into the house to get me some food and a drink of water. I felt very tired and had a little sleep.

Whilst I had been asleep the children had put a name on my hutch, they called me Snow, because my fur is very white. Later that day when I was playing with the children a big dog came along and frightened me, he chased me into my run and growled at me. The children told their dog off and said you are to make friends with Snowy. He has come to live with us. We all had a busy day and I am very tired so I am going to sleep.

Kathy Mills (9)
Ysgol Dyffryn Trannon

A Day In The Life Of A Bumblebee

Hi, I'm Buzzy and I'm a bumblebee. Today it's my turn to go and look for the wildest flower in Wales which is called Dreamer. Now Dreamer is the flower that bees over the centuries have found because she is a wild flower. So I spread out my wings and buzzed off out of the enormous beehive saying cheerio to the Queen bee. I had only been a little while when I saw some lovely flowers down below, so I flew down to have a look.

The wind was calm today so I decided to go and explore the group of flowers. When I got down there I nestled in the centre of the flower. After a little while I woke up and I collected some nectar from the lovely, sweet-smelling flowers. I flew a bit more when two children came towards me and started clapping their hands. Ouch, they caught me so I stuck out my needle and stung them. The children let me go and ran away crying.

After that I flew over Fox Wood to find Dreamer. I stopped over Bumble Wood because I thought I saw a group of weird-looking flowers. I swiftly flew down to have a closer look and there in front of my eyes was Dreamer. I snapped Dreamer off her stem and flew back to the beehive and when I got back we made lovely honey from lovely Dreamer.

Jamie Robinson (10)
Ysgol Dyffryn Trannon

A DAY IN THE LIFE OF HEIDI

I woke up on a prickly, straw bed overlooking a great valley below the Alps. I was in a small, wooden cabin in a straw loft. I looked at myself I was dressed in two, if not three frocks. I felt my hair and then I knew for definite who I was, I was Heidi.

I went down a few steps and I found myself in a rather large room and by the stove stood an old man. He had bushy, grey eyebrows and a long thick beard.
'Hello child,' he said wisely.
'Good morning Grandfather,' I said remembering the book.
'I want you to have some breakfast before you go out to play and help Peter with the goats, here have an apple and bring me back some goats milk, would you?' he asked.
'Yes Grandfather,' I said enthusiastically.
'Well, go on then, you've had your apple now go!'
And with that I went outside to find Peter. I thought about him and what he was like, I could hardly remember because it was such a long time ago since I'd read the book. I remember he lives in the Alps with his mother, but that's about all.

After about half an hour searching I eventually found him. We played all day and got buckets of milk. Finally, night drew in I said goodbye to Peter and went back to the cabin. I had supper and went to bed thinking so this is what it's like to be Heidi.

Carly Harris (10)
Ysgol Dyffryn Trannon

A Day In The Life Of A Six Month Old Baby

I awake with a nudge on my shoulder and a giant *waa, waa,* comes from me. My mum starts changing my nappy while I'm now sucking happily on a dummy. A giant puff of powder goes in my face and I start waving it away with my small, chubby hand. When that was over she started putting on that horrible, itchy vest, baggy trousers, my colourful, stripy jumper and a tight bib saying 'I'm a big boy.'

When she took me downstairs into the kitchen she sat me down in that 'very' high chair and I wondered what's for breakfast? I soon got my answer, a bowl of sloppy baby food. My mum sat down facing me, she started saying, here comes the choo-choo train. She stuffed it in my mouth but I spat it out in her face. I laughed joyfully.

She took me out of my chair and took me into the living room to watch the TV, it was the Teletubbies, oh not, this again, it was so boring I fell asleep for the next hour.

I was awoken by the doorbell and in came Aunty Liz saying where's my little nephew? She picked me up while I looked into her fat face. Oogh! I thought, I think I'm going to be *blaghaa,* too late I was sick right on Aunty Liz's face and jacket.

'Did you know this suit is dry clean only?' she said to me in a sweet, little voice. Then later when Aunty Liz had gone home I went to bed for another baby day.

Ryan Lane (11)
Ysgol Dyffryn Trannon

A Day In The Life Of A Dog

I woke up this morning after a good night's sleep. I sleep on my owner's bed - it's really soft and nice to sleep on. Every morning my other owner takes me outside, for a little walk and we go back in.

After a while he gives me some breakfast. The two girls and the boy and their mum come down for breakfast. Off they go I don't know where but they do go. I don't really like it, I get used to it after a while. Then the big man of the family takes me with him to put some glass in things without any glass in them. We do, I mean he does about five every day. Then we go home and he puts me in the kennel and goes off again. He brings the others home with him but not the female she comes home a bit later. We all have lots of fun again then we all have tea. Then a couple of hours later we go to bed. The next morning the people don't go off anywhere because the people's Nan died. They're all upset, so am I. Well bye for now, maybe we can talk some more another time. Bye!

Bethan Davies (11)
Ysgol Dyffryn Trannon

A Day In The Life Of Millie The Basset Hound

I woke up saying 'Daddy (her owner) I need the loo, it's potty time.' I barked and he came to put me out. I did my business. I barked 'Oh what a relief.' Daddy put me into the kitchen and the mummy, Rayn, Jamie (a girl) and Samantha they came and I jumped up on all of them.

Mummy gave me my breakfast and I ate it really fast then they let me out again because I like getting outside and I ran and my ears started flapping and I found a tennis ball to play with.

Then I smelt something, mmm, what's that smell? It was coming from the house, so I ran in, it was toast. I knew I'd get some because they always give me the last piece; they all had party hats on, they gave me a whole piece of toast then I realised it was my birthday and I was barking with my mouth full saying 'Happy birthday to me, happy birthday to me, happy birthday to me, happy birthday to me.' I was getting loads of hugs and I even had a birthday hat to wear, a blue one with purple spots and I had three new dog toys. I had fun but I was tired so I went to bed.

I woke up and somebody was trying to be silly, they had put a bright blue T-shirt on me. Every time I tried to walk I fell over but soon got angry so they took it off me. After that I played with my new toys with Jamie. Don't tell her I said this but I'm stronger than her.

But I then had to say goodbye to Rayn, Jamie and Sammy because it was their bedtime. They all gave me a kiss on the head. Soon after me and Daddy had been watching TV it was my bedtime. Who shall I go with? I know, I'll go with Jamie. So I said goodnight to Daddy and went on Jamie's bed to sleep. I woke Jamie up because I jumped on her. Ha, ha!

Kathryn Davies (11)
Ysgol Dyffryn Trannon

A Day In The Life Of A Blade Of Grass

One day in my field I was being bounced around by my friend Mr Wind. (I asked him a couple of days ago and he's obviously kept his promise of blowing me about!) Mr Wind was cooling down after a minute, but suddenly I was sucked into a black hole 'Sorry, pink hole, but I just found out that I was in a cow's stomach.'

It was very cold and lonely in there but then a little stick of some sort came over to me. He sounded very clever. The stick came up with an idea to get out of the pink hole. He said to me that he had some Hyoxide (powder to make you sick). So stick dribbled a bit of it on the cow's digestive system. Then an earthquake came and we came whooshing out with the other grass. So we hopped back into our places. But then the same thing happened again and I'm still in the cow's stomach. It's very boring here!

Sophie Wozencraft (9)
Ysgol Dyffryn Trannon

A DAY IN THE LIFE OF A CAR

I can be large or I can be small, sometimes I can be middle-sized. Sometimes I have got four, sometimes three and sometimes I have got only one. I can be shiny, I can be dull, sometimes very flashy. I can be any colour. I can be very dirty or clean. I can be slow or very fast if I want to. Sometimes I stay in my home and I don't come out for a long time. Sometimes I am out all the time, I can stay out all night even in the winter although I might be a bit slow if I stay out all night in the winter.

Richard Morgan (10)
Ysgol Dyffryn Trannon

A Day In The Life Of A Spider

As I watch the flies fly into my web covered in the early morning dew I get ready for a good breakfast. Slowly I begin to climb towards the struggling flies trapped in my web. After a tasty breakfast I hear a scream. It was the woman who owned the garden gate I built my web in. It was almost lunchtime but it looked like I would have to fast until tea.

I quickly abandoned my brand new web and fled from the garden. It took me at least three hours to find a new home. It was on a fence to a children's play park. Tired and hungry I built a quick web and settled down to think about my exciting day in the life of a spider.

Matthew Toms (9)
Ysgol Dyffryn Trannon

A Day In The Life Of A Flying Frog

On Christmas Day after eating the turkey we took the wishbone out and my dad and I both wanted to make a wish, so we pulled the wishbone and yes! I won! If you promise not to tell anyone, I'll tell you what I wished for. I wished to be an animal that could fly, swim and walk.

When I went to bed I fell straight to sleep and when I woke up the next morning I found myself in the body of a flying frog.

I went out of my hole and climbed a tree. When I got to the top, I could see for miles and then I remembered what I was - a flying frog. I decided to try flying and I jumped as far as I could and stretched as wide as I could. This is seriously *cool* I thought. And then I dived into the river and swam with all my might for about ten minutes. After I swam, I walked (well hopped then) through the jungle until bedtime. When I found a snug little hole I settled down and went to sleep.

Hours later, when I woke up, I looked like my normal self. My twenty-four hours as an amphibian had finally come to an end.

Eva Newton (10)
Ysgol Gynradd Penlôn Primary School

A Day In The Life Of Being A Hamster

One morning when I woke up, I was starting to grow hairs all over my body . . . it was very difficult for me to get changed because all of the hairs were making me look fat and they were pushing my clothes back down.
Finally I got changed but then I was shrinking very slowly.
Suddenly I was as small as a hamster but luckily for me I still had a hamster cage. Then my mum shouted,
'Stevie, breakfast is ready!'
'OK, coming now. Oh, actually I don't want any.'
My sister came in and saw me as a hamster and said:
'Stevie is that you?'
'Yes, it is me.'

Two whole hours had passed and I still looked the same. Then I went outside where everything looked really big, so I started to crawl downstairs. It took me ages.

When I got downstairs, the living room looked so big, the TV was like a mansion. I remembered that I was going to see what my mum was doing but when I got downstairs she wasn't there. I looked everywhere for her. Then I remembered that it was Thursday morning and she goes shopping. I was thinking in my head 'Now this is my chance to change back to normal, but how can I do that?' I tried changing back loads of times but then I gave up, so I went by the window and started to cry. Some kind of glitter came out of my tears and I was changing . . .

Stevie Waddington (11)
Ysgol Gynradd Penlôn Primary School

A Day In The Life Of A . . .

One summer morning I hatched out of a tiny little egg. I was trying to look for food. Where I had hatched there was a leaf. I started to eat the leaf. I was getting fatter and fatter because I ate loads of leaves.

I went to sleep for a couple of hours, and when I woke up I felt different. I thought to myself, 'I am going to explode any minute.'

I ate all of the cabbages in Mrs Whitfield's garden. Every time I was hungry, I always used to go there. But she had passed away one week ago. It was very sad for all the caterpillars because she always used to keep us as pets and feed us her cabbages. Soon I started to feel very funny. My whole body was changing shape, from being a normal happy caterpillar to being a chrysalis. I stayed as a chrysalis for a couple of hours, but soon I felt I was changing again. I felt free. I could see the sunlight ahead, and I flew into the sparkling sunlight as a beautiful butterfly.

Emma Coley (10)
Ysgol Gynradd Penlôn Primary School

A Day In The Life Of My Brother

I woke up one morning and looked around. Ugh! I was in my brother's room. I walked down the corridor and looked in the mirror.
'Oh my God! I've turned into my brother,' I said to the mirror.

When I went into my own bedroom, my brother was me. I woke him up. When he noticed what had happened he was shouting:
'Turn me back now.'
This did not happen. I had to go to my brother's school. The work was so hard. Because it was my brother's birthday, I got canned. It is when a person throws a can of Coke at you. At half-past three I was really glad when school was over. I was drenched. When I got home, everybody jumped out in front of me and shouted:
'Happy Birthday.'
When I went in the kitchen it was full of presents. Mum ordered me to open them.
'No, it's not my birthday, it's Mathew's,' I said to my mum.
Mathew opened all of the presents. Some were big and others were small. I went to bed at 11 o'clock and at midnight *bang!*
I woke up in my brother's bed. I ran down the corridor and looked in the mirror. Phew!

Luke Thomas (10)
Ysgol Gynradd Penlôn Primary School

A Day In The Life Of Tony Blair

That morning I woke up and I was in a king-sized bed. That is funny - how can I have a king-sized bed if I went to sleep in a normal bed, I asked myself.
'Tea and biscuits this morning, Tony?' asked the waitress.
'Tony? What are you going on about?' I thought to myself. Oh my God! I've got to be Tony Blair. *Cool!* Wow! A shirt and tie - it's a bit more tasty than the boring old Penlon school uniform every morning.

'Tony, the limousine's outside.'
'Coming!'
Blwch!
There's another egg wasted on my limo.
'We want some fuel now!' said the crowd.
I thought to myself, if they could just wait for a few hours then everything will be back to normal again. And off I went to the Houses of Parliament.
Eventually I arrived at The Houses. I walked in and felt really important because I am the Prime Minister of Britain.
'We want the prices of fuel lowered,' said the Scottish.
'I will lower the prices to 78 pence a litre, alright?'
'I want petrol back in the pumps or otherwise I'll never get my car running,' said the judge.
The crowd were starting to call me names and booed at me.
'Okay, maybe you all think I'm a bit of a loser, but you'll see after the election, if I lose my job or not.'
I know I will get the last laugh, I thought to myself.

Aaron James (10)
Ysgol Gynradd Penlôn Primary School

A Day In The Life Of Winnie The Pooh

One fine day in Hundred Acre Wood, Winnie the Pooh wanted an adventure . . .
Rabbit suggested 'a stroll in the park'.
'No, that's not an adventure,' Tigger said. 'Why don't you go and bounce to bounce land?'
'No, that's not an adventure either.'
In the end he went to go and live in the woods. Before he went Tigger, Rabbit, Eeyore and Piglet threw a massive going-away party. Piglet nearly flooded his house out by crying because he didn't want him to go! Everyone gave him a pot of honey, except Rabbit who gave him some carrots, so he swapped Tigger's honey for carrots.
When the party was over, Pooh started his journey. After five minutes he came back but Eeyore was living there so he had to go and live with Piglet but it was a nightmare. He kept on breaking things, so he had to go. He made sure that he moved out and they had a nice little party to welcome him home. Christopher Robin had to read him a story to get him to bed.
And that's the story of Winnie the Pooh in Hundred Acre Wood.

Katy Fawcett (10)
Ysgol-Y-Castell Primary School

A Day In The Life Of A Bin

I sit all day in the sun,
I have no money and I have no fun.
I stink and smell of spare food,
If I stink too much I get in a mood.
A plastic bag is put on my head,
I wish those children would go to bed.
I'm kicked and scuffed all day long,
I want to kick back but I know it's wrong.
I've got pens, paper, scissors and books,
This girl called Zoe gives me the dirty looks.
The teacher's the worst, he shouts a lot,
The boys in class are little swats.
The girls always squeal and scream,
Please wake me up and tell me it's a dream.
At dinner time I'm filled with paper bags,
I'm sure it's better than being filled with fags.
At night I'm cleaned with smelly stuff,
Then she tickles me with this stick of fluff.
She cleans me up for the day ahead,
Then tucks me into my comfy bed.
A couple of hours later when I've woke,
I've found out that overnight I've broke.
Do not worry or have a fright,
Because she'll fix me up and I'll be alright.
It's the same again as happened yesterday,
And the same will be tomorrow and today.

Zoe Butterworth (10)
Ysgol-Y-Castell Primary School

A Day In The Life Of My Dog Lily

At about 7.30am I start my daily schedule by doing my best to wake up the neighbours and my family. Sarah lets me out to go to the toilet, but instead I usually have a nose around in the garbage.

When I come back in, I have some breakfast (probably salmon and plaice), yum!

Now it's about 8.15am and I go to look out of the window in the lounge. I wait at the window until Daniel goes to school with Sarah (or Nan). I mostly doze around and play with my toys while Daniel's gone. Sometimes, I might steal the odd curler from Nan. If I'm good I get a Bonio or a treat. I run around and chase my tail to pass the time.

When Daniel comes home (about 3.30pm), I go mad and start jumping about until I get really tired. Then I have a nap for about half an hour. Then it's snack time, yay! I play until it gets dark. Then I sleep on my cushion in front of the fire for a quarter of an hour.

Then I have my supper before I say goodnight to Daniel. Next I go to bed to get the energy I need for the next day.

'Woof!'

Daniel Ostanek (10)
Ysgol-Y-Castell Primary School

A Day In The Life Of A TV

Today it's all alone by the couch doing nothing but sitting there. Chris and Dave are going to be home soon and feel its powerful goodness. Nothing can turn it on except the goldfish. It has no fun on its own all day. Mike is happy because it saves on the bill. It lounges around all day. It always feels sorry for itself. It gives a brilliant picture, first time, every time. It stares into the sky wondering and wondering. Its favourite part of the day is night-time. They all gather as a family because they all watch till about 2am. The TV is a very special part of all their lives. Without it they couldn't watch World Wrestling Federation and International Football and all of their favourite soaps, like Coronation Street and so on. It sits there and does nothing. It can't do acrobatic tricks but it can when you flick through the channels.

Christopher Rothwell (10)
Ysgol-Y-Castell Primary School

A Day In The Life Of A Dolphin

A dolphin swims around all day thinking of what to do.
Thumper, Kipper and herself (Flipper) go to school to learn to swim and catch their prey on the Great Barrier Reef of Australia.
Flipper and friends have to watch the waters in case of pollution and the humans in case they use them for bait, food or to get money to show them off and make them do things.
Flipper and Kipper are best friends. Flipper's mom spends most of her time looking out for them. She tells Flipper to stay away from the shallow waters in case the humans catch them and sell their skin.
Flipper's boyfriend, Wacky, drinks the polluted water. He's gonna die and that's what Flipper keeps telling him, but he doesn't listen. He drinks too much pollution and dies.
Flipper is heartbroken and kills herself by letting a shark eat her.
Disgusting or what? To let a shark eat her!
Her mom and dad try to find the shark and kill it. A boy called Sean kills the shark and throws it back in the water.

Katy Morris (10)
Ysgol-Y-Castell Primary School

A DAY IN THE LIFE OF MY PET DOGS

Today they run around fast after a ball, but they give up because they're lazy and to chew on a bone so crunchy. Then after, they have a nice relaxing rest.
Poppy eats the grass while Laddie just lounges around staring at the fluffy clouds in the sky wondering and wondering.
Poppy plays with her tail while Laddie just lounges around staring into the endless sky wondering and wondering.
After a while they start to fight with a bite here, a roll there and kicks.
Then, here comes lunch. Yummy! A drink of healthy water does the trick. Another nap clears their heads while they have dreams of food, bones and treats. Then a nice run around refreshes the body. Their tails wag, full of happiness. Their tongues stick out letting off heat. Their big fur coats and the sun makes them extremely hot, so a nice bowl full of cool water cools them down. They both stare into eternity as they jump about woofing. Poppy does tricks and runs around happily. Then they start waiting for the back door to be opened. Then comes tea. A gulp makes them full and ready for bed. A little run around before their bed time. Goodnight.

Elliot Fox-Byrne (10)
Ysgol-Y-Castell Primary School

A Day In The Life Of A £1 Coin

Hi, I'm called Notey. I live, well I don't know where I live. One day I get dropped in this thing with a slot. Mrs Ponto (my owner) told her daughter that she would put her pocket money in her money box. I don't personally know what a money box is. Now someone is taking me out of the money box and I'm going in something called a purse to Cool Stuff supermarket. I'm now getting out and being put on a glass thing above. Sorry, hang on, I think I'm going to sneeze. *Aaaachooo!* Bless me! Anyway, where was I? Oh yes, a lady is putting me in with a load of other money and notes. Why am I called Notey when I'm a £1 coin?
'Hi, I'm Notey, what's your name?'
'I'm Penny. I've been in about 100,000 people's hands today. Oh look, the lady is taking me out again.'
'£1.50 change, Hope you come back soon. Bye,' said the shopkeeper.
I wonder what this person's called. He's not as nice as Mrs Ponto because I haven't got a purse to sleep in. Oh well. I'm now on another glass thing in the bank and being put in a big safe. Oh, here he comes again to get me out. Oh no! He's got my brother Notes out (he's a £20 note).
'Hey Notey, sneak in my pocket and I'll take you home with me.'
I'm at my new home in another money box with my brothers and sisters and I hope it stays like that.

Kate Rylance (9)
Ysgol-Y-Castell Primary School

A DAY AS A HAMSTER

Once again, the sun shone in Gizmo's cage and woke her up.
'Not again, Mr Sun, why do you always wake me up?' moaned Gizmo.
He was always in a mood when woken up. He went down his ladder to get some breakfast.
'Right,' said Gizmo in a deep voice, 'today is hamster's escape day.'
Every day was the same. He would try to escape.
One day he got really close to freedom but he saw a plum on the floor and started nibbling it. His owner caught him and put him in his cage.
'Exercise,' shouted Gizmo, 'on the wheel *now!'*
Spin, spin, spin, the wheel was going so fast, it nearly came off.
He started to climb the cage, then he started chewing where he chewed yesterday.
'Freedom, freedom, freedom!'
He made a little hole and squeezed through it. He ran under the table.
'Next stop . . . the cat flap,' he said.
He knew where to go because he had planned it yesterday.
'Ahhhhh!' Gizmo cried because he saw the cat. Good job it went in the living room. Gizmo leapt through the cat flap.
'Wahoo! Las Vegas here I come!' Gizmo cried in joy but was he free yet? There, in the middle of his path, lay an apple.
'Yummy, yummy for my tummy!' he said.
Gizmo leapt at the apple and started nibbling it. Then all of a sudden his owner came and picked up Gizmo and put him back in his cage.
'Well,' said Gizmo, 'There's always tonight!'

Eleanor Donkin (10)
Ysgol-Y-Castell Primary School